WHATEVER YOU LIKE

WHATEVER YOU LIKE

MAUREEN SMITH

WHATEVER YOU LIKE

Recycling programs for this product may not exist in your area.

ISBN-13: 978-0-373-83198-2

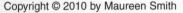

www.kimanipress.com

Printed in U.S.A.

Acknowledgments

My utmost gratitude to Executive Editor
Glenda Howard, whose vision for Kimani Nights
and editorial suggestions helped bring this
tantalizing tale to life.

A very special thanks to crime fiction author
R. Barri Flowers, who answered my questions
about the earnings of professional escorts—
which left me wondering if I'm in the
wrong line of work!

To my husband, Lorrent…he knows why

Chapter One

"Are we almost there?"

The uniformed chauffeur met Lena Morrison's gaze in the rearview mirror. "About five more minutes."

Nodding briskly, Lena slid a tube of MAC lipstick across her mouth and surveyed her reflection in the compact mirror she'd removed from her evening purse. The lustrous red color made her full lips look as juicy and inviting as ripe mangoes dangling from the bowed branches of a tree. Smoky eye shadow accentuated her wide, dark eyes and high cheekbones. She'd exchanged her conservative office attire for a sexy black dress that hugged her curves and had a plunging back. Diamonds glittered at her ears, throat and wrists.

She looked like a million bucks. Felt like it, too.

So it was only fitting that tonight she was escorting one of Chicago's most eligible bachelors to a glitzy party aboard his private yacht. Roderick Brand, president and

CEO of a multinational energy conglomerate. Educated at MIT. Recently named Businessman of the Year by Forbes. Net worth $2.4 billion.

Lena had done her research, of course. As a professional escort, it was her job to learn as much as she could about her wealthy clients. The more she knew and understood about them, the better she could serve their needs.

"Here we are."

The Bentley limousine had glided to a stop in front of a sleek glass high-rise located on Lake Shore Drive. At the canopied entrance to the building, a doorman greeted elegantly dressed couples heading out for a night on the town.

From the backseat of the limo, Lena watched as the driver spoke into the car phone. After a few moments, he hung up and met her eyes in the rearview mirror. "Mr. Brand will be down shortly."

Lena nodded, smiled. "Thank you."

As a rule, she never entered her clients' residences. While most of them understood that she was paid to accompany them to social events, there were always a few who expected more from her. After being groped, propositioned—even cornered in a bathroom—Lena had decided it'd be easier to maintain professional boundaries if she never stepped foot inside her clients' homes.

Her need for boundaries was what prompted her to get up and move to the opposite seat. She felt more comfortable sitting face-to-face to her clients rather than side by side. And it worked out great for the ones who enjoyed ogling her legs across the aisle, hoping for a glimpse up her dress. Wryly she wondered if tonight's client—

Suddenly Lena gasped, staring out the window.

The most gorgeous man she'd ever seen had just emerged from the building. At least six foot three and powerfully built, with wide, muscular shoulders and endlessly long legs that carried him forward with purpose. Lena had escorted some of the richest men to countless black-tie affairs, but she'd never known any man to wear the *hell* out of a tuxedo. Until tonight. Roderick Brand couldn't have looked finer if he'd just completed a cover shoot for *GQ*.

As he reached the waiting limo, Lena mouthed to herself, *Oh. My. God.*

The driver had gotten out to open the back door for Roderick. Lena's stomach clenched as he lowered himself into the plush leather seat across from her.

Their eyes met.

It was as if all the oxygen had been sucked out of the car—or out of Lena's lungs, at the very least. Suddenly she had difficulty breathing.

For several moments neither of them attempted to speak.

As Roderick's dark, glittering gaze traveled over her face and body, Lena shamelessly returned the favor. None of the photos she'd seen of him could begin to do the man justice. He was devastatingly handsome, with black slashes for eyebrows, sculpted cheekbones and a square jaw. His skin was a deep, molten brown that made her think of the most decadent chocolate dessert she'd ever eaten. But what had her mouth watering were his full, sensual lips that brought to mind all sorts of erotic images—skin moving on skin, limbs entangled, mouths and tongues working, two bodies thrusting between hot, twisted sheets.

A slow, legs-spreading smile curved Roderick's lips. As if he'd hijacked her thoughts.

"Hello." His deep, dark voice was as sexy as the man it belonged to. "You must be Lena."

She smiled. "Either that, or you've climbed into the wrong limo."

He laughed, a husky sound that made her nipples harden. "A sense of humor. I like that."

Her smile widened. "I aim to please."

"Oh, you do," Roderick murmured, giving her another one of those slow once-overs. "You please me *very* much."

His words sent an illicit shiver down her spine. Her loins tightened, and her clit pulsed and tingled until she had to shift in her seat to alleviate the pressure.

"Would you care for a drink?" she offered abruptly.

Roderick smiled. "I'd love one."

The limo was equipped with a fully stocked minibar. Roderick watched as Lena went to work fixing him a dirty martini with three olives. As she passed him the glass, their fingers brushed. Heat shot through her veins, making her skin tingle.

"Mmm," Roderick murmured after sampling his drink.

"Good?"

"Very." He held her gaze over the rim of the glass. "You seem to know exactly what I like."

Lena smiled demurely. "If I didn't," she said, settling back against her seat, "I wouldn't be very good at my job. And I am."

Something hot and wicked flashed in his eyes. "How good?"

She returned his gaze, pulse thudding. "Good enough to know better than to answer that question."

He chuckled, raising his glass to her in a mock toast. "Well played."

Lena grinned. It went through her mind that Roderick, with his heavy-lidded eyes and bone-melting smile, could easily pass for Idris Elba's brother. *Have mercy.*

As Roderick sipped his martini, she stared at his hand holding the glass. His fingers were long, broad and masculine. He oozed testosterone, confidence and power, and possessed an unmistakable swagger. Wearing an expensively tailored tuxedo, a gold Breguet wristwatch and John Lobb loafers, he looked right at home in the luxurious limousine. Yet even in his fancy threads he exuded danger, a ruthlessness that warned Lena that Roderick Brand would be formidable in a heartbeat if ever crossed. He hadn't gotten where he was without having a street fighter in him, courtesy of his South Side roots.

"It doesn't seem fair."

Lena's eyes snapped to Roderick's face. "What?"

"This setup. The fact that you know so much about me, and I don't know nearly enough about you."

Lena gave him an amused look. "What would you like to know?"

"Your last name, for starters."

"I can't tell you that."

"Can't? Or won't?"

"Both."

"Why?"

Lena couldn't help smiling. "You know why. Those are the rules."

"Whose?" he challenged. "Yours or the agency's?"

Torn between laughter and exasperation, Lena shook her head at him. "Are you always this persistent?"

"Absolutely." His voice dipped low. "And the more I want something, the more relentlessly I pursue it."

Lena's mouth went dry at the thought of being pursued by this virile, gorgeous man. And what would he do to her once he caught her? she wondered, even as she imagined being tied to a bed, naked and spread-eagle as Roderick took her roughly from behind.

She swallowed hard, giving herself a mental shake to erase the erotic image. "All you need to know about me, Mr. Brand, is that I take my work seriously and I'm committed to serving your needs." At the suggestive gleam that entered his eyes, she added, "Not *those* kind of needs. You hired me to be your companion this evening, so that's what I intend to be. Nothing more, nothing less."

His lips curved in a lazy half smile. "In that case, I have a request to make."

Lena was almost afraid to ask. "What is it?"

"I'm feeling kinda lonely over here. I'm sure that wasn't your intention."

"Of course not," Lena murmured.

Roderick patted the seat beside him. "Then come join me."

Lena knew it wasn't a request. This was a powerful man who was used to giving orders and being obeyed. She doubted anyone ever refused him. And the reality was that he was paying good money for her company. The least she could do was sit beside him—even if doing so tested every ounce of her self-control. Because if ever there was a man she needed to keep at arm's length, it was Roderick Brand.

"Much better," he said approvingly as she moved to his side. "See? I'm perfectly harmless."

At Lena's skeptical look, he laughed. They both knew he was about as harmless as a bloodthirsty wolf on the prowl for its next meal.

As he set aside his drink and leaned back against the seat, she watched the way the fabric of his pants stretched over his muscular thighs. She could feel the heat radiating from his body. The subtle, woodsy scent of his cologne teased her senses, tempting her to lean closer and inhale deeply. Somehow she managed to resist.

"So," Roderick began conversationally, "how long have you been with the agency?"

Lena hesitated. "Three years."

He nodded slowly. "Zandra tells me that you're twenty-nine, you have a master's degree in communications and you speak fluent Italian and Japanese."

"That's right."

As the owner of Elite For You Companions, Zandra Kennedy prided herself on hiring escorts of the highest caliber. The women she selected were not only beautiful; they were intelligent, polished and able to discuss politics, world affairs and a variety of other subjects in any social or business setting. The wealthy clients who anted up for one of Zandra's escorts knew that they were getting more than just arm candy. They were getting a companion who'd be admired for her beauty *and* brains.

"I can definitely see why you're one of Zandra's most popular employees," Roderick drawled.

Lena arched a brow at him. "Is that what she told you?"

He grinned. "Are you denying it?"

"Oh, no," Lena said with mock solemnity. "Far be it from me to call my boss a liar."

Roderick's grin broadened. "Especially after she said such nice things about you."

Lena's lips twisted wryly. "If she had to resort to bragging about her escorts, you must have been a hard sell."

"Let's just say I needed a little, ah, convincing."

"Oh, I see." Lena gave him a knowing smile. "You're a virgin."

He chuckled softly. "If that's what you call clients who've never hired escorts, then yeah, I'm a virgin."

Lena's belly quivered. "So I'm your first."

"You're my first." He smiled, slow and sensual. "Lucky me."

As they stared at each other, the air between them crackled with the kind of raw, scorching energy generated by two people who wanted to screw more than anything, but knew they shouldn't.

After several moments Lena dragged her gaze away and stared blindly out the window. The limo was gliding smoothly through downtown traffic, busy even at this time of night. Soon they'd reach their destination.

The sooner, the better, thought Lena.

Chapter Two

The party was in full swing when Lena and Roderick arrived.

At least two hundred people filled the elegant ballroom aboard Roderick's mega yacht on Lake Michigan. Colorful evening gowns were accentuated by jewels twinkling at ears, throats, fingers and wrists. Light scattered like falling diamonds from the crystal chandelier. A battalion of white-gloved waiters circulated through the crowd, serving hors d'oeuvres and champagne. A live orchestra serenaded the guests.

Roderick tucked Lena's arm through his, and together they made their way through the sparkling sea of partygoers. By working for an upscale escort agency, Lena had gained an encyclopedic knowledge of Chicago's movers and shakers. Not surprisingly, many were there that night. She recognized the mayor and his wife, a prominent senator, a judge and a famous media mogul.

With Lena at his side, Roderick mingled with his guests, greeting everyone by first name and remembering to ask about their children, their golf games and their summer homes in St. Tropez and Monte Carlo. He had a way about him, a cool charm and magnetism, that made people melt in his presence. Powerful men were reduced to grinning idiots, while their wives became blushing sycophants who batted their eyelashes and giggled at everything Roderick said. Even after he'd moved on, the women's admiring gazes followed him around the room. Lena couldn't say she blamed them. Roderick was so damn fine that even *she* found herself wondering what it'd be like if she were there as his woman instead of his hired companion. Crazy, dangerous thoughts.

The most important guest in attendance that night was Ichiro Kawamoto, a Japanese businessman Roderick had been wooing for weeks in order to acquire his struggling energy corporation. Understanding what was at stake, Lena turned on the charm, impressing the man with her fluency in Japanese and her knowledge of issues impacting his country's economy.

As they proceeded to their table for dinner, Kawamoto clapped Roderick on the shoulder and told him, "If I were you, Mr. Brand, I wouldn't let this beautiful woman out of my sight."

Roderick smiled languidly. "Believe me, I don't intend to." When he met Lena's gaze, the possessive heat in his eyes made her shiver.

Over dinner she kept up the charm offensive, determined to do her part to help facilitate Roderick's business deal. Strategically seated between him and Ichiro Kawamoto, she wasted no time engaging the Japanese businessman in a conversation about Kawamoto Energy, the company he'd founded nearly forty years ago. She broke the ice by asking him friendly, nonthreatening questions about how he'd gotten started. His keen dark eyes glowed with pride as he warmed to his subject, reminiscing about the challenges he'd faced and overcome while trying to establish an energy company during Japan's oil crisis of the 1970s.

Natsumi Kawamoto, a soft-spoken woman with elegantly coiffed hair and porcelain skin, wore an indulgent smile on her face as she listened to her husband speak. Roderick seemed equally riveted by Kawamoto's account of the past, interrupting occasionally to ask the man to expound on certain details.

When Roderick and Mrs. Kawamoto were lured into separate conversations with the guests seated beside them, Lena took advantage of the opportunity to steer the discussion with Kawamoto in a new direction.

Speaking in Japanese, she ventured carefully, "I understand that your company's nuclear capacity was drastically reduced after the closing of your power plant."

Kawamoto nodded, looking grave. "The facility was severely damaged during an earthquake three years ago. There was a major leak of radioactive wastewater."

"I'm very sorry to hear that," Lena said sympathetically. "You must have suffered a tremendous loss of revenue."

"We did," Kawamoto grimly acknowledged. "And we've never quite recovered. As a result, we've been unable to restart commercial operations because we don't have the capital needed to repair the power plant and upgrade safety measures."

"But Mr. Brand does," Lena gently reminded him.

"He can invest the one-point-six billion dollars required to restore the facility. And he's already established the right connections to obtain approval from the authorities to resume commercial operations."

"This is true." Smiling enigmatically, Kawamoto sipped his wine.

Reaching for her own glass, Lena added casually, "Mr. Brand told me that one of his top priorities would be to make Kawamoto Energy one of Japan's most important companies by increasing its share of the electricity sector. Eventually he'd like to see it replace one of the ten powerhouses currently included in the Federation of Electric Power Companies."

Kawamoto met her steady gaze. "That would be quite an accomplishment." Although he looked very impressed, Lena detected a wistful note in his voice that gave her pause.

And suddenly she understood why Ichiro Kawamoto was so resistant to Roderick's business proposal. He'd poured blood, sweat and tears into building his company from the ground up. The idea of surrendering the reins to someone else was anathema to him. What made matters even worse was that Kawamoto Energy was in dire financial straits. On some level, the man probably felt like a failure.

"Even though you'd no longer be at the helm of Kawamoto Energy," Lena told him in a gentle, conciliatory tone, "you can take pride in knowing that any future success the company experiences was made possible by the solid foundation you laid. That's your legacy, Mr. Kawamoto. And no one can ever take that away from you."

His expression softened, and he eyed her with newfound admiration and respect. "Maybe if one of my three daughters had a head for business—as *you* obviously do—I would not have to sell my company."

Lena laughed. "You flatter me, Mr. Kawamoto. I make no claim to having a head for business."

He smiled slightly. "Then you underestimate yourself. Part of being a shrewd businessman is having the ability to read people. It's a rare gift, which you obviously possess." He raised his wineglass in a toast to her. *"Kanpai."*

Lena smiled warmly, reciprocating the gesture. *"Kanpai."*

After dinner, Lena and Roderick were conversing with Kawamoto and his wife about their upcoming holiday plans. Or at least that's what Lena *thought* they were discussing. She was having a hard time concentrating on anything with Roderick's thumb idly stroking the bare skin on her lower back, right above her ass. His touch inflamed her, fueling the hungry ache between her thighs until her panties were completely soaked. By some miracle she managed to keep talking, laughing and behaving as though she had no clue that her nipples were thrusting brazenly against her bra or that she was in serious danger of climaxing right in her seat.

When she stole a sideways glance at Roderick's face, he appeared to be utterly engrossed in the conversation with the Japanese couple.

Needing a reprieve from his marauding touch, Lena excused herself from the table to go to the ladies' room.

Inside the luxuriously appointed bathroom, she smiled politely at the attendant passing out hot towels and made a beeline to the nearest empty stall. She removed a feminine wet nap from her purse—she never left home without one—and wiped away the moisture between her legs. When she'd finished, she flushed the toilet and made her way to the row of marble sinks to wash her hands.

The attendant, a middle-aged black woman with a friendly smile, handed Lena a hot towel. "Having a good time?"

Lena smiled at her. "I am, thank you."

"That's good. Mr. Brand sure knows how to throw a party."

"Yes, he does," Lena agreed, surrendering the towel so that she could retouch her lipstick.

"He's such a nice young man. Works too hard, though."

Lena met the woman's gaze in the mirror. There was a conspiratorial gleam in her eyes.

"I saw the two of you arrive together. You make such a beautiful couple."

Blushing, Lena opened her mouth to tell the woman that she and Roderick weren't dating, then quickly reconsidered. As an escort, it was her professional duty to protect her clients' privacy. So telling a complete stranger that she was Roderick's hired companion was out of the question.

She smiled warmly at the attendant. "I'm thoroughly enjoying Mr. Brand's company this evening."

The woman beamed with pleasure.

When Lena tried to give her a tip, she shook her head vigorously. "Oh, no. You don't have to tip me, baby. Mr. Brand is paying me *very* well."

That makes two of us, Lena thought wryly.

Ignoring the woman's protests, she tucked the large bill into the front pocket of her uniform and grinned at her before leaving the restroom.

When she emerged she bumped right into Roderick,

who'd apparently been waiting for her. Before she could open her mouth, he took her hand.

"I haven't given you the grand tour of the yacht," he said silkily.

"But your guests—"

"Can keep themselves entertained for a while."

He guided her away from the ballroom, where the orchestra had struck up a soft, bluesy number that had couples swaying across the mahogany dance floor. Others had spilled out onto the deck and gathered at the railing to enjoy the cool breeze and gaze out at the glistening, moonlit waters of Lake Michigan.

Roderick led Lena up the curved double staircase to the upper-level sky deck, which was perfect for open-air mingling and stargazing. Surprisingly, no one else had wandered up there yet.

As they leisurely started across the deck, Lena remarked, "Mr. and Mrs. Kawamoto seem like a lovely couple."

"They are," Roderick agreed. "They've been married for over forty years, and they're incredibly devoted to their children."

"I can tell. Their eyes light up whenever they talk about their daughters." Lena hesitated. "I can sense, however, that Mr. Kawamoto wishes he had a son to take over running the company."

Roderick smiled ruefully. "I guess I'm fortunate that he doesn't."

"I guess you are." Lena chuckled dryly. "But when has something like that ever stopped a corporate raider from pursuing an advantageous acquisition?"

Roderick grimaced. "The term 'corporate raider' has such negative connotations, thanks to all the hostile takeovers that happened during the eighties.

I don't consider myself some greedy vulture circling overhead, waiting to feed on the carcasses of bankrupt companies."

"But you *do* profit from their financial misfortunes," Lena pointed out.

"That's true," he admitted. "But I only pursue acquisitions that will be mutually beneficial to both parties. I've never made a business deal that caused me to wrestle with my conscience afterward because I knowingly exploited the other party."

"Congratulations," Lena murmured.

Roderick gave her an amused sidelong glance. "I don't know you well enough to tell whether or not you were being sarcastic."

She chuckled. "I wasn't being sarcastic. I meant what I said. I commend you for not being a soulless corporate shark who ruthlessly preys on the weak and downtrodden."

Roderick threw back his head and laughed. "Damned with faint praise!"

Lena grinned, enjoying the sound of his deep, masculine laughter. "All joking aside, I don't think there's anything wrong with the way you're trying to rescue Kawamoto Energy from bankruptcy. The earthquake that shut down their power plant was nobody's fault, but since then, some executive-level decisions have been made that negatively impacted the corporation's bottom line. It's pretty clear to me that Kawamoto Energy needs a complete overhaul. And I think your strategies for increasing the company's nuclear capacity and sales are brilliant." She smiled softly. "In time, I can see Mr. Kawamoto thanking you."

Roderick smiled. "You can?"

Lena nodded. "Absolutely. Of course, he'd need time

to adjust to the reality of someone else running his beloved company. But once he sees what a good steward you are, I don't think he'd be too proud to express his gratitude to you."

Roderick stopped walking and turned to face her, searching her features in the silvery moonlight. "You know what I think? I think you're absolutely amazing."

Lena blushed demurely. "That's kind of you to say—"

"Kindness has nothing to do with it. I'm just speaking the truth. You're an amazing woman, Lena. No matter what happens with Kawamoto, I'm so glad I had an opportunity to meet you tonight."

Lena warmed with pleasure. "I'm glad you feel that way," she said softly. "I've enjoyed meeting you as well, Roderick."

They stared at each other.

Although they weren't touching, Lena felt a tangible connection between them, an ever-present electric energy that vibrated in the air that separated them. Intoxicating. Dangerous.

Averting her gaze, she glanced up at the starry sky and sighed deeply. "What a beautiful n—"

Without warning Roderick drew her into a dark alcove and pinned her against the wall. Her pulse thudded as she stared into his glittering eyes.

"I've been dying to do this all night," he murmured before slanting his mouth over hers.

Lena gasped. Reflexively, she raised her hands to push him away. Instead her arms wrapped around his neck and pulled him closer. A low, guttural sound rumbled up from his throat. He deepened the kiss—a scorching, ravenous kiss unlike any Lena had ever experienced before.

He cupped her face between his big hands as his lips parted hers. The sensation of his hot, wet tongue sliding against hers made her moan. It didn't occur to her that someone might stumble upon them. She was too busy reeling from the pleasure of his kiss, from the pressure of his hard, heavy body imprisoning hers. She writhed against him as he ran his hands down to her hips, slid them over her ass and squeezed. She bit his bottom lip, and he bit her back. They kissed in raw urgency, tongues dueling, mouths suckling.

He shoved a muscular thigh between her legs, flattening her against the wall. She shivered as he kissed her behind her ear, down her throat and across her collarbone. Her nipples hardened until they ached. She could feel his erection against her belly—hot, huge and gloriously hard. Her clit throbbed with lust, and wetness leaked from her pussy.

Panting, she hooked her leg over his waist and cupped his bulging shaft. He groaned and thrust against her hand as she rubbed him, reveling in the way his breathing grew louder and faster. She was about to unzip his pants and fall to her knees when suddenly he grabbed her hand. Their eyes met in the moonlit darkness as he took both of her wrists and pinned them to the wall above her head, holding them in place with one hand. Lena moaned, arching desperately against him.

In the heat of the moment, it didn't matter to her that she was crossing the line with a client, something she'd vowed she would never do again. It didn't matter that she'd probably hate herself in the morning for being so weak. She wanted Roderick more than her very next breath, and nothing else mattered.

Using his free hand, he dragged her dress up to her waist, exposing the garter belt and thigh-high stockings she wore. His husky murmur of approval made her tremble with need. He slipped his hand between her legs, grazing the inside of her thigh with his fingertips. Her breath snagged in her throat. Every part of her body was primed, ready and aching, a delicious tingling running from her head to her toes.

He nudged aside her drenched panties and found her throbbing clitoris. Lena shuddered, leaning her head back against the wall. He stroked her, teasing and tormenting her as he ran his fingers along her clit and the swollen folds of her labia. She moaned, wanting his whole hand inside her, knuckles-deep. But he took his sweet time, fingers dancing and circling, coming close but never actually dipping inside.

When Lena couldn't take it anymore, when her hips were bucking and twisting frantically against him, when her entire body was a tightly wound knot of sexual frustration, Roderick relented and plunged two fingers inside her. She almost screamed.

As her clitoris swelled, she rocked against his hand. He pushed deeper, his fingers curling upward and sending jolts of electricity to her G-spot. She groaned, closing her eyes and spreading her legs wider. He pressed harder and faster, his thumb working her clit like he'd been pleasuring her all his life.

Her thighs began to shake. She could feel an orgasm building, could feel every muscle in her body grow taut with tension and desire.

When Roderick's hot mouth closed over one breast, she gasped. He continued fingering her as he sucked her nipple through her silk dress, making her squirm from the onslaught of erotic sensation.

And then he thrust a third finger inside her.

This time she couldn't hold back her scream.

As her body convulsed, Roderick released her wrists and wrapped his arms around her, holding her tightly against him.

Long moments later, she let out a deep, shuddering breath and dropped her head onto his shoulder. She could feel the hot length of his erection straining against his pants, demanding release. Her belly quivered with fresh arousal.

He stroked a hand down her bare back, sending delicious shivers through her body. "What do you say we find a bed and finish this?" he whispered into her ear.

Yes! Lena wanted to shout. *Yes, yes, yes!*

But as tempting as Roderick's offer sounded, she knew it'd be wrong to sleep with him. She'd already gone too far as it was, breaking not only the agency's policy but her own rule about becoming intimate with clients. Once she had sex with Roderick, there'd be no turning back. Because after one night with him, she'd be whipped. No doubt about it.

"If you're still worried about my guests," he murmured, "we can wait until the party's over. The master stateroom's on the lower deck. There's a Jacuzzi, a fireplace. A bed big enough for me to spread you out, taste you all over, take you from one corner to another."

Lena must have whimpered, because he laughed softly. Wickedly.

"Say yes," he urged her.

"I—I can't," she mumbled against his shoulder. "This was a mistake. You're my client—"

"Only for a few more hours."

"That's not the point. I shouldn't have—"

She was interrupted by the sound of approaching

voices. Her head snapped up, and she stared wild-eyed into Roderick's face. Damn it! The last thing she wanted was to be caught making out with him, though everyone at the party probably assumed they were already lovers—or would be by the end of the night.

Roderick watched her intently. "Lena—"

She clapped her hand over his mouth and quickly backed him farther into the darkened alcove.

The voices belonged to a man and a woman who'd probably sneaked up to the sky deck to have some privacy. Lena hoped and prayed that the couple wouldn't decide to find a hiding place—namely, hers and Roderick's.

"…could have sworn I heard someone scream just a minute ago," the female was saying, her voice slightly slurred.

Her companion chuckled. "I think you've had too much wine."

"Probably, but I *did* hear something. It sounded like a woman's scream."

Lena grimaced, cursing her own lack of self-control. A bar of moonlight slanting across Roderick's face revealed the laughter glittering in his eyes. She pressed her hand harder over his mouth, her deadly gaze warning him that there'd be hell to pay if he so much as *breathed* the wrong way.

"Sounds like an Agatha Christie novel," came the man's amused response. "A dark, starry night. A bunch of wealthy socialites partying the night away aboard a luxury yacht, blissfully oblivious to the gruesome murder taking place above deck."

The woman let out a breathy giggle. "What if Roderick Brand isn't what he appears to be? What if he's really a sadistic psychopath who lured us to this party so he could kill us one by one, like the killer in *And Then There Were None?*"

"Oooh, scary." The man laughed.

Lena felt Roderick's lips curve into a smile against her palm. She rolled her eyes.

The couple had neared the opening to the alcove. Lena held her breath, silently willing them to keep walking. Although she and Roderick were both dressed in black, the shadows might not conceal them for very long. All it'd take to blow their cover was a sliver of moonlight catching and reflecting the diamonds she wore.

"If Brand's a psychopath," the man joked, "he sure knows how to throw one hell of a party."

"And he's sexy as hell, too," drawled the woman.

"Hey!" her companion protested.

Lena shook her head at Roderick, whose gaze had turned downright wicked. As she eyed him suspiciously, his lips parted. She felt his warm breath against her skin, and then he slid the tip of his tongue across her palm. Jolts of sensation shot through her veins. She snatched her hand away as if she'd been scalded by a hot burner. Strong white teeth flashed in the moonlight, and she realized that she'd done exactly what Roderick wanted. She skewered him with a look that ordered him to remain quiet, but he clearly had other ideas.

Keeping one arm firmly around her waist, he curled his other hand around her nape and slanted his mouth over hers. Instant heat swamped her body. Summoning all her willpower, she tore her mouth free and twisted away from him, turning her back on him. Big damn mistake. Now she could feel every hard, mouthwatering inch of his erection nestled between her butt cheeks.

As if that weren't bad enough, the annoying couple

had stopped at the railing—less than ten feet away from the alcove where Lena and Roderick silently grappled in the darkness. But she could no longer make out what the man and woman were saying. Their voices had been drowned out by the blood pounding against her eardrums as Roderick nuzzled the back of her neck, running his tongue up and down her nape.

When his hands snaked over her rib cage and cupped her breasts, she nearly moaned aloud. Her nipples hardened as he gently stroked them, the heat of his skin penetrating her silk dress. One moment she was struggling to break free of his hold. The next moment she was pressing herself against him, craving as much contact as she could get.

Roderick rolled his hips, grinding his erection against her butt. Her clitoris swelled, and she bit her lip hard to stifle another moan. She wanted to bend over, spread her legs and take him deep inside her. She wanted him to ram into her until her juices ran down the inside of her legs, until her throat was raw from screaming with ecstasy.

"Spend the night with me," he whispered, sucking her earlobe.

She shivered, electric fire sweeping over her skin. Somehow she managed to shake her head.

"Please." He dipped his tongue into her ear, making her gasp.

"Did you hear something?" asked the woman at the railing.

Lena froze, heart thudding.

Roderick lowered his smiling mouth to her bare shoulder.

"I didn't hear anything." The man sounded amused.

"Remind me not to let you have any more wine tonight."

"Very funny. I'm not drunk. I heard a noise."

"Of course you did. Come on, let's go."

"Where?"

"I heard this love boat has twelve guest staterooms. Let's go see if any of them are unlocked."

"Mmm," the woman purred in delight. "You naughty boy, you."

Lena didn't draw an easy breath until the couple's footsteps had receded into the distance. Then she sprang out of Roderick's arms before he could trap her again.

"It's time to return to the party," she told him. "You've neglected your guests long enough."

He chuckled, the sound curling around her like a drift of smoke. "Did those two sound neglected to you?"

They hadn't, but that was beside the point.

Pinning Roderick with a direct gaze, Lena said firmly, "Look, I'm not going to sleep with you. What we did tonight was a mistake. A huge mistake. I'm not blaming you. I take full responsibility for my own actions. Which is why I'm telling you that this—" she motioned to encompass both of them "—can't happen again. Do you understand?"

Roderick regarded her for a long, assessing moment.

Defiantly she stared back at him, holding her ground.

After what seemed an eternity, he heaved a deep, resigned breath. "Okay."

Lena blinked. "Okay?"

He nodded. "I don't want to pressure you into doing something you're not comfortable with. That'd be selfish of me, not to mention barbaric—two things I generally try not to be when dealing with women."

Lena eyed him warily. She couldn't believe he was giving up so easily. Correction: She *didn't* believe it. He was up to something, she was sure of it.

He stepped forward, brushing an almost brotherly kiss across her forehead. "Come on," he murmured, gently taking her hand. "Let's not keep our guests waiting any longer."

Lena's insides warmed with pleasure at the words he'd used. *Our guests.*

She shouldn't have liked the way it sounded. But she did.

And that's when she knew she was in serious trouble.

Chapter Three

For Lena, getting through the rest of the night was an exercise in discipline. Trying to maintain her composure, trying to smile and make conversation with strangers, trying to erase the memory of Roderick's fingers stroking deep inside her—all took sheer self-control.

When they left the party after midnight, she didn't know whether to be relieved or terrified at the prospect of being alone with him. Despite what he'd told her about backing off, she wasn't entirely convinced of his sincerity. If he tried to seduce her during the ride home, she honestly didn't know if she'd have the willpower to resist him.

Once inside the plush dark cocoon of the limo, Roderick tugged off his tie and grabbed a bottle of Moët from the minibar. Lena watched as he poured each of them a drink and handed her a glass.

"I'd like to propose a toast," he said, smiling broadly. "The evening was a huge success, thanks to you."

"Me?"

"Yes, you. On Monday morning I have a meeting with Ichiro Kawamoto to discuss my acquisition of his energy company."

"That's great news," Lena exclaimed warmly. "Congratulations."

"Thanks. As I told you earlier, I've been courting Kawamoto for weeks, with little success. I don't think it's a coincidence that after meeting *you* tonight, he's suddenly more amenable to negotiating with me."

Lena chuckled, crossing her legs as she settled more comfortably into the plush seating. "I think you're giving me too much credit. Maybe Mr. Kawamoto was just playing hardball," she suggested, though she'd reached a different conclusion over dinner. "Or maybe he just needed more time to weigh the pros and cons of your business proposal before he reached a decision."

Roderick grinned. "I think you underestimate what an incredible impression you made on him, how thoroughly you charmed him." He raised his glass to her. "A toast. To one of the most beautiful, fascinating women I've ever had the privilege of meeting."

Lena blushed with pleasure. They clinked glasses and sipped their champagne, never taking their eyes off each other.

"Zandra was right," Roderick murmured.

"About?"

"You. She said you'd be perfect for me. She was right."

Lena's pulse did a weird fluttering thing. "Well, she told me that you preferred an escort who spoke

Japanese. I happened to be the only one who met that qualification."

"I'm glad you were." Roderick held her gaze. "But that's not the only reason you're perfect for me, Lena."

Her mouth went bone-dry. She gulped more champagne, needing something stronger to steady her nerves.

"I'd like to see you again," Roderick said quietly.

Lena shook her head. "I don't think that's a good idea."

"Why? Because we're attracted to each other?"

She gave a short, humorless laugh. "*That's* an understatement if I ever heard one."

Roderick smiled wryly. "So you're refusing to see me again because we have such amazing chemistry. Is that what you're telling me?"

"That's *exactly* what I'm telling you."

"And how would Zandra feel about you turning away a paying customer?"

Lena shot him a narrow look. "She's not my pimp."

Roderick frowned. "I wasn't suggesting—"

"*I* choose which clients I want to go out with. Zandra has never forced anyone on me. It doesn't work that way."

A muscle clenched in Roderick's jaw. He downed the rest of his drink, set aside the empty glass, then turned in the seat to face her. His gaze was piercingly direct. "I know I promised not to pressure you—"

"Look how long *that* lasted."

He scowled. "Damn it, Lena. I'm trying to figure out a way to make this work."

"And I'm telling you that—"

Without warning, the limo swerved sharply. Lena's

glass flew from her hand as she hurtled across the seat and slammed into Roderick, who was pinned against the door.

"Shit!" he swore, catching her by the shoulders as horns blared furiously behind them. His concerned gaze swept over her face. "Are you all right?"

She nodded jerkily.

Straightening from the door, Roderick lowered the privacy glass and barked at the driver, "What the hell happened?"

The man's anxious gaze appeared in the rearview mirror. "Sorry about that, Mr. Brand. Some crazy asshole just cut me off. Are you two okay? Miss Morrison?"

"I'm fine." Lena was so shaken up that she barely registered that he'd used her last name.

Roderick pulled her onto his lap, brushing her hair off her face, passing his hands over her body as if to check for broken bones. "Are you sure you aren't hurt?" he demanded.

"I'm okay," she mumbled. "Just a little rattled, that's all. And grateful."

"Grateful?"

She nodded, exhaling a shaky breath. "It could have been worse. If I hadn't used your body as my landing pad, I might have gone headfirst through the window. And that wouldn't have been a pretty sight."

Roderick wasn't amused. Scowling ferociously, he growled at the driver, "Take it easy up there."

"Yes, sir."

Though touched by Roderick's concern for her, Lena felt compelled to defend her employer's newest chauffeur. "It's not his fault some Chicagoans are lousy drivers. No offense."

"None taken." Roderick smiled wryly at her. "So you're not from Chicago?"

Lena hesitated, then answered truthfully, "No, I'm not."

"Am I allowed to ask where you're from?"

"You can ask. Doesn't mean I'll tell you."

"I'll try anyway. Where are you from?"

"Transylvania."

Roderick laughed. "Transylvania?"

"That's right." She grinned.

"I wouldn't have guessed it. Especially since you don't even have a Romanian accent."

"Oh, that." Lena shrugged dismissively. "I've been living in the States for so long that I lost my accent."

"I see." Roderick nodded, playing along. "And what do you miss the most about, ah, Transylvania?"

"Oh, that's easy. The scenic mountains and legendary castles."

"Yeah? Ever visited Dracula's castle?"

"Of course. It's a national monument and a popular tourist attraction."

Dropping his voice to a hushed whisper, Roderick asked, "Any sightings of the undead one?"

"Now that you mention it," Lena whispered back conspiratorially, "I *did* have a chance encounter with—"

Roderick leaned closer.

And she promptly lost her train of thought.

"Well?" he prodded after several moments, his eyes glimmering with mischief. "You had a chance encounter with…?"

"I, uh…" Lena floundered. She'd been enjoying their playful exchange so much that she'd completely forgotten she was draped across his lap. Until he moved, and the muscles in his thighs flexed beneath her butt. She tensed, even as heat bloomed between her legs.

"Lena." There was an unspoken question in Roderick's husky voice.

She stared at him.

He stared back.

She didn't know who moved first.

The next thing she knew their mouths were fused, tongues tangling frantically. Roderick stabbed a button on the armrest, raising the tinted privacy glass that shielded them from the driver's view.

And then his hands were sliding up Lena's thighs, deftly removing her panties. Her dress rode up as she straddled his lap, a leg on each side of his waist. He ripped off his tuxedo jacket and she clawed at his shirt, desperate to get at his skin, frustrated because she couldn't wait long enough.

He gripped the straps of her dress and yanked them down, releasing her breasts with a soft bounce. She groaned at the heat of his mouth on her nipples, the wet lash of his tongue.

He unzipped his pants and reached inside, freeing himself. Lena's breath quickened at the sight of his long, dark penis jutting straight into the air. He dug into his pocket, pulled out a condom and tore open the foil packet with his teeth. He'd barely covered himself before he was reaching for her again, grabbing her hips and guiding her down onto his thick erection.

She moaned with pleasure as he filled her, stretching her all the way. Her muscles convulsed and tightened around him.

He groaned, a rough, masculine sound that made her walls clench again. Already on the verge of coming, she lifted off him with a shudder, then slowly eased back down, taking him back inside her dripping wetness.

His hands gripped her butt as he began moving with deep, steady strokes. She held on to his big shoulders, her fingers digging into the hard, springy muscles beneath his shirt. Her head fell back as his greedy mouth raked over her exposed throat.

When he reached between their joined bodies and pressed his thumb against her clit, she cried out. He rubbed her in slow, sensual circles, spreading heat from her belly to her trembling thighs down to her curling toes.

All her fears and misgivings had dissolved. Nothing else mattered but her insatiable desire for Roderick and his for her. Although she was on top, he dictated the pace, pounding into her with a desperate fury that sent her breasts bouncing up and down. With every thrust, her clit grazed the short black curls surrounding his shaft, the friction unbearably tantalizing.

Their breathing grew heavier, a loud, harsh sound in the insulated confines of the limo. The tinted windows were soon covered with steam.

Heart thundering, Lena leaned down to kiss Roderick's jaw and throat, then his lips. They kissed each other hard, bruisingly. Lena broke away, panting, and leaned back on his thighs, giving him a deeper angle of penetration. He plunged faster, every stroke hitting her harder, stronger. Driving her over the edge.

She came with a broken sob, spasms of ecstasy rocketing through her body, wrenching Roderick's name from her throat.

Without missing a beat, he surged off the seat and bore her down to the floor. Her legs tightened around his waist, her ankles locked behind his broad back. She thrust her hips at him and he thrust his hips at her—again and again, deeper and harder and faster, until white-hot pleasure exploded, ricocheting from her body to his. They climaxed together, shuddering violently and clutching each other.

Their ragged breathing was the only sound that penetrated the ensuing silence. Neither of them moved a muscle.

Within moments, the inevitable recriminations flooded Lena's conscience like water gushing from a breached levee. She closed her eyes, channeling her thoughts outward. She focused on the gliding motion of the limo, the sound of her discarded champagne glass rolling across the floor as the driver turned a corner, the thin shards of light from the minibar that seeped through her eyelids.

She focused on anything but what she and Roderick had just done.

She didn't know how much time passed before he lifted his head and looked down at her. Their eyes met. His were gentle, hers guarded. As he lowered his mouth to hers, Lena averted her face so that he only caught a corner of her lips. He gazed at her a moment longer, then slowly rolled away from her and sat up.

Lena didn't look at him as he disposed of the condom and zipped up his pants. Even when he handed her panties to her, she avoided eye contact with him.

Returning to the seat, she went through the motions of slipping on her underwear, adjusting her stockings, straightening her dress and making a halfhearted attempt to repair her wrecked hairdo. She couldn't possibly *look* any worse than she felt.

Roderick moved to the minibar, poured himself a shot of vodka and downed it in one swallow. When he offered Lena a glass she shook her head, though a stiff drink might have done her a world of good right about then.

As Roderick sat down beside her, she turned her head and stared out the window. Feeling his intent gaze on her, she braced herself, waiting for him to speak.

She didn't have to wait long.

"I'm not going to apologize for what just happened," he said quietly.

"I don't expect you to." Her tone was self-deprecating. "You didn't exactly force yourself on me."

He reached over and caught her hand, threading his strong fingers through hers. "I want to see you again, Lena."

Steeling her emotions, she pulled her hand free. "My answer hasn't changed."

He sighed harshly and swore under his breath.

The limo came to a stop. They had finally reached Roderick's downtown residence.

The driver got out, but he didn't immediately open the backseat door. He stood with his back discreetly to the window, giving his passengers their privacy.

Suddenly struck by the realization that she'd never see Roderick again, Lena blurted impulsively, "For what it's worth, I had a wonderful time tonight. But I can't go out with you again. I hope you understand."

He gave her a long, brooding look. Then—to her surprise—his mouth curved in a slow, lazy smile. As if he knew a secret she didn't.

"I meant what I told you earlier," he murmured.

Lena frowned, puzzled. "About what?"

He leaned over and kissed her, a soft, tender kiss that left her aching for more. Drawing back, he winked at her. "I'll let you think about it."

Frustrated, she glared at him. "I don't know what—"

But he'd already climbed out of the car.

It was only as Lena watched him walk away that she remembered what he'd said to her on the ride to the party. *The more I want something, the more relentlessly I pursue it.*

Closing her eyes, she leaned back against the seat and exhaled a deep, shaky breath.

God help her if Roderick Brand ever decided to pursue her.

God help both of them.

Chapter Four

"There she is! There's my precious baby girl!"

The sight of Cleveland Morrison's broad, toothy grin did wonders for Lena's mood the next afternoon. Her smile widened as she crossed the flagstone terrace to reach the table where he sat with a book on his lap, a magnifying glass resting over an open page.

"Poppa." She bent, planting an affectionate kiss on his upturned cheek. The rasp of his beard tickled her lips, making her smile. "Nurse Jacobs must be on vacation."

"How'd you know?" her grandfather asked in surprise.

"Because you need a shave, and she's the only one you let anywhere near you with a razor."

Grinning sheepishly, Cleveland rubbed his bristly chin with his good hand. "Not my fault she's the only one who knows what she's doing."

"Uh-huh." Lena chuckled, joining him at the table.

Everyone knew that her grandfather had a crush on Margaret Jacobs, one of his caregivers at the assisted-living facility he'd called home for the past three years. The woman had become a permanent fixture at his side while he underwent therapy for a massive stroke that had left him paralyzed on one side of his body. She'd been a godsend to Lena, who'd agonized over the decision to place her grandfather in a nursing home. She'd found fault with every establishment she'd visited until a coworker recommended Lakeview Manor, one of Chicago's most expensive assisted-living residences. It boasted an elegant facility that overlooked a pretty lake and had a state-of-the-art rehabilitation center, beautifully landscaped grounds and caring, professional staff who catered to the residents' every need. Moonlighting as a high-end escort was the only way Lena could afford such a place, but it was more than worth it. Her grandfather deserved nothing but the best.

"When does Nurse Jacobs get back from vacation?" she asked him.

"Tomorrow."

"Good." Lena grinned playfully. "You go another day without a shave, Poppa, and folks might start mistaking you for Wolfman Jack."

That earned her one of Cleveland's hearty, barrel-chested laughs. When she was a little girl, she'd loved climbing into his lap and pressing her ear to his sturdy chest just to feel the deep vibration of his laughter. After his stroke, she'd feared she would never hear—or feel—that wonderful sound again.

Setting aside his book and magnifying glass,

Cleveland nodded at the covered cake dish Lena had placed on the table. "What you got there?"

"Oh, just a little something I whipped up for you this morning." With exaggerated casualness she removed the lid.

Her grandfather's face lit up like fireworks launched into a night sky. "German chocolate cake! My favorite!"

Lena grinned. "I know."

On cue, a staff member appeared with the cake knife and plates Lena had requested when she first arrived.

"Sherry, look what my baby girl brought me," Cleveland bragged to the smiling woman. "Am I the luckiest man in the world or what?"

"You sure are, Mr. Morrison. Spoiled rotten, too," Sherry teased, winking at Lena.

She laughed, cutting into the cake. "I'm just returning the favor. Poppa gave me and my sister everything we wanted when we were growing up. He could never say no, and we took full advantage of that."

Cleveland guffawed at the notion of being manipulated in any way by the two granddaughters he and his wife had raised following their mother's death. Because their biological father had been nothing more than a sperm donor, Cleveland was the only father Lena and her younger sister, Morgan, had ever known. They owed him everything.

After Lena had cut slices of cake for herself, Cleveland and Sherry, her grandfather sent the woman back inside to share the rest of the dessert with the other residents. Since Lena frequently brought him goodies, he didn't mind sharing—on most days anyway.

By the time Lena reached for her fork, he'd already devoured half of his piece. She enjoyed watching him eat, because she knew how hard he'd worked in rehab to regain the ability to feed himself after the stroke. His ultimate goal was to walk again, grim prognosis be damned.

"I sure do love it when you make your grandma's German chocolate cake. It always tastes just like hers, God rest her sainted soul."

Lena smiled softly. "All those years of watching her in the kitchen definitely paid off."

Cleveland grinned. "As I always say, baby girl, you're gonna make some lucky man an excellent wife one day."

Inexplicably, Lena thought of Roderick Brand. Of course, thinking about him only forced her to remember what they'd done the night before, which was the *last* thing she needed to be thinking about while sitting across from her eighty-year-old grandfather, who probably believed she was still a virgin.

As her face heated with renewed shame, she averted her gaze to stare out across the wide expanse of lawn that sloped down to the lake. The bright afternoon sun lit a shimmering path across the water. Lena could use a good, cold swim right about now.

"How's work?" her grandfather asked.

Lena cut into her cake. "Work's good."

By day she was a grant writer for a private liberal arts college in Evanston. Her grandfather had no idea that she moonlighted as an escort, and she intended to keep it that way.

"Got any major projects in the works?"

"Sure do." Lena told him about the million-dollar grant proposal she'd recently submitted on behalf of the college's performing arts center. "This could be the largest grant we've ever received," she explained.

"Really?" Cleveland arched two snowy eyebrows. "Sounds like you've got a lot riding on your shoulders."

"You could say that. Ever since the economy tanked, endowments at colleges and universities across the country have practically dried up. We really need the research funds. Not to mention that securing this grant will make me a shoo-in for a promotion."

"That's wonderful, sweetheart," Cleveland said warmly. "As hard as you work, you definitely deserve a promotion. But I'm just wondering…" He trailed off, looking thoughtful as he scratched his jaw.

Lena ate a bite of cake. "Wondering what?"

"Truth be told, baby girl, I've been a little worried about you."

"You have?" *Uh-oh.* "Why?"

"Well, you already work such long hours. If you get a promotion, that means even more responsibility and longer hours. Am I right?"

"More than likely," Lena admitted.

Cleveland frowned. "Doesn't seem like you have much time for a social life."

"I do," she assured him. It wasn't exactly a lie. If hobnobbing with the rich and powerful at glitzy yacht parties didn't qualify as having a social life, what did?

Her grandfather looked skeptical. "Visiting your crippled grandpa in a nursing home every week doesn't count."

Lena gave him a reproving look. "Stop calling yourself crippled. And aren't I always telling you about new restaurants and museums I've visited?"

"Alone," he pointed out.

She shrugged. "I like my own company."

"You're wonderful company," her grandfather agreed. "You know I always look forward to spending time with you. I just worry that you're not getting out there enough, meeting other young folks like yourself. Your sister's always talking about the new man in her life." He peered at Lena over the rim of his bifocals. "When was the last time *you* went on a date?"

She choked out a laugh. "Poppa!"

"What? It's a fair question."

She smiled ruefully. "No offense, Poppa, but I don't exactly feel comfortable discussing my, uh, love life with you."

Truthfully, there wasn't much to discuss. Her love life was nonexistent because she hadn't figured out a way to balance being a professional escort and somebody's girlfriend. She knew that very few men would understand or accept her decision to work as an escort, and giving it up wasn't an option for her as her grandfather's sole support. Nor was she willing to keep her side gig a secret from any man she was dating. She had friends who sneaked around behind their boyfriends' backs and lied to them all the time. She didn't want that kind of relationship, and judging by her girlfriends' constant complaints, she wasn't missing much by remaining single. But a girl had needs, so for the past three years she'd enjoyed brief but satisfying flings with guys who were as commitment-phobic as she was.

But after one night with Roderick Brand, she realized how sexually deprived she'd been.

"I just want to make sure that your job doesn't become your life," her grandfather was saying.

Incredulous, Lena shook her head at him. "I can't

believe I'm hearing this from the man who devoted fifty years of his life to the Los Angeles Metropolitan Transit Authority, working tirelessly to support his family and put three dependents—me, Morgan and our mother—through college. *You're* going to lecture *me* about working too hard?"

"It's not the same thing," Cleveland grumbled. "You're too young and beautiful to be a workaholic, Lena."

"I'm not a workaholic. Believe me, I have a life outside of the college." *If only you knew!*

Her grandfather studied her in shrewd silence a moment longer, then grunted. "As long as you're happy—"

"I am."

"Then that's the most important thing." He hesitated, looking as though he wanted to say more.

Lena waited.

"You know I always worry about how you can afford to put me up in this Shangri-la. I know it ain't cheap—"

She frowned. "Poppa—"

He held up a hand, forestalling her protest. "All I was going to say is that maybe a promotion's not such a bad thing. You know, if it makes it easier for you to...take care of me."

A lump rose in Lena's throat. He was thanking her without actually saying the words, because she'd rebuffed him every time he'd tried to express his gratitude in the past.

Smiling tenderly, she said, "When I get the promotion, Poppa, I'm taking you to dinner and a show to celebrate."

He winked at her. "It's a date." His gaze strayed to

her slice of cake, which she'd barely touched. "Are you gonna eat that or stare at it?"

Laughing, Lena slid her plate across the table. *"Buon appetito."*

Chapter Five

Lena's cell phone rang as she stepped through the front door of her downtown Chicago condo. She dug the phone out of her handbag and answered, "Hello?"

"Hello, there," Zandra Kennedy's smooth, friendly voice greeted her. "Did I catch you at a bad time?"

"Not at all. I just got back from visiting my grandfather."

"How's he doing?"

"He's doing great," Lena replied, setting her handbag on the foyer table and stepping out of her stiletto boots. "When I left, he and his friend Abraham were about to play chess. I warned the staff to be on standby in case they get into one of their blood-pressure-raising arguments."

Zandra chuckled. "Isn't Abraham the feisty old Jewish guy who always begs you to sing 'Stormy Weather,' then critiques your performance by pointing out which notes you should hold longer to sound more like Lena Horne?"

Lena laughed. "That's him."

Thanks to her grandfather, she'd been named after the late, legendary songstress and had grown up listening to her music and watching her films. When she was a little girl, she'd enjoyed donning a wig and regaling her grandparents with her off-key but heartfelt rendition of "Stormy Weather." Though her singing had improved over the years, she now limited her "performances" to the annual holiday party at the retirement home, where most of the attendees wore hearing aids anyway.

"I'm glad your grandfather's doing well," Zandra said warmly. "I know how much you worry about him."

Lena smiled. "No more than he worries about me."

As she stepped down into the living room, her feet sank into plush carpeting. Carpeted floors had been a requirement when she'd first begun her apartment search after moving to Chicago. Though she appreciated her condo's spacious rooms, high ceilings and scenic view of the downtown skyline, she couldn't have survived her first Chicago winter without carpeted floors, as well as a fireplace and heated parking.

"So," Zandra said, getting to the reason for her call, "how'd things go with Roderick last night?"

Lena gulped hard, dropping weakly onto the sofa. She'd hoped to put off talking to Zandra for as long as possible. But she should have known better. Zandra had been unusually excited when she'd contacted Lena about going out with Roderick. She'd been so eager to reach Lena that she'd even broken protocol by calling her at work after leaving two messages on her cell phone. Lena had chalked up Zandra's urgent behavior to Roderick's billionaire status, though he certainly wasn't the agency's first billionaire client, nor would he be the last.

"Lena?" Zandra prompted. "Are you still there?"

"Yes, I'm here," Lena said, striving for a normal tone. "Things went well last night."

"Really?"

"Really. We, uh, had a great time."

"That's wonderful!" Zandra exclaimed. "I knew you and Roderick would hit it off!"

You don't know the half of it, Lena thought with a grimace.

"I told him you'd be perfect for him," Zandra crowed.

"Yeah, he may have mentioned that."

"Clearly I was right." Zandra sounded way too pleased with herself.

Lena swallowed. If she weren't such a damn coward, she'd tell Zandra the truth about what she and Roderick had done. After all, she'd violated the agency's policy—again—by having sex with him. Her lack of self-control could cost Zandra her business, her reputation—hell, her freedom—if the agency ever came under investigation for prostitution. She owed Zandra the truth, no matter the repercussions.

Plucking a speck of lint off her jeans, Lena asked very casually, "So, um, you haven't spoken to Roderick?"

"Not yet. He left a message for me this morning, said he was on his way to Japan on business but he'd be in touch soon."

"Oh." Lena's stomach knotted. She wondered if Roderick would complain to Zandra about her refusal to see him again. But once Zandra learned what had happened between them, she'd understand why Lena had taken that stance.

"I assume he's going to Japan to close the deal with Ichiro Kawamoto, which means things must have gone even better than I expected last night." Zandra chuckled with satisfaction. "He owes me *big-time*."

Lena smiled weakly. "How well do you know Roderick?"

There was a pregnant pause. "We know each other pretty well."

Lena felt a sudden stab of jealousy at the realization that Zandra and Roderick may have been lovers. And why not? Zandra was a smart, gorgeous woman who epitomized confidence, sensuality and glamour. Lena had watched her work a room, batting her long eyelashes and flashing a sultry smile that reduced grown men to drooling adolescents. Many of her clients had initially contacted the agency hoping to score a date with *her*.

"It's not like that," Zandra said wryly.

"What?" Lena pretended not to know what she was talking about.

"Roderick and I have known each other for over twenty years. We grew up together on the South Side, went to the same schools, hung out at the same places. But we've never been more than just friends."

Lena frowned. "So you've never—"

"Fucked him?" Zandra sighed. "Can't say I've ever had the pleasure."

"Oh." Lena didn't know whether to be relieved or baffled.

Zandra chuckled dryly. "Now you're probably wondering what the hell's wrong with me. Believe me, I'm not blind or comatose. I know how unbelievably hot Roderick is. I can't tell you how many times I've been approached by friends and relatives who wanted me to fix them up with him. And they've always wondered the same thing about me and Roderick. It's hard for them to believe that we've never so much as kissed, but it's true. We've always been more like brother and sister than anything else. I cherish his friendship, and I'd never do anything to jeopardize it."

Lena smiled. "He's very lucky to have you in his life."

"That's what I keep telling him." Zandra laughed.

Lena couldn't imagine having a platonic relationship with a man like Roderick Brand. Every time he just glanced her way, she'd want to get sweaty and naked. But if Zandra claimed that they were just friends, she'd have to take her word for it. Not that it really mattered. Roderick was nothing more to Lena than a one-night stand. Sure, the sex had been phenomenal. Out of this world. But that's all it had been. Sex. Exhilarating but meaningless sex.

Or so she kept telling herself.

"When Roderick mentioned a party he was throwing for Ichiro Kawamoto," Zandra explained, "I suggested that he hire one of my escorts to be his date for the evening. He looked at me like I'd started speaking in tongues. The idea of paying for a companion was a foreign concept to him."

"No surprise there," Lena muttered. Roderick probably couldn't take two steps without tripping over females trying to lure him into bed. Women would pay *him* to take them out on a date.

Zandra continued, "I told him that none of the women he normally dates would impress Ichiro Kawamoto the way one of my girls would—specifically, you. He was still skeptical, so I started telling him about you. I could tell he was impressed by your educational background; your fluency in Japanese sealed the deal for him. When he asked to see your photo, I refused to show it to him. I knew you'd knock his socks off, so I just told him to trust me. I'm so glad he did."

Speak for yourself, Lena thought darkly.

"So," Zandra said, drawing out the word, "are you going to see him again?"

Lena swallowed hard. "No."

"No?" Zandra sounded surprised.

"No. I'm not."

In the ensuing silence, Lena could hear Zandra's unspoken questions, could hear the wheels turning in her mind. She was speculating about whether Lena had slept with Roderick, but she was reluctant to come right out and ask. Probably because she didn't want to know.

"Are you sure you don't want to see him again?" she gently probed. "If he asks for—"

Lena closed her eyes. "I can't."

"Oh." A lengthy pause. "I see."

Lena waited tensely.

Zandra heaved a deep, frustrated breath. "Damn it, Lena."

Guilt assailed her at once. "I'm so sorry, Zandra. I don't know what the hell I was thinking."

"You obviously weren't," Zandra muttered.

Lena didn't argue. She couldn't.

"I don't have to tell you what a bad position you're putting me in," Zandra continued. "The agency means everything to me. I can't afford to lose it over some sex scandal."

"I know." Lena felt like shit for betraying Zandra's trust. Her guilt was compounded by the fact that Zandra was the one who'd come to her rescue three years ago when she'd needed extra money to put her grandfather in a retirement home.

They'd met at a social function hosted by the national chapter of their sorority. After explaining that she owned and operated an upscale escort agency, Zandra had asked Lena whether she'd ever considered working as a paid companion.

"Can't say that I have," Lena had replied.

"You should," Zandra told her. "With your looks, poise and level of education, wealthy men would pay top dollar for the pleasure of your company. I can guarantee that you'd make a killing if you worked for me."

If the conversation had occurred at any other time, Lena wouldn't have given Zandra's proposition a second thought. But finding another source of income had been weighing on her mind lately. So she was undeniably intrigued by the idea of "making a killing" in *any* capacity.

Sensing her receptiveness, Zandra passed her a glossy business card. "Give me a call. I'd love to have you on board."

Lena did call her. And true to Zandra's word, she *did* make a killing as one of the agency's top escorts. Working for Zandra, she made more in one month than she earned as a grant writer for an entire year. Although she'd hate to forfeit the extra income, she wouldn't blame Zandra for considering her too much of a risk.

"Do you want me to quit the agency?" she asked quietly.

Zandra sighed in resignation. "Of course not. You're one of my most popular escorts. It wouldn't make business sense for me to let you go. Besides, maybe this is *my* fault. I'm the one who set you up with Roderick, knowing how irresistible he is to women."

"No," Lena argued, "that's a cop-out. It's not *your*

fault that I didn't use better judgment. I'm a professional. I'm supposed to know better."

Again Zandra sighed. "Well, it's not as if you'd be the first of my escorts to violate the no-sex policy. One girl, in particular, made a regular habit of sleeping with clients until I was forced to show her the door. I hated having to lose her, but she'd been warned several times. So I had no other choice."

Lena gulped. "I'll consider myself forewarned."

"Good," Zandra grumbled. "But with the holiday season approaching, I really can't afford to get rid of you anyway."

Lena smiled ruefully. "Good, 'cause I need the money. Not just for Poppa, but Morgan's been hinting that she wants new bedroom furniture for Christmas."

"I keep forgetting that you have more than one dependent," Zandra said dryly.

Lena chuckled. Taking care of Morgan was second nature to her, something she'd been doing since they were children. She felt responsible for her younger sister, who'd only been a baby when their mother died. Now, as an underpaid public relations specialist, Morgan earned just enough to cover her rent, utilities and the credit card debt she'd incurred as a result of being a shopaholic. Which was why she was unable to help pay for their grandfather's care.

"Well, I'd better run," Zandra announced. "I've got company coming over for dinner, and I haven't even decided what to wear. Enjoy the rest of your weekend, Lena."

"You, too."

After hanging up the phone, Lena got up and padded to the wall of windows that overlooked the Chicago skyline. The sun had disappeared, leaving behind an overcast day that matched her mood.

She'd made a huge mistake last night. There was no sugarcoating the truth. She'd fucked up—literally and figuratively. But it didn't have to be the end of the world. She'd been down this road before.

Shortly after she started working as an escort, she'd gone out with a wealthy real estate developer named Glenn Donahue. Glenn was handsome, smart and charming. He and Lena had hit it off right away. When he requested her company again, she'd gladly accepted. By the end of their third date, she was convinced that they shared a special connection. So when Glenn took her into his arms and kissed her, it felt right. One thing led to another, and they wound up in bed together. The sex was satisfying, so satisfying that she let herself be talked into spending the night.

But when she woke up the next morning, Glenn was already gone. On the nightstand she'd found a wad of cash and a note hastily scrawled on hotel stationery. Glenn had thanked her for a great time and told her to buy something nice for herself with the two-hundred-dollar tip he'd left her. To add insult to injury, he'd misspelled her name, using an *i* instead of an *e*.

Lena had never been so humiliated in her life. For a long time she'd just sat in bed clutching the covers to her chest, feeling utterly cheap and used. The next time she ran into Glenn, he was with another escort. He'd looked right through Lena, as if she'd been nothing more to him than a faceless prostitute.

As hurt as she was, Lena knew she had only herself to blame for foolishly mistaking sexual attraction for something deeper. She was so afraid of repeating the same mistake with another client that she'd seriously considered getting out of the escort business. When she told Zandra what had happened, Zandra was disappointed but still managed to be sympathetic and supportive. She'd counseled Lena to take some time off and clear her head before she made up her mind about leaving the agency. Ultimately, Lena's responsibility to her grandfather had taken precedence over everything else. So she'd remained an escort.

But after her humiliating experience with Glenn, she'd vowed never to become sexually involved with another client. For three years, she'd had no trouble keeping that vow.

And then along came Roderick Brand.

He hadn't needed three dates to seduce her. Three hours into their evening, he was finger-fucking her. Before the night was over, they were screwing like their lives depended on it.

As the scorching images tumbled through Lena's mind, her cheeks burned with shame. Closing her eyes, she leaned her forehead against the cool windowpane and muttered a curse.

Yeah, she'd made a big mistake. She'd let her libido override the painful but valuable lesson she'd learned three years ago. She should have known better. She should have been stronger.

But she couldn't dwell on it forever. She had to move on, or she'd drive herself crazy. Just as she'd survived the episode with Glenn, she would survive this one.

And the sooner she forgot about Roderick Brand, the better off she'd be.

Chapter Six

A week later, Lena was in her office working on a report when the department secretary poked her head through the open doorway. "You're wanted in the conference room."

"By whom?" Lena asked, without glancing up from her computer.

"Ethan."

Lena stopped typing. Ethan O'Doherty was the director of foundation and corporate relations. In other words, he was her boss.

"Tell him I'll be right there," she told the secretary.

Before leaving the office she saved her file, then grabbed a pen and a notepad. As she headed down the corridor, she passed a quick hand over her hair and smoothed down her black pencil skirt to make sure she looked presentable.

Reaching the conference room, she strode purposefully through the door.

And pulled up short.

There, seated at the conference table as though he had every right, was Roderick Brand.

Lena's heart slammed against her chest.

He was conversing with Ethan, but he glanced up when she entered the room. Their gazes caught and held, the shared voltage between them nearly knocking Lena off her feet.

"Ah, here she is now," Ethan announced, rising to greet her. Roderick followed more slowly. "Thanks for joining us, Lena. I'd like to introduce you to Roderick Brand, president and CEO of Brand International Corp."

Recovering her composure, Lena plastered on her best professional smile and stepped forward, hand extended. "Mr. Brand."

"Miss Morrison."

They exchanged a brief, impersonal handshake. But there was a glint in Roderick's eyes that brought a hot flush to Lena's skin. Or maybe his touch was to blame.

What was he doing there? she wondered frantically. How had he uncovered her real identity? Where she worked? Didn't he realize that she could lose her job if anyone at the college found out about her secret night life?

Ethan volunteered, "Lena, I was just explaining to Mr. Brand that you're responsible for developing, writing and submitting all of the college's grant proposals. He was very impressed with the one you recently submitted on behalf of our performing arts center."

"So impressed, in fact, that I wanted to meet you

in person to discuss the proposal," Roderick added smoothly.

"I don't understand." Lena was proud of the fact that her voice didn't come out in a croak. "I don't recall submitting anything to your company."

"You didn't." A smile lurked in one corner of Roderick's mouth.

Lena grew even more agitated.

"Why don't we all sit down?" Ethan suggested.

Lena sat in a chair across from Roderick while Ethan reclaimed his seat at the head of the table. He was grinning like a kid who'd received an early Christmas present. A moment later, Lena discovered why.

"Before you arrived, Lena, Mr. Brand was telling me about his company's recent acquisition of Midwest Arts Foundation."

"Really?" Stunned, Lena stared at Roderick. This time there was no mistaking the wicked gleam in his eyes. "I didn't even realize that the foundation was up for sale."

"It wasn't," Roderick drawled, leaning back comfortably in his chair. He wore a designer suit, a beautiful dress shirt and an expensive watch. The cut of the dark suit accentuated his broad shoulders and powerful build. Lena wondered if it was possible for him to be even yummier than she remembered.

Swallowing hard, she forced her mind back to the matter at hand. "So even though the foundation wasn't up for sale, you bought it anyway?"

Roderick smiled slowly. "I made them an offer they couldn't refuse."

Ethan laughed heartily. Lena could muster only a tepid smile. Though she knew she was pushing her luck, she couldn't resist pointing out, "I thought Brand

International Corp was an energy conglomerate. When did you start buying charitable foundations?"

Roderick looked amused. "I'm always interested in acquiring good companies and expanding into new markets. I'm sure you realize that Brand International Corp already controls businesses as diverse as oil refineries and software providers."

Of course she realized. She'd thoroughly researched his billion-dollar empire in preparation for their date, and he knew that. But *she* knew that there was nothing coincidental about his "recent" purchase of Midwest Arts Foundation, one of the corporations she'd solicited for funds. He'd done it for one reason and one reason only: to get Lena in his clutches.

Dismayed by the accusatory tone of her questions, Ethan quickly intervened, "The bottom line, Lena, is that Mr. Brand is in a position to reward us the performing arts grant. Isn't that wonderful?"

"Of course," Lena said with another forced smile.

"Based on the needs outlined in your proposal," Roderick told her, "I'm prepared to approve an additional five hundred thousand."

Lena gasped. Ethan beamed ecstatically, all but jumping onto the table and doing the Riverdance.

As Lena gaped at Roderick, his eyes glinted wickedly. He had her over a barrel, and he knew it.

Bad metaphor, she immediately thought as her mind conjured an image of him literally bending her over a barrel and having his way with her.

"However," he continued, looking appropriately apologetic, "I met with my funding team yesterday, and they raised a few concerns that weren't addressed in the proposal. I'm afraid you'd have to make some revisions before I could authorize the release of funds."

"Of course," Ethan hastened to assure him before Lena could open her mouth. "We appreciate the opportunity you're giving us to revise the proposal. Lena's going to make it her top priority."

"Good." Roderick met her gaze, a smile lingering on his lips. "If you're free for lunch, I thought we could go over the suggested revisions."

"Today?" Lena shook her head, panicking. "I can't, unfortunately. I have back-to-back meetings—"

Ethan shot her a look that questioned her sanity. "I'm sure we can rearrange your schedule to accommodate Mr. Brand. Especially after he took time out of his busy schedule to pay us a personal visit."

"Of course," Lena muttered. She knew Roderick was enjoying every second of this, damn him.

Ethan said decisively, "I'll have Carmen move things around on your calendar this afternoon so you can have lunch with Mr. Brand."

"Great." Lena smiled at Roderick through clenched teeth. "I'll get my purse."

She didn't say a word until they were seated inside his car—a sleek, luxurious Maybach with an engine that purred as they pulled away from the picturesque campus.

Rounding on Roderick, she demanded furiously, "How the hell did you find me?"

He sent her a lazy glance. "Did you think I wouldn't?"

"I thought I made it clear that I didn't *want* you to." Her eyes narrowed suspiciously. "Did Zandra—"

"No. She didn't tell me anything." His lips twisted wryly. "She's immune to bribes."

"You tried to bribe her?"

"I would have, but I didn't have to."

"Then how…?" Lena trailed off as a memory surfaced from that night. The chauffeur had called her by her last name after the near-collision with another car. "The new guy. Damn it."

Roderick chuckled softly. "Having that piece of information about you helped me track down the rest."

Lena scowled at him. "What is it with you? What part of 'I can't see you again' did you not understand?"

Ignoring the question, he asked idly, "Do you have a taste for anything in particular?"

"No," she snapped in exasperation. "I don't care where we eat. I shouldn't even be going anywhere with you! Do you have any idea what could happen if my colleagues find out that I'm an escort?"

"Don't worry," Roderick murmured. "Your secret's safe with me."

Lena crossed her arms and glared through the windshield, too incensed to appreciate the vivid splashes of yellow, orange and red that transformed the tree-lined landscape into a Thomas Kinkade painting.

"I hope you're not leaving Evanston," she grumbled. "I only have one hour for lunch."

Roderick slanted her an amused glance. "I seriously doubt your boss is gonna be watching the clock," he said dryly. "He was more than eager to rearrange your schedule to accommodate me."

"Tell me about it," Lena grumbled. "If you'd sweetened the pot with another half a mil, he might have driven us to the nearest hotel and slipped us a credit card. And I'm pretty sure *you* wouldn't have objected."

"Hell, no." Roderick's wolfish grin made her toes curl inside her kitten-heel pumps.

She crossed her legs and watched his eyes follow the hem of her skirt as it rose to tease him with a glimpse of her smooth bare thighs. His gaze lingered long enough to send heat sizzling through her veins, burning a path to her groin. All of a sudden, checking into a hotel room didn't sound like such a bad idea.

She was more than relieved when Roderick's cell phone rang. He reached inside his breast pocket and pulled out the sleek BlackBerry, then gave her an apologetic look. "I'm sorry, I have to take this. It's the office."

She waved a hand. "Go ahead. I don't mind."

She stared out the window as he spoke into the phone, his deep, dark voice pouring over her like melted honey. He was by far the sexiest, most compelling man she'd ever encountered in her life. She wished they'd met under different circumstances, or never met at all. He made her want things she shouldn't want. Things she couldn't have.

When she realized that they'd left Evanston, she shot a dirty look at Roderick, who merely grinned.

He drove into downtown Chicago, maneuvering through midday traffic with the skilled ease of a native. Their destination was an upscale restaurant that catered to an exclusive clientele, the kind of place that required reservations a month in advance.

As the car glided to a stop under the canopied entrance, a valet opened Lena's door and helped her out while another retrieved the keys from Roderick. The maître d' waiting near the front entrance greeted Roderick by name, bowed gracefully to Lena and escorted them through the busy restaurant to an opulent private dining room.

They were seated at a table for two near a cozy fireplace. The intimate setting made Lena feel like they were on a date, which she suspected had been Roderick's intent.

Once the waiter had taken their orders and departed, she raised a brow at Roderick. "You're obviously a regular here, but how did you get this room—especially during the lunch rush—without a reservation?"

His eyes met hers. "I had a reservation."

"What, a standing reservation or—" As comprehension dawned, her eyes widened with angry indignation. "Mighty presumptuous, aren't we? How the hell did you know I'd agree to have lunch with you?"

His lips quirked into a half smile. "You're here, aren't you?"

Heat stung her face. "I didn't have much of a choice," she fired back. "You made sure of that."

They were interrupted when the waiter materialized with their drinks and appetizers. Lena ignored her oyster bisque and went straight for the wine, hoping it would help calm her nerves.

Deep down, she acknowledged what an incredibly enviable position she was in. What woman in her right mind wouldn't love to be pursued by a virile, gorgeous, wealthy man—a man so determined to have her that he'd bought a company, for God's sake? Lena knew she should feel flattered to be courted by Roderick. Under normal circumstances she *would* have been flattered. But there was nothing "normal" about this situation. Not even close.

"Easy," Roderick murmured, watching with an

amused expression as she gulped down her wine. "I still have to return you to work, remember?"

"I can hold my liquor." She gave him a sardonic look. "Or are you worried that I might embarrass you in this nice restaurant?"

He chuckled. "I don't get embarrassed very easily."

"No?" Lena was perversely tempted to find out what would happen if she slurped her soup, chewed with her mouth open, belched loudly *and* got stumbling drunk. Would Roderick be so repulsed that he wouldn't want her anymore? Could she get rid of him that easily?

As if he'd read her mind, Roderick grinned slowly. "Nothing you could say or do would embarrass me—or turn me off."

"Damn," Lena muttered darkly, and he laughed.

After sampling her bisque, she asked, "So, what are these revisions you wanted to discuss with me?"

Roderick picked up his glass and took a languid sip of Bordeaux. "There weren't any."

Lena blinked at him, convinced she'd heard wrong. "Excuse me?"

"There were no revisions to your proposal. I just made that up to get you alone."

Incredulous, Lena shook her head at him. "I don't believe this. Did you even *read* my proposal?"

"I did. It was excellent. Very comprehensive and well written. I had no follow-up questions or suggestions for improvement."

"What about your funding team?" Her eyes narrowed suspiciously. "Do you even *have* a funding team?"

"I do now." His mouth twitched. "But I haven't had a chance to meet with them yet."

"Are you kidding me?" Torn between exasperation,

disbelief and anger, Lena glared at him. "Have you lost your mind?"

He grinned unabashedly. "Not at all."

"I beg to differ. First you buy a foundation that was established to give away money, when you're in the business of *making* money. Then you show up at my workplace to personally offer the grant funds, but *only* on the condition that I make revisions—revisions that you don't really want! Doesn't any of that strike you as crazy?"

"Not crazy," Roderick countered silkily. "Determined."

Lena's stomach clenched, and a flush stole over her body. She was spared from responding when the waiter returned with their meals. She waited until he'd settled their plates on the table, topped off their wine, draped a linen napkin across her lap and left the room before she returned her attention to Roderick.

"What do you want?" she asked tightly.

"I think you already know what I want." A hot, possessive gleam filled his eyes. "I want you."

A shiver raced down Lena's spine, and her nipples puckered against the silk of her bra. She swallowed with difficulty. "Look, I don't know what you have in mind, but—"

"Let's eat first," Roderick suggested smoothly. "Then we can talk."

Eat? How could he possibly expect her to eat at a time like this? Food was the absolute last thing on her mind. But she'd ordered the most expensive entrée on the lunch menu—out of pure spite—so it'd be a shame to let it go to waste.

Drawing a deep, calming breath, she picked up her fork and cut into her braised lobster. As the smoky, succulent flavor burst in her mouth, she couldn't help sighing a little.

"Good?" Roderick murmured.

"Very." She nodded at his steak. "Yours?"

"Top-notch."

They ate in silence for a few minutes. When Lena glanced up again, she found Roderick watching her thoughtfully.

"What made you leave Los Angeles?" he asked curiously.

She gave him a mocking look. "You mean you didn't learn everything there is to know about me when you conducted your background check?"

He smiled faintly. "Sweetheart, I barely even scratched the surface."

That disarmed her. She hesitated, then answered, "I grew up in L.A., but I wanted a change of scenery. I moved to Chicago after landing a job at the college."

Roderick nodded slowly. "Do you ever miss home?"

"Sometimes." She smiled wryly. "Mostly during the winter."

He chuckled. "Our winters take some getting used to."

"That's what people keep telling me."

"They're right." His eyes glinted with mischief. "You just have to find someone to keep you warm during those cold, windy nights."

Lena's stomach quivered. "I'm sure *you* have no problem finding volunteers."

"Nor should you." His voice deepened seductively. "I'm more than ready, willing and able to keep you warm, Lena. And not just during the wintertime."

She flushed all over, heat gathering beneath her

clothes, inside her pumps, between her thighs. She glanced toward the fireplace, half wondering if she should summon the waiter to put out the flames before she overheated.

Resisting the urge to fan herself, she reached for her glass and took a long sip of wine.

Roderick watched her, his eyes dancing with amusement. He enjoyed rattling her, damn him. To prove her point, he announced casually, "We've been invited to Japan."

Lena nearly choked on her wine. Coughing, she gaped at him. *"We?"* she croaked.

"Yeah. You and me. When I was in Japan last week, I had dinner with Ichiro Kawamoto and his wife. They asked about you, told me how much they'd enjoyed meeting you at the party. They made me promise to bring you during my next trip to Japan. They even invited us to stay at their home in Tokyo."

Lena arched a brow at him. "Do they know that I was your paid escort, not your girlfriend?"

"Kawamoto figured out our arrangement," Roderick admitted.

"Really? How?"

"He sensed a certain restraint between us. Even though we were clearly attracted to each other, he could tell that we were, ah, holding back."

Lena snorted derisively. "Some holding back. We couldn't keep our hands off each other."

Roderick smiled a little. "He also said that you referred to me as 'Mr. Brand' throughout your conversation with him."

"Oh." Lena grinned wryly. "Yeah, I suppose that *would* be a dead giveaway."

Roderick chuckled. "He came right out and asked me

the nature of our relationship, so I told him the truth. He called you my beautiful American geisha."

"He did?" Lena smiled. "Well, geisha were once celebrated in Japanese culture, so I guess I'll take that as a compliment."

"You should. He definitely meant it as one." Roderick held her gaze. "So will you go with me?"

"Where?"

"To Japan."

She stared at him. "You were serious about that?"

"Very serious."

She frowned. "Roderick—"

"I've already sent my transition team over there to evaluate Kawamoto's company and begin the restructuring process. I'll be joining them in a few weeks to check their progress. I'd like you to go with me."

Even before he'd finished speaking, Lena was shaking her head emphatically. "I can't, Roderick. It's out of the question."

"Why?"

"*Why?*" she echoed in disbelief. "Do you even have to ask? First of all, we're not a couple. And even if we were, it'd be hard for me to just drop everything and go flying halfway around the world with you. I have responsibilities. I have a job. Speaking of which," she said, glancing pointedly at her watch, "I should really be getting back to the office. I've been gone over an hour."

Roderick gave her a look of exaggerated patience. "Didn't we already establish that your boss won't care how long you're gone?"

"Well, I care. I have a lot of work to do."

He smiled indolently. "Securing this grant is supposed to be your top priority," he reminded her.

He had her there. "Fine," Lena conceded, heaving a resigned breath. "Name your terms."

"You're ready to negotiate?"

"Yes." Even as the word left her mouth, her nerves tightened. Why did she have a feeling that negotiating with Roderick Brand would be as dangerous as negotiating with the devil?

"All right. Here are my terms." He leaned forward in his chair and pinned her with his dark, penetrating gaze. "I'll approve the grant on one condition."

"What is it?" Lena's voice was barely above a whisper.

"You have to agree to spend the next three weeks as my personal companion."

His meaning didn't register at first. "Your... companion?"

"Yeah." He smiled, slow and sinfully wicked. "To put it bluntly, Lena, I'm asking you to be my sexual companion—one who will fulfill my every need."

Chapter Seven

As Roderick's words sank in, fury erupted in Lena's chest. Fury combined with a nauseating sense of déjà vu.

With as much dignity as she could muster, she rose from her chair and stared down at Roderick with a look of icy disdain. "I think you'd better take me back to work now."

He shook his head. "We're not finished yet."

"Oh, yes, we are!" As she spun away from the table his hand shot out, seizing her wrist.

"Let go of me," she hissed furiously. She tried to yank her arm free, but his grip was too strong.

"Wait," he said, jumping to his feet. "Just hear me out."

"I don't need to! You're out of your damn mind!"

The waiter appeared, took one look at them and beat a hasty retreat, closing the curtained doors behind him.

Roderick rounded the table and pulled Lena roughly into his arms. She struggled against him, but she might as well have been wrestling an eight-hundred-pound Siberian tiger. Even in her anger she was no match for Roderick's strength or his fierce, focused determination.

"Listen to me," he growled, cradling her face between his big hands. "Let me explain—"

"I'm not a damn prostitute!" Lena raged.

"I know, sweetheart. I'm sorry, I wasn't trying to offend you. I just—*hell*." He lowered his head and fastened his mouth to hers, smothering her startled gasp.

When she put her fists between them his arms went around her, holding her so tightly she couldn't escape. His warm, delicious taste invaded her senses as his tongue sank into her mouth. Her entire body shook, an explosive combination of anger, adrenaline and arousal pounding through her veins. She'd expected the kiss to be urgent and bruising. But Roderick kissed her with a slow, deep hunger that was just as powerful, just as devastating. Even as her mind rebelled, she felt herself weakening against him, drowning in sensation and need.

She almost whimpered when he broke the kiss, dragging his mouth along her throat. "I can't stop thinking about you," he muttered raggedly, his hot breath on her skin sending jolts of pleasure to her groin. "Ever since that night, you've been on my mind twenty-four seven. I don't blame you for thinking I'm crazy. The thought's crossed my mind several times over the past week. I've never wanted another woman as badly as I want you, Lena. I'll do anything—*anything*—to have you again."

Oh, God. Lena closed her eyes and inhaled deeply, struggling to get her choppy breathing under control. No man had ever talked to her this way before. No man had ever wanted her with this kind of raw, primal intensity that left her reeling with frustration and desire.

"Say yes," he coaxed huskily. His lips reclaimed hers, parting them so that their breath mingled hotly. "Say yes, Lena."

Reaching deep, Lena summoned her last ounce of willpower and wrenched her mouth away from his. "No. *No.*"

He swore under his breath, then reluctantly released her and stepped back. He looked dangerously aroused, and frustrated as hell.

"I'm not for sale, Roderick." Lena fought to sound resolute when her insides were quaking uncontrollably. "You can't just acquire me the way you acquired Midwest Arts Foundation."

He blew out a ragged breath. "I know that."

"Do you?" she challenged. "You just tried to bribe me for sex in exchange for a monetary donation. Obviously you *do* think I'm for sale."

He scowled. "I don't, damn it."

"No? Then what do you call it?"

"I call it proposing an arrangement that'd be incredibly beneficial to both of us. Your college gets the funds it desperately needs, and I get—"

"A sexual companion to be at your beck and call," Lena said caustically.

He paused, his mouth quirking at the corners. "Maybe I could have phrased it differently."

"Why?" she taunted. "A sex slave is essentially what you want, isn't it? Someone to cater to your every sexual whim, to give you blow jobs on demand and call you master at the crack of a whip."

Roderick smiled lazily. "It doesn't have to be that one-sided."

"Yeah, right."

"I'm serious." His eyes darkened with illicit promise. "Believe me, Lena, I have every intention of giving as much pleasure as I receive."

Her nipples tightened and heat swelled between her legs at the memory of just how much "pleasure" he'd given her the night of the party. The thought of being his sex slave was so damned tempting, it was all she could do not to pounce on him and rip his custom-made suit from his sexy body.

Keeping her voice and expression neutral, she said, "Sorry. I'm not interested."

"The hell you aren't," Roderick growled. "You sure as hell seemed 'interested' when I kissed you a moment ago. If I'd lifted your skirt and spread you out on that table you wouldn't have uttered a word of protest. Deny it all you want, Lena, but I know damn well you want me as much as I want you. So why are we standing here arguing when all we both want is to fuck each other's brains out?"

Lena congratulated herself for not flinching at his deliberate crudeness. "You have a real problem taking no for an answer," she said coldly.

His expression darkened. "Damn it, Lena, what are you so afraid of? It's not as if we haven't already made love. We have, and it was—"

"A mistake," she said sharply. "One that I don't intend to repeat."

He regarded her in silence for several long, tense moments. Lena held her ground, staunchly resisting the urge to squirm or adjust her blouse, which suddenly felt too tight.

When her nerves were stretched to the breaking point, Roderick pulled out his cell phone and pressed a button. "Send the car," he instructed someone on the other end.

He disconnected and shoved the phone back into his breast pocket. Without sparing Lena another glance, he rounded the table, picked up his glass and drained the rest of his wine.

As if on cue, the waiter returned to clear away their dishes and settle the bill. He made a point of avoiding eye contact with Lena, even when she asked him for directions to the restroom. She wondered how much he'd overheard of her confrontation with Roderick. The convenient timing of his arrival made her suspect that he'd been eavesdropping at the door.

When she and Roderick emerged from the restaurant minutes later, a gleaming Rolls Royce was idling at the curb.

"My driver's taking you back to work," Roderick told her.

"Why?"

A small, crooked smile curved his lips. "I don't trust myself to be alone with you anymore."

Lena blushed.

He walked her to the car and helped her into the luxurious backseat. Before he could shut the door, she blurted, "What am I supposed to tell Ethan about the grant?"

"That's up to you," Roderick said mildly.

She bristled with anger. "I hope you realize how wrong you are for waltzing into my workplace, meeting with my boss and getting his hopes up about money that came with strings attached."

"I regret that," Roderick murmured. "I had really hoped we could work something out. But you made your choice, Lena, and I have to respect that. I guess it's a good thing you submitted the proposal to other companies, huh?"

When she just glared at him, he grinned. He knew as well as she did that no other company would offer an additional five hundred thousand, as he'd done. Given the economy, she'd be lucky to get any takers at all.

"If you change your mind about my offer," Roderick drawled, passing her a business card, "give me a call."

Lena scowled. "When hell freezes over."

Chuckling softly, he glanced up at the drab gray sky. "Speaking of freezing, it's supposed to be a brutal winter this year. Even worse than usual. I hope you're prepared."

Remembering their earlier conversation about Chicago winters, Lena said coolly, "I've stocked up on electric blankets. But thanks for your concern."

Roderick gave her a slow, knowing smile. "When you've had enough self-deprivation, you know where to reach me."

Before Lena could respond, he closed the car door and stepped away from the curb. Holding her gaze through the window, he mouthed, *I'll be waiting.*

Chapter Eight

"How was your date last Friday?"

Reclining on a plush suede bench, Lena watched as her younger sister pulled on a knit jumper dress and smoothed the fabric over her slim thighs. "That looks really good on you," Lena remarked.

"Think so?" Standing in front of the dressing room's three-way mirror, twenty-five-year-old Morgan Morrison twirled around to get a better look at herself from all angles. A slight frown tugged at her full lips. "It doesn't make me look chunky?"

Lena chuckled dryly. "Considering that you're all of a size four, I don't think that's possible."

Morgan stuck her tongue out at her. "Not everyone can be a voluptuous bitch with D-cup titties and an apple-bottom ass that men drool over."

Lena laughed. "Don't hate. *You've* never had to worry

about your weight or had your food rationed for you at Thanksgiving dinners, so just hush."

Morgan grinned sheepishly, flashing dimples in a pretty, caramel-toned face. It was the first time she'd smiled since Lena had picked her up that morning to go shopping. Morgan had just returned from a public relations conference in Baltimore, where she'd apparently bumped heads with some of her coworkers. She'd called that morning to vent to Lena, who'd suggested lunch and a day of retail therapy along Chicago's Magnificent Mile.

"You didn't answer my question," Morgan said, her voice muffled as she tugged the dress up over her head.

Lena feigned ignorance. "What question?"

"I asked how your date went last Friday. You know, the one you were racing off to when I called you from my hotel room."

"You mean we haven't spoken since then?"

"No." Morgan's face emerged, her dark eyes narrowed. "And why do I get the feeling that you're stalling?"

"I'm not," Lena lied. "I just thought I'd already told you about it."

"Nope. You were rushing to get ready that night because you'd stayed late at work, so you promised to call me during the week to tell me how the date went. You never did."

"Oh. Well, I meant to." Another lie.

"So?" Morgan prompted, reaching for another garment on a hanger. "How'd it go?"

"Great. I really enjoyed myself."

"Yeah?"

"Yeah. It was…fun." Lena blushed, and was glad her sister's head had disappeared through the neck hole of the shirt she was trying on.

"Where was the party held?" Morgan asked.

"On his yacht."

"Champagne and caviar?"

"Of course."

"Did you see Oprah?"

Lena smiled. "Not this time."

Morgan sighed dramatically. "My big sister, companion to the rich and famous. I'm so jealous."

"That's funny," Lena said wryly. "You were singing a different tune when I first told you I was going to become an escort."

Morgan met her gaze in the mirror. "That was before you explained the agency's no-sex policy. I didn't want you selling your body just to keep Poppa in that fancy retirement home, and *he* wouldn't have stood for it either. But once you told me that you wouldn't be having sex with your clients, I was okay with it."

Lena suddenly became absorbed in an inspection of her Jimmy Choo suede ankle boots. She'd never told her sister about her experience with Glenn Donahue. Morgan had always looked up to Lena as a role model. She would have been disappointed to learn that Lena had slept with a client, violating not only the agency's policy but her own personal values as well. Needless to say, Lena had no intention of telling her sister about Roderick.

Morgan struck a pose in front of the mirror, modeling a leopard-print designer shirt. "What do you think?"

Lena wrinkled her nose. "Too loud."

Morgan laughed. "I agree. It looked better on the mannequin." As she began removing the rejected shirt, she asked, "So who was the lucky guy this time?"

"Lucky guy?"

"Your client. The one you just went out with."

"Oh." Lena dug out her cell phone, pretending to check for missed calls. "His name's Roderick Brand."

Morgan's eyes widened, and she spun around to gape at her sister. "You went out with *Roderick Brand?*"

"Yeah." Lena affected a nonchalant tone. "You've heard of him before?"

"*Hello?* He only happens to be one of the richest men in Chicago! Didn't you see him on that episode of *Oprah* last year that featured movers and shakers in the world of business and entertainment? Oprah couldn't stop gushing over Roderick because he's a hometown boy."

"I must have missed that show," Lena said dryly.

"I think you were out of town that week." Wearing only her bra and panties, Morgan hurried over and plopped down beside Lena on the bench. "So, dish. What was he like?"

Lena laughed. "Can't you talk and try on clothes at the same time? There's probably a long line of women waiting to use this dressing room."

"Let them wait," Morgan said, waving a dismissive hand. "As much money as we're about to spend in this store—"

Lena snorted. *"We?"*

"—I have every right to shop at my leisure. Besides, it's not as if this is the only dressing room. Now give me the scoop on Roderick Brand. Is he as sexy in person as he was on TV?"

"I didn't see him on TV," Lena reminded her.

"Girl, you know what I mean."

Lena chuckled. "Roderick is very sexy. Stop-your-heart sexy."

"Oh, man." Morgan groaned. "Does he smell good, too?"

Lena grinned. "Delicious."

Her sister squealed. Some women got turned on by great abs. A good-smelling man did it for Morgan every time.

She sighed deeply. "You're so lucky, Lena, going on a date with Roderick Brand."

"Sure." Lena smiled weakly. "Lucky me."

"So how'd the date end?" Morgan demanded excitedly. "Did he ask to see you again?"

Lena glanced toward the dressing room's closed door. "I really think you should finish trying on those outfits, Morg. You haven't even gone through half the pile you brought in here."

"In a minute. I want to hear more about your date with Roderick."

Lena swallowed. "You know," she evaded, "the agency's clients are wealthy, influential men who expect discretion from the escorts they hire. Technically I'm not even supposed to discuss who they are, let alone what happens on our dates."

"But I'm your sister," Morgan protested. "It's not as if I'm going to tell anyone."

"That's not the point. It's a matter of privacy."

Morgan huffed out an exasperated breath. "Fine. Keep your client-escort confidentiality." She paused. "But I must point out that this is the first time you've ever been so protective of a client."

"That's not true," Lena protested.

"Yes, it is."

"Well, maybe that's because this is the first time you've ever taken such an interest in one of my clients."

"Maybe." Morgan studied her, a speculative gleam in her eyes. "Or maybe you're hiding something."

Because Morgan was four years younger, it was easy for Lena to forget just how perceptive she could be. "I'm not hiding anything," she said with a straight face. "Roderick and I had a great time, but I'm not going to see him again."

Morgan frowned. "Why not? You have repeat customers all the time."

"Not this time." Before Morgan could press the issue, Lena playfully slapped her bare thigh. "Now get your ass up and finish trying on those damn clothes before I change my mind about footing the bill for this little shopping trip."

Laughing, Morgan jumped up and scrambled across the dressing room. But she wasn't quite ready to drop the subject of Roderick. As she shimmied into a designer skirt, she said offhandedly, "If Roderick stopped using the agency, he'd no longer be a client. Right?"

Lena hesitated. "That's right."

"Then you wouldn't have to worry about breaking any rules with him. You'd be free and clear to date him."

Lena frowned. "It's not that simple, Morg. Roderick Brand isn't the kind of man who'd be cool with having his girlfriend work as an escort."

"So quit." Morgan winked at her. "Let him be your sugar daddy."

"*Excuse* me?" Lena sputtered in disbelief. "Aren't you the one who's always preaching the importance of female empowerment and independence? Isn't that the main reason you broke up with your last boyfriend? Because he was pressuring you to move in with him and you weren't ready to give up your own space?"

Morgan sucked her teeth. "I broke up with him because he was an asshole. Trust me, if Roderick Brand had asked me to move in with him, my stuff would've been packed up and loaded onto a moving truck before he could say *Baby, please*."

Lena chuckled, shaking her head. "Girl, you're crazy."

Morgan snorted. "You're letting a gorgeous billionaire get away, and *I'm* the one who's crazy?"

Lena rose from the bench. "Let's go. We've been in here so long my butt's falling asleep."

Morgan sighed, reaching for her skinny jeans. "I don't think I'm in the mood for shopping anyway. Although I *did* see a cashmere coat I wanted to check out in Macy's. It's supposed to be a really bad winter."

"So I've heard," Lena grumbled darkly.

Chapter Nine

Over the following week, Lena made phone calls to the remaining organizations she'd solicited for funds. She offered to provide more information if necessary. She offered to travel to their offices and do presentations. She did everything but barter her firstborn child.

To keep her boss off her back, she assured him that she was working on the "revisions" Roderick had requested. Fortunately, Ethan took her at her word and didn't press her for details. Although she felt guilty for lying to him, she had no other choice. If she told him the truth about Roderick's outrageous ultimatum, she'd also have to explain how she'd met him—and that was out of the question.

But as the week wore on, the rejections began to arrive. The reasons given reverberated through Lena's mind like the sound of doors being slammed in her face, one right after another. *We're experiencing severe* *budget cuts...mandatory funding freeze until the economy stabilizes...limited resources due to corporate downsizing...*and so on and so forth.

By the time Lena heard from the last prospective donor on Friday, she was beyond dejected. She'd exhausted all her options and come up empty.

So there was only one thing left for her to do.

She had to swallow her pride and make a deal with the devil.

She had to give Roderick what he wanted: her.

Heat washed over her at the thought of spending the next three weeks as his lover. She would be at his complete mercy, his for the taking and commanding. She would be expected to satisfy his every sexual need and desire, no matter what he demanded of her.

Could she really agree to such an arrangement?

What other choice do you have?

"I don't," Lena muttered aloud to her empty office. The choice had been taken out of her hands the moment Roderick set his sights on having her. All that was left for her to do was surrender.

Surrender to the sexiest, most compelling man she'd ever met in her life.

Surrender to the most amazing lover she'd ever had.

Who are you kidding? she asked herself. *There are far worse fates than becoming Roderick Brand's sexual companion. Hell, most women would kill to trade places with you right now!*

With a sigh of resignation, Lena got up and closed the door to her office. After returning to her desk, she retrieved her cell phone and Roderick's business card from her handbag. Taking a deep breath to shore up her courage, she punched in the number to his private line.

He answered on the third ring, his deep voice spreading heat through her limbs. "Roderick Brand."

"You win," Lena said as calmly as her pounding heart would allow.

His soft chuckle drifted through the line. "I must have missed it."

"Missed what?"

"Hell freezing over."

"Very funny," Lena grumbled, chafing at the reminder of what she'd said to him after lunch that day. "You just couldn't resist, could you?"

"When it comes to you," he drawled, "I don't know the meaning of the word *resist*."

"So I've noticed." She dragged in a shaky breath. "So how do you want to do this? We need to discuss the details, establish some ground rules."

"I agree," he said silkily. "Are you still at work?"

"Yes."

"What time do you get off?"

"Four, but I usually don't leave until after five."

"I want to see you tonight." It wasn't a request, and Lena knew it.

She swallowed. Twice. "Tonight's fine."

"Good," he murmured. "I can't wait to see you again. It's been too damn long."

Her stomach bottomed out. "It's only been a week."

"Like I said, too damn long."

She closed her eyes, leaning weakly against her chair. "Roderick, I—"

"Leave now. I'll send my driver over to pick you up at five-thirty. That should give you enough time to get home and get ready for me."

The words echoed through her mind, seductive and dangerously alluring. *Get ready for me.*

"I'm heading into a meeting," he told her, "so I'll see you tonight."

"Wait." Her head was spinning. Everything was happening too fast.

"Yes?" Roderick prompted softly.

She licked her dry lips. "H-how do you know where I live?"

He laughed, the sound husky in her ear. "By the time our three weeks are up, I'm going to know everything about you, Lena. *Everything.*"

He ended the call, leaving her shaken and wondering what the hell she'd just gotten herself into.

Lena wasn't surprised that Roderick chose his yacht as the destination for their first rendezvous. The *Native Sun* was where it had all started, so for Lena, going back there was like returning to the scene of a crime. Admittedly, it was hard to think of crimes when confronted with the vision of Roderick's gleaming white yacht silhouetted against a spectacular sunset.

When she saw him sauntering down the ramp to meet her, her mind went blank and she forgot to breathe. He was devastatingly handsome in a black dress shirt, black slacks and black boots. Between the dark clothing, his cocky swagger and the backdrop of the massive ship, it was no wonder her mind conjured an image of a marauding pirate come to take her captive. Her heart began thumping as he neared her, and she wondered again if she could really go through with this secret arrangement.

"Lena." Just the way her name poured out of that deep, intoxicating voice sent her imagination into overdrive.

She strove for composure. "Hello, Roderick."

His slow, lazy gaze swept over her body, taking in her attire. A strapless sheath dress that skimmed the top of her knees and tall heels that accentuated her long, shapely legs.

The eyes that traveled back up to her face glittered with pure male appreciation. "You look beautiful," Roderick said huskily.

"Thank you. You didn't tell me where we were going, so I wasn't sure how to dress."

"You're perfect."

Her insides tingled with pleasure.

Glancing over her shoulder, Roderick nodded at his driver, who waited on the pier beside the Rolls Royce. "Thanks for delivering her safely, Ed."

The man tipped his dark head with a smile. "Enjoy your evening, boss. Miss Morrison."

"Good night, Ed." Lena smiled, fighting an irrational urge to beg the friendly driver to take her back home.

Roderick looked down at her. "Ready to go inside?"

Mentally she squared her shoulders to bolster her courage. "Lead the way."

A brush of electricity sparked along her veins as he tucked her hand under his arm and guided her down the ramp. They boarded the yacht and were greeted warmly by the captain, who looked spiffy in a nautical dress uniform. After assuring them that everything was on schedule, he strode off toward the wheelhouse at the top of the yacht.

"My chef's putting the final touches on dinner," Roderick told Lena. "In the meantime, I thought I'd give you the grand tour, since we didn't get around to it last time."

Lena's face heated at the memory of how they'd gotten sidetracked, and what had followed later that night. "A tour sounds good."

Keeping her arm securely tucked through his, Roderick escorted her to a double staircase at the stern, which led them up to the main deck.

The night of the party, Lena had been too distracted by her raging libido to fully appreciate the magnificence of Roderick's mega yacht. The *Native Sun* was a mansion on water, four stories of sheer luxury suitable for cruising around the world. In addition to the grand ballroom where the party had been held, the ship featured a spacious salon, a huge formal dining room, a bar on every level, a gym, an aquarium, an observation lounge, a private movie theater with an enormous plasma screen, a spa and sauna, and a pool with a retractable roof. Lena admired crystal chandeliers, gleaming onyx countertops and rich mahogany walls and floors offset by plush carpeting. The guest staterooms were large and elegantly furnished, complete with Jacuzzi bathrooms and private balconies. Each deck boasted high ceilings surrounded by huge picture windows that overlooked the water. There was a helicopter, as well as a remote-controlled vehicle below deck for guests who wanted to see the ocean floor.

Three years of hobnobbing with the rich had not immunized Lena from being awed by Roderick's luxurious yacht, which surpassed anything she'd ever seen.

"Wow," she breathed as they neared the end of the tour. "This is absolutely amazing, Roderick."

He inclined his head modestly. "I'm glad you like it."

She laughed. "What's not to like? It has everything. And I mean *everything*. Do you spend a lot of time on the yacht?"

"Not personally, no. I mostly use it for entertaining clients and chartering cruises for my family."

"You must have a big family."

He smiled. "Five siblings and a slew of nieces, nephews and cousins."

Lena gave him a knowing grin. "I bet they're all spoiled."

"Rotten. Every last one of 'em."

They shared a quiet chuckle.

Holding her gaze, Roderick reached out and trailed a finger down her cheek. Heat suffused her skin, and she found herself leaning into his touch as he pushed a tendril of hair away from her face and tucked it behind her ear.

"Are you ready for dinner now?" he murmured. "Or should I take you to the last stop on the tour?"

"What would that be?" Lena whispered.

"The master stateroom."

Her stomach quivered. There was no mistaking the seductive gleam in his eyes. He intended to have her before the night was over.

Lena gulped. "I think I'm ready for dinner," she said, hating the tremor in her voice.

Roderick smiled slowly. He'd heard it, too. "Dinner it is, then. We have a lot to discuss."

Chapter Ten

They dined by candlelight on the sky deck.

It was unbelievably romantic, with soft music playing in the background and a warm breeze blowing across the glistening waters of Lake Michigan. Instead of jumping right into negotiations regarding their arrangement, they broke the ice with small talk that gradually deepened into more personal subjects.

Relaxed by good food and wine, Lena found herself answering Roderick's questions about her childhood. She told him about growing up in south L.A. and being raised by her grandparents after losing her mother to breast cancer that was detected too late. When Roderick murmured his condolences, she said ruefully, "I guess the only consolation is that I was only four. Too young, really, to remember her. And my sister was just a baby."

"Morgan, right?"

"Right." Lena gave him a wry look. "Did I already mention her name, or did you uncover it during your background check?"

A faintly amused smile touched his mouth. "Both."

Lena just shook her head at him.

"So how did you talk your sister into following you to Chicago?" Roderick asked, raising his wineglass to his lips.

Lena chuckled softly. "It wasn't easy. Unlike me, Morgan wasn't necessarily looking for a change of scenery. She'd just graduated from college and landed a good job. She was about to move out of our grandparents' house and get her own place. And then our grandmother died, and we both became consumed with looking after our grandfather and making sure he was all right. Ultimately we agreed that he'd be better off with me in Chicago. Morgan stayed behind for a few months, but not having her family nearby was really hard on her. So she packed up and joined us, and the rest is history."

Roderick nodded, digesting her response. "How did your grandfather adjust to the move? It couldn't have been easy for him."

Lena grimaced. "No, it wasn't. He was still grieving, and trying to get acclimated to a new environment didn't help. The stress took a toll on his health."

She told Roderick about her grandfather's stroke, confessing the tremendous guilt she'd felt because she was on a business trip at the time. Three years later, she was still haunted by what could have happened if Morgan hadn't come home early that day and found their grandfather collapsed on the floor. The fear of not being there during the next emergency finally convinced

Lena to place him in an assisted-living facility, where he'd receive round-the-clock care and attention.

As Lena talked, Roderick listened and watched her with focused absorption, as if her words had the power to unlock the secrets of the universe. As an escort, she'd grown used to one-sided conversations where *she* asked most of the questions, stroked egos and served as a sounding board for her clients. It was nice to be with a man who seemed genuinely interested in her as a person, not just as arm candy.

Before she knew it three hours had passed. Moonlight reflected off the rippling surface of the lake. In the distance, the glittering Chicago skyline lit up the shore.

Lena sighed contentedly. "It's so beautiful up here on the sky deck. Perfect for stargazing."

"Sweetheart," Roderick drawled softly, "all I'm interested in gazing at is you."

She laughed, giving him a look. "Do you get far with lines like that?"

He chuckled. "You'd be surprised."

"Actually, I wouldn't. You could recite ads from the phone book and still make women swoon."

"Yeah? I'll have to try that sometime."

They shared teasing smiles across the table.

"Why aren't you married?" Lena blurted before she could stop herself.

His eyes danced with amusement in the candlelight. "Maybe I haven't found the right woman."

"Have you been looking?"

"Can't say that I have."

"Too busy conquering the world?"

He laughed. "You sound like my mother."

Lena grinned. "Does she hound you about getting married?"

"Only every other day." He smiled a little. "But I know she means well. She wants me to be happy."

"Meaning you aren't?"

"I don't know." A shadow fell over his eyes, and he shrugged one broad shoulder. "I don't give it much thought."

Lena didn't believe him, but before she could probe further, he turned the tables on her. "What about you, Lena? Are you happy?"

"We weren't talking about me," she countered smoothly.

He chuckled softly and glanced out at the star-speckled water.

As silence lapsed between them, Lena watched as his finger absently traced the rim of his wineglass. Her clit twitched at the memory of his fingers buried deep inside her, bringing her to a screaming orgasm.

She flushed as his dark gaze returned to hers. He pushed his glass aside, then reached across the small table and captured her hand in his. Her breath lodged in her throat and refused to slip past her lips. As his thumb stroked the top of her knuckles, currents of electricity raced up her arm and made her shiver.

"Cold?" he murmured.

She shook her head, though the temperature had probably dropped by a few degrees.

"I'm glad you're here, Lena," Roderick said huskily. "I've been looking forward to this night all week."

Her lips twisted sardonically. "So you knew I'd have to swallow my pride and accept your ultimatum."

"I didn't know," he corrected. "I *hoped*."

"Well, congratulations. You got your wish."

"Come now," he murmured, turning her hand over and rubbing slow, sensual circles into her palm. "This doesn't have to be an adversarial arrangement. In fact, I intend to make this experience very enjoyable for both of us."

Lena's pulse thudded. An erotic tingle snaked from her pelvis to her breasts, squeezing her nipples into taut points. "Name your terms," she whispered.

"For starters," he said silkily, "I want to see you every day for the next three weeks."

"Every day?"

"Every day."

"But I have other obligations," she protested. "I see clients at least twice a week!"

Roderick's expression hardened. "Not for the next three weeks you won't."

"*What?* You can't dictate—"

"Oh, yes, I can." Something dark and uncivilized flared in his eyes. "For the next three weeks you pretty much belong to me, Lena. Every day, and for as long as I want your company. That's nonnegotiable."

She withdrew her hand from his, bristling with anger and resentment. "You're interfering with my livelihood."

"Actually," he countered calmly, "I thought I was helping it. Your boss mentioned to me that you're up for a promotion. Securing this grant will make it a slam dunk. So don't sit there and pretend you're not getting something out of this arrangement. You wouldn't be here if you weren't."

Lena glared at him, wanting to slap the arrogant look off his face. Seething with fury, she leaned forward. "Let's get something straight right now," she said in a low, controlled voice. "You're giving that money to the college, *not* to me. You know damn well that I earn way more as an escort than I do as a grant writer. So don't pretend to misunderstand me when I say that you're interfering with my livelihood by costing me three weeks of work. Not to mention the money that Zandra will lose as a result of my absence."

Roderick leaned forward as well, his eyes glittering fiercely. "I had every intention of compensating Zandra for any lost revenue. As for you, I'll double whatever you would have earned during that time period. There. Problem solved."

They stared each other down, the air between them crackling with challenge and sexual tension.

Lena flashed a cold, narrow smile. "You sure do like to throw your money around, big spender."

"It's not about the damn money," Roderick growled, latent heat and frustration simmering in his gaze. "It's about me wanting you so bad I can't see or think straight. It's about me having you, no matter what it takes."

Her nipples hardened in a rush. "You want me?"

"Yes, damn it."

Lena stood, snatching her napkin off her lap and tossing it onto the table. "Then let's get down to business."

Chapter Eleven

They got as far as the private elevator that led down to the master stateroom.

As soon as the doors closed Roderick grabbed Lena and crushed his lips over hers. She threw her arms around his neck and thrust her tongue into his mouth. He groaned, a rough, guttural sound that she felt down to her toes.

As he lifted her off the floor, she wrapped her legs around his waist. Her back hit the wall. Without breaking the kiss, Roderick reached between their bodies and quickly unzipped his pants before slipping his hand under her dress. His fingertips grazed her clit as he pushed aside her thong. She was already wet for him. So slick that her body offered no resistance as he shoved into her. She cried out.

Their gazes locked as he began thrusting into her, fast and hard and furious. She clung to him, delicious pleasure running through every ounce of her being.

The elevator arrived on their floor with a ding. The sound went completely ignored as Roderick's hips continued pummeling Lena's like a jackhammer. It was animalistic, it was raw, and moments later it was over as they both came with hoarse cries.

Roderick shuddered and dropped his face onto her shoulder, both of them breathing hard. Lena closed her eyes and silently counted out her heartbeats. When they slowed to normal she tapped Roderick's arm, indicating that he should release her. He hesitated, looking like he wanted to refuse before he thought better of it. She unwrapped her shaky legs from his waist as he eased her down and stepped back, refastening his pants.

His eyes were hooded, his voice pitched low as he said, "I'm sorry. I should have used—"

Lena pressed a finger to his lips. "I'm on the Pill. Do you get regular checkups?"

He nodded, understanding the reason for her question. "Had one last month. Clean bill of health, HIV negative."

"Good. Me, too."

A hopeful gleam lit his eyes. "Does this mean—"

"We won't be needing any condoms." Her lips curved in a sultry smile. "I don't want anything between us but skin."

Hunger, hot and swift, darkened his gaze.

As he reached for her she turned away and pressed the elevator button. The doors opened to reveal a private foyer, beyond which was an enormous, lavishly appointed suite. Purring with approval, Lena sauntered off the elevator to enter the cabin, peeling off her dress and dropping it to the floor as she went.

Roderick's sharp intake of breath sent a thrill of pure feminine satisfaction through her. It was time to restore the balance of power. Roderick may have started off with the upper hand, but he wouldn't be calling the shots for very long. Not if *she* had anything to say about it.

She took a slow turn around the luxurious suite, which occupied the entire lower deck and boasted sweeping views of the water from a private terrace. She made a show of admiring everything in sight, deliberately taking her time before facing Roderick.

He was still standing in the foyer near the elevator, as if his feet had been cemented to the floor. She smiled to herself, relishing his awestruck expression. She knew the picture she made—generous breasts spilling over the cups of her skimpy lace bra, legs sheathed in a black garter belt and thigh-high stockings, feet encased in strappy black stilettos with razor-sharp heels. She'd dressed provocatively on purpose, knowing Roderick would want to commence their arrangement as soon as possible.

Recovering his composure, he came toward her with a slow, predatory stealth that made her heart pound with excitement and anticipation. Her nipples tightened, straining against the lace of her bra. Between her legs, her clit pulsed and throbbed.

When Roderick stopped before her, she reached up and stroked his face, a tender caress that belied the snap of authority in her next words. "Tonight I'm in charge. You will do everything I tell you, and you will *not* touch me or make a move unless I say you can. Do you understand?"

Roderick hesitated, an internal struggle waging behind his dark, glittering eyes. She knew how hard it was for such a strong alpha male to relinquish control to anyone. He wanted to keep her under his command, wanted to dictate the pace of their seduction just as he'd dictated the terms of their arrangement.

Well, that's too damned bad.

"Do you understand?" Lena repeated herself.

He nodded obediently.

"Good boy," Lena crooned with satisfaction.

His mouth twitched, but he had the good sense to keep quiet.

She reached up and unbuttoned his black shirt and peeled it off, revealing broad shoulders and a wide mahogany chest ridged with muscle.

"Mmm," she purred appreciatively. She ran her hands over his smooth, hot skin, basking in the way he shivered at her touch. "*Very* nice."

Transfixed, his eyes followed her as she knelt before him and removed his leather boots and socks. Watching his face, she unbuckled his belt and slowly unzipped him. His breath quickened as she gripped the waistband of his pants and briefs and pushed them down his long, powerful legs. He stepped out of them and impatiently kicked them aside.

His engorged penis bobbed hungrily toward her face. She leaned forward and flicked her tongue over the swollen head, catching a silky drop of precum.

Roderick jerked and swore hoarsely under his breath.

Licking her lips as if she'd just sampled the most decadent dessert, Lena glided to her feet. With a seductive smile that promised more to come, she backed Roderick slowly toward the king-size bed and shoved him down.

"Lie back," she commanded.

He gave her a slow, sexy-as-hell smile and did as he was told.

Standing with her legs provocatively splayed apart, she reached up and unpinned her hair from the elegant twist on top of her head. She combed her fingers through the dark, relaxed strands and shook them loose until they fell softly to her shoulders. Roderick was riveted.

Suppressing a satisfied smile, Lena turned around and leaned over to unbuckle her stiletto heels, deliberately treating him to a long, enticing look at her shapely ass in a lace thong.

He let out an agonized moan. "Damn, baby, you're killing me."

Her lips curved in a naughty smile. Slowly she straightened, turned and hooked her thumbs into her panties, as if she were trying to decide whether to take them off now or later.

"Now," Roderick whispered raggedly. "Let me see you."

She gave him a stern look. "Have you forgotten who's in charge here?"

He licked his lips. "No, I—"

She gave the waistband of her panties a sharp little snap. "Just for your disobedience, I'm leaving them on."

He groaned in protest.

She smiled inwardly and ran an admiring gaze over the dark, powerful length of his body stretched out on the bed. His muscled arms were folded behind his head, showing off curly tufts of black armpit hair. His long, dark penis lay erect against his taut stomach, swelling even more beneath her bold appraisal. He was beautiful, so breathtakingly male it was all Lena could do not to pounce on the bed and devour him.

"Oh, my," she murmured, biting her lower lip. "You, Mr. Brand, are one magnificent work of art."

His hot, hungry gaze raked over her body. "I've been thinking the same thing about you."

She smiled, the sultry smile of a femme fatale.

He stared at her as she slithered onto the bed, crawled over to his side and curled her legs underneath her. When he reached for her, she batted his hand away.

"Ah, ah, ah," she admonished, wagging her finger at him. "Did I give you permission to touch me?"

He moaned. "Lena—"

"I didn't say you could touch me." She cut him off in her best dominatrix-inspired voice. "Now, do I need to tie you up, or are you going to be a good boy?"

He growled something obscene that made her laugh.

"I'll take that as a yes," she said.

He nodded and closed his eyes as she leaned over him and trailed her lips down his sculpted chest and abdomen, feeling his muscles clench as her tongue ran over him. He smelled and tasted delicious, a heady combination of skin, sweat and desire.

She kissed his pubic bone and licked sensually around his penis before easing it into her mouth. He made a harsh animal sound deep in his throat. Her body tightened with pleasure.

He was achingly hard and thick, his skin like velvet on her tongue. She worked her lips and tongue from tip to base, caressing his engorged sac with her fingers. He swore hoarsely, shoving his hand into her hair and gripping her head as it bobbed up and down over him. He pushed his hips upward, thrusting into her mouth as she sucked him harder and faster, aroused by his guttural moans of pleasure.

Moments later he came with a deep shudder, his shaft pulsing spasmodically in her mouth. Smooth, salty fluid spilled over her tongue and rolled down the back of her throat. She swallowed hungrily, and didn't stop sucking until she'd milked every last drop of come from his penis.

Roderick was still shuddering as she pulled away, wiping a trickle of wetness from the corner of her mouth. Her clit was hard and throbbing, screaming for attention. She reached down and stroked herself, trying to relieve some of the pressure. But that wasn't good enough.

Dazed, Roderick stared at her as she stood and grasped the waistband of her panties. Slowly and provocatively, she tugged them over her hips and down her thighs, revealing her smooth-shaven mound. Roderick sucked in a sharp breath, his eyes blazing with fierce arousal as he beheld her nudity.

She gave him a slow, sensual smile. "My turn."

She stood over him, her feet bracketing his shoulders as she sank to her knees and lowered her aching sex to his mouth. She felt the heat of his breath, then gasped at the touch of his lips on her. He kissed her, an erotic, openmouthed kiss that made her shiver. His tongue slid up and down her labia, circling her swollen clit until she moaned in agony.

His eyes glinted wickedly. "Payback," he whispered.

Before Lena could retaliate—not that she could have, not right then—he sucked her clit into his mouth. She arched backward, her hips jerking violently. He palmed her butt and pressed his face deeper into her pussy, inhaling her scent, lapping at her with slow, sensuous licks. And then he did something extraordinary with his tongue that made her see fireworks. She cried out wildly as she erupted, waves of pleasure crashing through her until she thought she'd pass out.

Gasping and trembling, she stared down into

Roderick's smoldering eyes and wondered where he—and his tongue—had been all her life.

His hands gently kneaded her butt. "Let me make love to you," he whispered, husky and urgent.

She bent and kissed him, tasting herself on his warm, wet lips. "You will."

But only on my terms.

Smoothly she rolled away from him and climbed off the bed. He surged up into a sitting position, watching as she sauntered across the cabin to reach the panoramic picture windows. During her earlier perusal of the suite, she'd noticed a pair of silk sashes used to tie back the tall custom drapes. She removed them quickly and efficiently, then turned and retraced her steps to the bed.

"I didn't bring handcuffs," she drawled coyly, "so a girl's gotta improvise."

Roderick frowned as she rejoined him on the bed. "Lena—"

"Shh. *I'm* in charge, remember?"

A muscle clenched in his jaw. Broodingly he watched as she positioned his arms over his head and went to work tying his wrists to the mahogany bedpost.

"This isn't fair," he grumbled darkly. "I won't be able to touch you."

"I know." She smiled. "Give it a tug. I want to test the knot."

His lips quirked as he pulled halfheartedly at the silk restraint. "You do realize," he murmured, "that this won't hold me if I really want to get at you."

Lena shivered at his words, at the dark, dangerous undercurrents in his voice. Of course she knew that her little makeshift bond was no match for him. He was a big, powerful man. A man who didn't surrender control very easily. She'd have better luck trying to restrain a wild lion.

Holding his gaze, she said evenly, "You agreed to my terms. If you try to free yourself, you'll totally ruin the mood. Is that what you want?"

"Hell, no," he muttered.

"I didn't think so." She leaned over and kissed him, a long, deep, provocative kiss. His breath quickened, fanning against her lips. She could feel the coiled tension in his body, knew that he wanted to tear himself free and ravage her. It thrilled and aroused her to know that she could have such an effect on him, could push him to the limits of his endurance.

Drawing away, she murmured seductively, "Now relax and enjoy the ride."

He looked at her, nostrils flaring.

When she reached down and unclasped her lace bra, he groaned and squeezed his eyes shut, tortured by the sight of breasts he could see but not touch. "Damn you, woman. You're really trying to kill me."

She laughed, soft and naughty.

And then she straddled him and lowered herself onto his thick, jutting penis.

His eyes flew open, locking onto hers with searing intensity.

Poised over him, Lena felt an overwhelming sense of power. She could do anything she wanted to him, could have her wicked way with him. And there wasn't a damn thing he could do about it.

Staring down into his eyes, she said in a voice like cool silk, "This time *I* get to dictate the pace. You don't move until I say you can move. Understand?"

His expression darkened with displeasure. "Fuck," he growled savagely.

"Oh, I intend to," she purred.

She began to ride him, long, gliding strokes up and down his length. She could feel every ridge on his penis, every swollen inch as she took him deeper. She loved the hard solidity of his body beneath her, the scorching heat of his skin.

Easing herself up, she watched in fascination as her body slid from his dark, glistening shaft. She hovered right at the tip, feeling her walls grip and contract around him. And then she slid back down, glorying in the erotic friction. Roderick groaned, sweat beading on his forehead, his muscles quivering as he fought the urge to thrust into her.

She leaned down and brushed her breasts across his parted lips, teasing and tormenting him. His tongue darted out to taste her nipple just as she pulled away with a throaty laugh. Frustrated, he swore and growled deep in his throat. She'd never felt more powerful.

She reveled in the harshness of his breathing as she leaned back, giving him a full view of her bouncing tits as she rocked up and down on him. She cupped them and imagined his big, strong hands caressing her nipples. The image was so tantalizing that she was tempted to release him from his restraint just so he could really touch her. But she resisted, reminding herself not to surrender control. It was all about control. Empowerment.

So she lifted her breasts, flicked out her tongue and licked her taut nipples.

When Roderick made a rough, strangled sound of hunger, she laughed. She felt wicked, wanton. Completely uninhibited.

She started riding him harder and faster, arching her

back and shoving her hips forward so that his penis hit her at the deepest angle, sending waves of mind-blowing sensation through her groin and up her back. Her clit quivered and convulsed, and she ached for release.

"Now," she cried in a dark, husky voice. "Move now."

It was like releasing a raging bull from its pen. Roderick's hips surged upward, and he began thrusting into her so violently she had to squeeze her thighs around his to remain astride him.

Their bodies slapped together, flesh striking flesh. Her thighs were hot and slick, slipping and sliding against his as their tempo increased. She could hardly breathe, her heart pounding like a racehorse's as it galloped toward the finish line. Gasping, she ground her hips against Roderick's, her pussy full and aching. He pushed back at her, trying to get as deep inside her as possible.

And then she was coming. And so was he. His body arched as he exploded inside her with a shout, flooding her with his scalding heat.

She threw back her head and closed her eyes. Gripped in the throes of ecstasy, she almost called out his name. But at the last second she held back, refusing to cede any power to him, even in that electrifying moment.

She collapsed on top of him, her sweat mingling with his, sealing their hot skin together. She lay on his chest and listened to his ragged breathing, her head lifting with every deep inhalation.

She must have dozed off. When she felt his arms go around her she jumped slightly, startled at how quietly and easily he'd loosened the restraint. The fact that he hadn't freed himself during their fevered lovemaking showed just how much willpower he possessed.

He'd allowed her to call the shots tonight, which begged the obvious question: Had she ever really been in control?

Chapter Twelve

It was the absence of Roderick's body that awakened Lena the next morning.

After spending the night wrapped around him, their bodies joined from shoulder to thigh, it was jarring to roll over and encounter nothing but empty space. Jarring enough to pull her out of a deep, satiated slumber.

She sat up quickly, clutching the sheets to her chest as she swept a look around the cabin.

It was empty.

Roderick was nowhere to be found.

Fighting a sick sense of déjà vu, she swung her gaze to the bedside table, half expecting to find a wad of bills and a thank-you note. When she saw nothing there, she wilted against the headboard and blew out a shaky breath.

Get a grip, girlfriend. He didn't skip out on you. He "owns" you for the next three weeks, remember?

Lena grimaced, dragging an unsteady hand through her disheveled hair.

She hadn't meant to spend the night with Roderick. After the disaster with Glenn Donahue, she'd sworn off sleepovers with men—clients or otherwise. She'd had every intention of asking Roderick to summon his driver to take her home. But when he'd folded her into his arms and whispered an endearment against her mouth, she couldn't bring herself to leave him.

You really are a glutton for punishment, her conscience mocked.

The ding of the elevator sounded from the foyer. Her nerves tightened, twisting her stomach into knots. She schooled her features into impassivity just as Roderick sauntered into the cabin.

If she thought he couldn't look any better than when he was wearing one of his expensively tailored Italian suits, she was dead wrong. The man was fine and divine in dark jeans that hung low on his hips and a T-shirt that molded his muscled arms and chest. Even his bare feet were mouthwateringly sexy in a pair of black flip-flops.

"Good morning," he murmured, gazing at her as he approached the bed. Her pulse thudded with each step that brought him closer.

"Why didn't you wake me up?" Hearing the note of accusation in her voice, she inwardly cringed.

Roderick smiled. "You were sleeping so peacefully, I didn't want to disturb you. Especially since you didn't get much rest last night," he added meaningfully.

Her cheeks heated. She wet her lips, rolled them inward, and averted her eyes from his as he plopped down on the edge of the bed and leaned back on his elbows. The intoxicating musk of their lovemaking wafted up from the sheets, taunting and tempting her.

"Why, Miss Morrison," Roderick drawled, sounding distinctly amused, "unless my eyes are deceiving me, I *do* believe you're blushing. I wouldn't have expected that from the naughty little vixen who tied me up and had her way with me last night."

"I'm not blushing," Lena muttered, even as her face grew hotter.

Roderick laughed.

Hoping to distract him, Lena asked abruptly, "What time is it?"

"Just after ten."

She gasped. "Ten!"

Roderick shrugged a shoulder, unconcerned. "Saturdays are meant for sleeping in."

And yet *he'd* apparently been up for a while. "I need to get home," Lena told him. "Can you send for your driver?"

"I could," he said indolently, "but it wouldn't do you much good."

"Why not?" Suddenly she went still. "Wait a minute…. Why is the boat moving? Aren't we docked at the pier?"

Roderick's eyes glinted with mischief. "Not quite."

She frowned at him. "What does that mean?"

"It means that you're not going home today. Or tomorrow either, for that matter."

"Why not?"

"Because we're taking a two-day cruise down Lake Michigan."

"What?" Lena exclaimed, bolting upright. "You can't be serious!"

"I am, actually. I woke up this morning, stepped out

on the terrace and decided this was a perfect weekend for a relaxing, scenic trip down Lake Michigan." He smiled lazily. "I realize it's not Belize or the South of France—we can do that next time."

Lena stared at him in outraged disbelief. "Have you lost your mind? I'm not going on a cruise with you! Turn this boat around!"

He chuckled softly. "I'm afraid I can't do that. We're already on our way to Michigan."

"Michigan!"

"Yep. Captain says our first stop is Holland, a quaint little Dutch village with cobblestone sidewalks—his description, not mine. After that we're off to Mackinac Island. Horse-drawn carriages, beautiful Victorian architecture, limestone bluffs. I've never been there, but it sounds charming, don't you think?"

"Lovely," Lena agreed through clenched teeth. "Tell me something, Roderick. While you were experiencing this moment of spontaneous inspiration this morning, did it once occur to you that I might have other plans this weekend?"

"What other plans?" There was a jealous edge to his voice.

It was on the tip of her tongue to tell him that she visited her grandfather every Saturday and Sunday. But when she opened her mouth, some perverse impulse made her say instead, "I have a date tonight."

Roderick frowned. "I thought I already told you—"

"It's not with a client."

Something dark and possessive flashed in his eyes. "Are you telling me that you're seeing someone?"

She didn't blink. "That's right."

His eyes narrowed. "I don't believe you."

She bristled. "Why not?"

"You're not the unfaithful kind."

"We have an open relationship," she flung back.

Roderick's expression hardened. "Then he's a damn fool. And so are you if you think this changes anything between us."

"Really?" she challenged. "So you'd have no qualms about banging another man's girlfriend?"

He laughed shortly. "You don't have a boyfriend, Lena."

"How the hell do you know?"

"Because you would have mentioned him last night during our negotiations." His gaze darkened, moving hungrily across her face. "And because no man in his right mind would willingly share you with strangers. *I* sure as hell wouldn't."

Lena's pulse jumped and raced. She tried to swallow, but her throat was too dry.

Roderick chuckled, soft and knowing.

Glancing around the cabin, Lena mumbled, "Where's my dress?"

"It's being dry-cleaned. It had a…stain on it."

She caught his meaning, remembered their explosive elevator encounter, and pulled the sheets up to her eyes to hide her flushed face.

Roderick threw back his head and laughed, which only made her blush harder.

As his laughter subsided, he smiled and shook his head at her. "What a fascinating contradiction you are, Lena Morrison. I'm going to *love* spending the next three weeks with you."

"I bet you are," she grumbled under her breath.

What Roderick didn't know about her was that no

matter how many seductions she performed, or how confident and worldly she seemed as an escort, a part of her would always be the shy teenager who'd struggled constantly with her weight and low self-esteem.

Dark eyes twinkling, Roderick straightened from the bed. "I have some important phone calls to make," he said apologetically. "I'll try to finish up as quickly as possible. In the meantime, make yourself comfortable." He nodded toward the connecting bathroom suite. "Take a hot shower. Or soak in the Jacuzzi, if you like."

"I don't have a change of clothes," Lena reminded him sourly.

"No problem. During our tour, you may have noticed the boutique on the third deck. I had it specially built for my sisters, who always forget to pack something whenever they travel. They appreciate the convenience of having a full-scale boutique on board, and not having to spend a dime is an added bonus. And they're both shameless clotheshorses, so of course I have to keep the shop stocked with the latest fashions. You'll find everything you need. Skirts, tops, jeans…lingerie," he added suggestively.

Lena congratulated herself for not blushing this time. Shaking her head in disbelief, she said, "You've thought of everything, haven't you?"

He grinned unrepentantly.

When the elevator chimed from the foyer, Lena shot him a questioning glance.

"Your breakfast is here," he told her, rising from the bed as a uniformed server rolled a linen-covered cart into the cabin. As Roderick motioned the woman forward, Lena pulled the heavy duvet up to her chest to make sure she wasn't flashing a nipple.

After the server had filled a glass with orange juice and fussed with the fresh-cut flowers arranged in a crystal vase, Roderick thanked her. She smiled shyly at him and Lena before departing.

Lena's stomach growled as the scent of hot food hit her nostrils.

If Roderick heard the embarrassing rumble, he gave no indication. "I hope you're hungry." Standing over the cart, he removed the silver serving lids to reveal an appetizing spread of thick Belgian waffles, bacon, scrambled eggs, grits, biscuits and an exotic assortment of fresh fruit.

Lena's eyes widened. "Please tell me I'm not supposed to eat all that food by myself."

Roderick chuckled softly. "We worked up quite an appetite last night. You should be hungry."

"Not *that* hungry." But her mouth was definitely watering as she watched him fix a plate from the dishes set out on the cart. "Have you already eaten?"

"Sort of. I had coffee and bagels during my videoconference this morning."

"Videoconference?"

He smiled wryly. "My new Japanese business associates don't recognize Saturdays as part of the weekend."

"So in addition to planning a spontaneous weekend getaway and taking care of my dry-cleaning, you had a business meeting? Just how long have you been up?"

"A few hours. Syrup?"

"Yes, please." She watched as he poured maple syrup over the Belgian waffle. "I can't believe I didn't hear you moving around. I'm usually a light sleeper."

"You were exhausted." His lips twitched. "Understandably so."

Lena couldn't argue. She was deliciously sore, her muscles aching in places she hadn't used in years, if ever.

Instead of passing her the plate he'd fixed, Roderick sat on the bed beside her and cut into the waffle. When he brought the fork to Lena's mouth, she was so startled that she opened without thinking.

Roderick watched as her lips closed around the fork, accepting the morsel of food. After she'd chewed and swallowed, he murmured, "Good?"

"Mmm. Scrumptious. My compliments to the chef."

Roderick smiled. "I'll pass that along."

He forked up another piece of waffle and held it to her lips. This time she hesitated before accepting it. She'd never been fed by a man before. It made her feel vulnerable...and cherished.

Over the next several minutes, he alternated between feeding her forkfuls of waffle, grits and eggs, and pinching off pieces of a biscuit to give to her. Their eyes held every time she bit into the moist, flaky warmth. She didn't know what delighted her more—the delectable food or eating from Roderick's hand.

When he offered her another bite of waffle, she belatedly remembered that he'd had only bagels that morning. She caught his wrist and redirected the fork, indicating that he should feed himself.

She watched as he drew the morsel of food into his mouth and closed his eyes. She didn't know whether he was savoring the waffle or the taste of her that lingered on the fork. She got her answer when his lids lifted to reveal dark eyes glittering with arousal. As he slowly licked the tines of the fork, her nipples puckered and her clit pulsed.

They stared at each other as he speared a chunk of mango and brushed it tantalizingly across her lips before sliding it into her mouth. She sighed with pleasure as the sweet, luscious flavor bathed her tongue. When Roderick fed her another piece, droplets of juice dribbled onto her chin. He wiped them away, then slid his fingers into his mouth and sucked them as if he were tasting her pussy.

Lena shivered, wetness pooling between her thighs. She'd never realized that the simple act of being fed by another could be so damn stimulating. She was seized with the sudden urge to knock the plate out of Roderick's hand, tear off his clothes and haul him back into bed with her. But she hadn't quite forgiven him for commandeering her weekend. That kind of arrogance couldn't be rewarded with hot, mind-blowing sex—at least not right away.

When Roderick reached for the fork to resume feeding her, she put her hand over his. "I can take it from here."

His mouth curved in a slow, sensual smile. As he settled the plate on her lap, she could feel the heat of his skin through the thick duvet. The brush of his fingers sent sparks of electricity shooting to her groin, making her clit throb until she had to squeeze her thighs together.

The devilish gleam in Roderick's eyes let her know that he was fully aware of—and pleased with—the havoc he was wreaking on her body.

As he stretched lazily from the bed, he said, "Tonight we can have dinner on the terrace. The view's great. Scenic and…inspiring."

Lena muttered darkly, "The last time you were inspired by that view, I wound up getting kidnapped."

He laughed. "I prefer the term 'whisked away.' It sounds more romantic. Less—"

"Criminal?"

He grinned. "Exactly."

Before Lena could respond, he plucked a tulip from the vase, broke the stem, then leaned down and gently tucked the flower behind her ear. As his soft gaze roamed across her face, he murmured, "Be still my heart."

Ignoring the way her own heart thumped, Lena gave him a surly look. "Don't you have phone calls to make?"

He smiled. "I do. And that's the *only* thing keeping me from climbing back into that bed and making love to you. I know that once I start, I won't be able to stop."

Lena's mouth went bone-dry. She could only stare at him as he swiped a slice of bacon off the cart, bit into it and winked at her as he sauntered from the cabin.

She waited until he'd boarded the elevator before she closed her eyes and released a deep, shuddering breath. She was trapped on a boat with Roderick Brand for the next two days, and there wasn't a damn thing she could do about it.

Suddenly the notion of being captured by a marauding pirate didn't seem so far-fetched after all.

Chapter Thirteen

After breakfast, Lena made a trip to the boutique on the main deck. Half an hour later, she emerged armed with enough clothes to get her through the weekend. As Roderick had promised, she'd found everything she needed inside the upscale shop, which rivaled anything the Magnificent Mile had to offer. Morgan would have been in retail nirvana, Lena mused as she returned to the master stateroom.

At the reminder of her sister, she retrieved her cell phone and composed a quick text message: *Something came up. Can't visit Poppa this weekend. When you see him, kiss him for me and tell him I'll drop by on Monday.*

She grimaced as she hit Send. She knew her vague explanation would raise more questions than it had answered, but she couldn't tell her sister the truth about where she was, and who she was with. So when Morgan wrote back promptly to ask what had come up, Lena paused for only a moment before typing back: *Had to go out of town on business.*

Guilt gnawed at her as she thought about her mounting lies. First she'd lied to her boss, now her sister. Before the three weeks were up, she wouldn't have anyone left to deceive.

Thanks a lot, Roderick, she thought resentfully.

Needing to channel her emotions into something productive, she decided to go for a swim.

After changing into a white bikini—one of the items she'd picked up at the boutique—she went in search of the pool, wishing she'd taken careful note of its location during Roderick's tour. On a boat this size, it was easy to get lost. Fortunately, she passed a crew member who kindly directed her to an upper deck, where the large pool awaited her with a swim-up bar and dual staircases that rose from the swim platform to the top deck.

She disrobed, kicked off her flip-flops and dropped her towel onto a lounge chair, then dove cleanly into the cold, invigorating water.

An hour later, she'd swum three miles. It was the most she'd completed in months, and it felt damn good. As her head broke the surface of the water, she heard applause. Blinking rapidly to clear her vision, she looked up to find Roderick standing above her at the edge of the pool. He was clapping, a broad grin stretched across his face.

"My Nubian mermaid," he said admiringly.

Lena accepted his proffered hand, and he pulled her effortlessly out of the water.

"Thanks," she murmured, smoothing back her wet hair. "How long have you been standing here?"

He smiled into her eyes. "Long enough to see what an amazing swimmer you are."

Lena smiled, not entirely immune to his flattery. "Thank you."

Sidestepping him, she padded to the lounge chair where she'd left her towel. She could feel the heat of Roderick's gaze on her butt, so hot that it chased away the goose bumps on her skin. She grabbed her towel and rubbed down her arms and legs as he walked over to her.

"Where'd you learn how to swim like that?" he asked.

"My grandfather taught me how to swim when I was four. He says I took to the water like a fish."

"I can believe it," Roderick drawled, dropping down onto the deck chair beside hers. "Why do you think I called you a mermaid?"

Lena grinned, wringing water out of her hair. "Poppa's the one who encouraged me to try out for my high school swim team."

"Which I'm sure you made with no problem."

She grimaced. "Not the first time. I wasn't as fast as the other swimmers." She hesitated, then surprised herself by confessing, "I needed to lose some weight."

She flushed as Roderick's gaze wandered down her flat stomach, trim waist and toned, healthy thighs.

"Don't be fooled by what you see now," she advised, interpreting his thoughts. "Unlike my sister, who can get away with eating anything she wants, I've always struggled with my weight. After not making the cut the first time, I trained really hard, changed my diet and shed the necessary pounds so I'd be ready for tryouts the following year. Joining the swim team helped me stay fit and keep the weight off. So I make every effort to get in the pool at least three times a week."

"Good for you," Roderick murmured.

"Thanks." As she stretched out on the lounge chair, his appreciative gaze raked over her body again, lingering on her breasts until her nipples tightened. She considered putting on her robe, then decided not to give him the satisfaction of knowing how much he affected her.

As if he doesn't already know.

Shoving the thought aside, she dug out a pair of sunglasses from her beach bag and slid them onto her face. The sun was warm, the sky a vivid shade of blue. Roderick had been right about one thing. It *was* a perfect weekend for being out on the lake.

"If you get cold," he told her, "let me know and I'll have the roof closed."

"I'm fine," Lena assured him. "There's a nice breeze blowing off the water."

"It is nice." Reclining in the lounge chair with his hands clasped behind his dark head, Roderick was the epitome of a man at leisure. A very sexy, dangerous man.

"Did you finish making your phone calls?" Lena asked, dragging her gaze away from him.

"I did," he murmured. "So now I can give you my undivided attention."

Lena's pulse quickened. She knew it was no accident that he'd made the seemingly innocuous words sound like a seductive promise. "What time are we supposed to arrive at our first stop?" she blurted.

"Whenever," came his lazy response. "I told the captain to take it slow, keep our speed under ten knots. We're in no rush."

Speak for yourself, thought Lena, suddenly eager for the company of other people to provide a buffer between them.

As if to taunt her, Roderick got up suddenly and sat down on her lounge chair, the fabric of his jeans rasping her bare thigh.

Lena jumped, staring at him. "What are you doing?"

His eyes glinted with amusement. "Are you thirsty? I could bring you something to drink." When she glanced toward the unmanned swim-up bar, he said, "I'll fix you something. Whatever you like."

Lena smiled. "A mojito would be nice," she said, as much to get rid of him as anything else.

He smiled. "One mojito, coming right up." But he lingered at her side, sweeping a look over her that ignited every inch of her bare skin. "God, you're beautiful," he said, low and husky. "I can't take my eyes off you in this bikini. You found it in the boutique?"

She swallowed hard. "Of course."

A slow smile curved his sensual mouth. "I couldn't have chosen better myself." He fingered the string tie at her hip. "Easy on…easy off."

Need throbbed between Lena's thighs. Abruptly she sat up and swung her legs over the opposite side of the chair. As she stood, she yanked off her sunglasses and tossed them onto the chair.

"I'm going for another swim," she mumbled.

"I'll join you."

She glanced over her shoulder and gulped at the sight of Roderick stripping off his T-shirt, muscles bunching and rippling in the sunlight. She quickly averted her gaze and launched herself into the pool. Moments later she heard a splash as he dove in after her. She swam away from him, doing a leisurely breaststroke that masked her sudden urgency to escape.

She gasped as a pair of strong hands grabbed her around the waist and dragged her underwater. She flailed her arms and legs, swallowing a mouthful of water in her struggle.

As she and Roderick surfaced together, she sputtered indignantly, "Hey, what the hell—"

He slanted his mouth over hers and kissed her. The feel of his warm, wet tongue sliding against hers sent electricity sizzling through her veins, instantly melting her resistance. Her arms wound around his neck as his hands framed her face, pulling her even closer. He kissed her until she was breathless, until she had to break away to drag vital air into her lungs.

His lips trailed a simmering line of kisses down her jaw, to the tender skin behind her ear and lower to her throat. She wrapped her legs around him as his hands slid from her waist to cup her breasts. She shivered, her nipples hardening as he lightly caressed them.

When that was no longer enough, he untied her bikini top, catching her breasts as they spilled into his hands. He made a husky sound of pleasure, then lowered his head and closed his mouth over a beaded nipple. Lena moaned and tilted back her head to give him better access. He sucked her nipples, first one and then the other, the wetness of his tongue mirroring the wetness of the water surrounding them.

As the throbbing ache deepened between her thighs, Lena shamelessly rubbed herself against his erection, wanting him inside her. Lifting his mouth from her breast, he deftly untied her bikini bottom, letting the scrap of fabric float away. And then he reached down, his fingers finding her clit and stroking it. It swelled instantly under his caress, making her groan. She arched her hips against his hand, begging him to go deeper.

He gave her a wickedly sexy grin, then disappeared underwater. His hands gripped her thighs, pushing her legs apart. Lena let out a shocked gasp of pleasure at the touch of his mouth on her sex. The cold of the water, and the contrasting heat of his tongue, was like nothing she'd ever felt before. She closed her eyes, moaning as he licked her swollen folds and sucked her clit until she climaxed with a wild cry.

Roderick came up for air, his eyes glittering with satisfaction as he cradled her shuddering body in his arms. Water dripped from his thick black lashes when he bent and kissed her, deeply and possessively. The brilliant blue sky faded away as her vision blurred.

Her head was still spinning as he quickly removed his briefs, turned her around and pulled her down onto his strong thighs. She cried out as his long, thick shaft slid inside her. She closed her eyes, curving an arm around his neck and leaning her head back against his shoulder. He felt huge inside her, wedged so high and deep she swore she could feel him in her chest. As he began to move she expected pounding—hard, fast and frantic. Instead he gently rocked, gliding in and out of her body with a slow, sensual rhythm designed to drive her completely out of her mind. A delicious sizzle began in her belly, pooled in her groin and spread rapidly through her veins.

He swept her wet hair over one shoulder and kissed her nape, scraping his teeth over her sensitized flesh. She shivered convulsively. His fingers slid up and over her stomach to palm her breasts and pinch her erect nipples. She whimpered, torn between pleasure and pain.

His strokes deepened, rippling the surface of the

water. She leaned forward on his thighs, spreading her legs wider to take in as much of him as she could. The friction between their joined bodies was so hot she was surprised the water around them didn't start boiling. She moaned as an unbearable pressure built inside her, straining to its breaking point.

"I want you to come for me, Lena," Roderick whispered in her ear, low and husky.

She groaned. "I'm—"

"Come now."

She exploded on command, screaming and convulsing with the force of her orgasm. He gripped her waist and held her tightly in place as he began thrusting faster and harder, his hips pummeling her ass. The harsh sound of his breathing filled her ears. And then he stiffened and groaned, shooting liquid heat into her womb.

Struggling for breath, he buried his face in the curve of her neck. "Damn, baby," he rasped. "That was hot."

Lena smiled dreamily. "Mmm-hmm."

A feeling of sated exhaustion had crept over her body. She was vaguely aware of Roderick nuzzling her throat and the side of her face and holding her in his arms as they drifted around the pool. The water lapped at her swollen sex, a soothing, intimate caress. She was so relaxed that she could have gone to sleep right then and there.

It was only when they reached the edge of the pool that reality intruded.

"Wait," she murmured as Roderick nudged her toward the steps. "We can't climb out of here naked. One of your crew members might see us, or people on the shore—"

"Wait here." Roderick stole a hot, wet kiss before swimming off to retrieve their discarded scraps of clothing. When he returned to her, they dressed quickly, smiling lazily at each other. As Lena climbed the steps ahead of Roderick, she provocatively gyrated her hips and laughingly darted out of the way when he reached for her.

As she sauntered toward the lounge chair to collect her things, he grabbed her from behind and tossed her over his shoulder in a fireman's carry.

"Hey!" she squealed, her sodden hair hanging like a curtain over her face. "I was going to—"

"Get them later," Roderick growled, slapping her soundly on the ass as he strode from the deck. "You need to be punished for teasing me like that."

Chapter Fourteen

And punish her he did.

Frontward, backward, sideways, up against the wall, down on the floor. He made her come so many times she thought she'd go blind from the light show that exploded behind her eyelids during each orgasm. He was insatiable. So was she, for that matter.

Hours passed before they finally collapsed in a heap, completely entangled, thoroughly spent. Every inch of the bed was drenched, and so were they.

"So much for seeing Holland," Lena panted, sprawled across Roderick's hot, heaving body.

He grunted. "Holland who?"

She tried to laugh, but didn't have enough air in her lungs. After several moments, she attempted to speak. "I'm surprised your captain didn't send a search and rescue team after us."

Roderick chuckled, a low, husky rumble that vibrated

through her body. "I'd already told him not to stop if he didn't hear from me at least half an hour before we reached port."

A wry grin curved Lena's mouth. "Such premeditation."

He laughed. "I prefer to think of it as good foresight. Premeditation sounds so—"

"Criminal?"

"Exactly."

They both laughed.

Pressing a kiss to her temple, Roderick murmured, "Does this mean you've forgiven me for—"

"Kidnapping me?"

"Whisking you away," he corrected.

"I suppose." She heaved a dramatic sigh. "It could be worse."

"Yeah? How so?"

"You could have me locked up in some dark, musty dungeon crawling with spiders and rats."

She felt him smile into her hair. "I don't have a dungeon."

"Why not? This mega yacht has everything else."

"Well, I'm not a pirate."

She snorted. "The verdict's still out on that."

His smile deepened. "If I'm a pirate, then you're—"

Lena choked out a laugh. "Oh, no! Don't say it."

"Don't say what?"

"Don't say anything about pirate treasure, or about me being the finest booty you've ever captured."

Roderick laughed. "Why not?"

She lifted her head from his chest to grin at him. "Because I'd have to dock you cool points for delivering such a corny line."

"Well, now, we can't have that." His eyes glinted

wolfishly. "Even if you *are* the finest booty I've ever captured."

Lena laughed. Smiling demurely, she fluttered her lashes at him and gushed in the breathy voice of an infatuated maiden, "Oh, Captain, I bet you say that to *all* the girls."

"Nah." His gaze softened. "Just you."

Her smile wavered. Their eyes held for a long, charged moment before Lena glanced away, resettling her head against the solid warmth of his chest and staring out the windows. The scenic Michigan shoreline was silhouetted against a sky ablaze with orange, red and purple.

"Oh, man," she murmured in wonder. "What an absolutely beautiful sunset."

"That it is," Roderick agreed, lazily stroking a hand up and down her back.

Lena struggled not to succumb to his touch. To the sense of peace washing over her. To the romantic perfection of this moment. But how could she *not* succumb? She was having a once-in-a-lifetime experience that most women could only fantasize about. She'd been whisked away—yes, whisked away—on a romantic luxury cruise with the richest, most gorgeous man she'd ever met. A heart-stoppingly sexy man who'd given her more mind-blowing orgasms in one day than she'd had in several years. Now she was lying in his arms, gazing out at a breathtaking sunset and contemplating three more weeks of pure sensual bliss. It was too good to be true.

Why, oh, why couldn't they have met under different circumstances?

Would it matter? her conscience challenged. *No matter where or how you met, you'd still be an escort, and he'd still be the type of man who'd refuse to share you with strangers, as he put it.*

"Hey."

Lena glanced up to meet Roderick's probing gaze. "I'm sorry. Did you say something?"

"Nothing important. Why were you frowning just now?"

"Was I?"

"Yeah. You were."

She shrugged, buying time. "I was just thinking."

"About…?"

She sighed. "I was wondering what I should tell Zandra when she calls to set me up with a client."

"Just tell her you're not available," Roderick said simply.

"For three weeks?" Lena was skeptical.

"Sure."

"And you think she's just going to accept that—no questions asked?" Lena snorted. "You must not know Zandra very well. But, wait, you *do*. So you should know better."

Roderick grinned. "Do you want me to talk to her?"

"No!"

He cocked an amused brow at her. "Why not?"

"Because."

He waited. When she offered no more, he said dryly, "That's not an answer."

Lena heaved an exasperated breath. "Do I have to spell it out? I don't want her to know about our arrangement."

"I see." He searched her face. "Are you embarrassed?"

She scowled. "Why should *I* be embarrassed? *I'm* not the one who bribed *you* with sex in exchange for money."

"Touché." Roderick grinned.

The man had no shame.

"I can't tell Zandra about our arrangement because you're a client," Lena explained, "and I've already violated the agency's policy by sleeping with you—"

"Sleeping? Is that what you call what we've been doing?" Roderick drawled, squeezing her butt.

Heat flooded her cheeks—the ones on her face *and* on her backside. "You know what I mean," she snapped, swatting his hand away.

He chuckled softly. "I think you're underestimating Zandra. If you told her the truth about our arrangement, I know she wouldn't pass judgment."

"That's not the point," Lena said, striving for patience. "The point is that I'm not supposed to get involved with clients, yet here I am sailing down Lake Michigan with you, coming off my gazillionth orgasm."

"Gazillionth?" he teased. "You mean you've been count-ing?"

Lena rolled her eyes in exasperation. "Why do I even bother?"

Roderick laughed. His arms, strong and heavy, wrapped around her, snuggling her closer to his warm body. "I'm just messing with you, baby girl. I understand what you're saying. If you don't want Zandra to know about us, I won't say a word."

The way he said "about us" made it sound like they were secret lovers. Which, Lena supposed, they were.

Sighing in resignation, she traced her fingertip along the edge of an amazing pectoral muscle that quivered in response to her touch. "So," she said casually, "Zandra tells me that you guys go way back."

"Uh-huh."

"You grew up in the same neighborhood, attended the same schools, et cetera, et cetera."

"Yep."

"She said you've been friends forever."

"Forever." His lazy voice had a hint of laughter in it. "Is there something you want to ask me, Lena?"

"Well," she hedged. "It's just that, well, Zandra's a very beautiful woman."

"Very," Roderick agreed.

"Men come on to her *all* the time."

"And you're wondering why I'm not one of them."

Lena bit her lower lip. "The thought *has* crossed my mind. Zandra told me that you've always had a platonic relationship—"

"And you find that hard to believe."

"A little," she admitted sheepishly. "I mean, Zandra's gorgeous—"

"She is." Roderick chuckled softly. "But you have to understand something. I knew her back when she had buck teeth, ashy knees and a headful of wild hair."

"That's mean!" Lena protested with a sharp poke to his ribs.

He laughed. "I wasn't trying to be mean," he insisted, capturing her hand before she could poke him again. "If you'd let me finish, I was going to say that Zandra knew *me* when I was just a scrawny kid who needed to grow into his big ears and even bigger head. The point is, she's always been like a sister to me. I'm proud of the smart, successful woman she's become, and I don't dispute that she's a knockout. But I'm not interested in her like that. To me, she'll always be sweet, scrappy Za-Za from around the way."

Lena lifted her head to smile at him. "Za-Za. Somehow that suits her."

Roderick smiled, sending shivers of warmth down her spine as he nibbled on her fingertips. "Why does any of this matter to you anyway? Would you be jealous if Zandra and I had slept together?"

"Of course not."

"Liar."

"I'm not," she argued, tugging her fingers from his marauding mouth. "I was just curious, that's all. Things are complicated enough between us. The last thing I need is to be looking over my shoulder because I'm encroaching on my boss's territory."

Roderick grinned broadly. "You're in luck. I happen to be unclaimed territory, so feel free to encroach away."

Lena laughed. "In your dreams."

"You have no idea." He angled his head to nip at her throat, his warm breath tickling her skin. "My last word on Zandra—"

"Yes?" Lena prompted eagerly. Too eagerly.

Roderick drew back, a knowing gleam in his eyes. "Just curious, huh?"

Lena blushed. "What were you going to say?"

He chuckled. "If there's ever any doubt in your mind about the nature of my relationship with her, just talk to my brother Remy."

"Remy?"

"Short for Remington." His lips quirked. "My mother named him after a character from one of her favorite soap operas. Poor guy's heard every joke under the sun about Remington brand products."

"Remington...Brand—oh." Lena grinned sympathetically. "He must have developed a great sense of humor."

"That, and a mean left hook."

Her grin widened. "So why should I ask Remy about you and Zandra?"

"Because he's crazy about her. He staked his claim a couple years ago, and he knows I'd never, as you say, encroach on his territory."

Lena smiled softly. "That's very sweet of you. And loyal."

Roderick shrugged. "We're twins. We've always looked out for each—"

"Good Lord!" Lena burst out, staring at him in wide-eyed shock. "You mean there are *two* of you?"

He laughed, amused by her reaction. "You make that sound like a bad thing."

"Not bad." *Just dangerous,* she mentally added. It was scary enough that God had unleashed Roderick Brand on the female populace. But a double dose of him? It was inconceivable.

She wanted to ask more questions about his twin brother, but Roderick suddenly rolled out of bed, leaned down and swept her into his arms with an astonishing ease that took her breath away and reminded her of just how physically outmatched she was.

Looping her arms around his neck, she murmured teasingly, "Where are you taking me, pirate captain?"

He slanted her a roguish grin. "It's time for a bath, my buxom wench."

"Splendid," she purred. "I'm very eager to show you how good I am at washing backs."

He wiggled his brows suggestively. "Fronts, too?"

She gave him a coquettish look beneath her lashes. "Of course, master."

His grin widened. "Then I just might decide to feed

you before I ravish you again. And just for the record, Lena," he added, his eyes glimmering with wicked triumph, "it only took me a day to get you to call me master."

Chapter Fifteen

Later that evening, they disembarked at Mackinac Island and had dinner at a romantic waterfront restaurant that boasted the best views of the island. Not that it really mattered. They spent more time staring at each other and trading intimate smiles across the table than actually enjoying the scenery.

After dinner they strolled hand in hand along the picturesque downtown streets, where the delectable scent of fudge wafted out from every other shop that lined the sidewalks. Lena didn't protest too much when Roderick tugged her into one of the candy shops to get a sample of Mackinac Island's world-famous fudge. It was divine, hand-paddled morsels of heavenly decadence. One taste just wasn't enough. At the shopkeeper's urging, they sampled a variety of flavors, everything from butter pecan to double chocolate fudge. They laughed quietly as they fed each other, licking fingers and sharing heated looks that made even the shopkeeper blush.

Before they left, Roderick bought a pound of several different flavors to take home to his nieces and nephews. But once he and Lena had boarded the horse-drawn buggy that would deliver them back to the yacht, he dug into the stash, broke off a piece of fudge and slid it into Lena's mouth. As he withdrew, she closed her lips around his fingers and sucked them clean. Roderick inhaled sharply, his pupils flaring and dilating in the moonlit darkness of the enclosed carriage.

She fed him a morsel of fudge, then licked into his mouth, stealing the melted sweetness off his tongue.

He groaned, dragging his lips from hers to nuzzle her throat. The rasp of his unshaven jaw sent electric bolts of sensation down to her stomach. "I want you, Lena," he whispered huskily.

She trembled hard. "I want you, too. But we have to wait. We're almost at the marina."

"I can't wait that long."

She pulled away reluctantly. "You have to."

"Then touch yourself for me."

Her mouth went dry. "What?"

"You heard me." His low, velvety voice was an invitation to sin. "I want to see you pleasure yourself. For my eyes only."

She shook her head, darting a glance outside at the coachman. "Not here. When we get back to the yacht."

A devilish gleam filled Roderick's eyes. He leaned close and whispered in her ear, "If you don't touch yourself, I'll do it for you."

A shiver of desire rippled through her. She stared at him, and had no doubt that he'd make good on his threat if she refused to do as he'd asked. His hand was already easing up her skirt, the heat of his touch igniting every molecule in her body.

She'd never masturbated in front of anyone before. She'd done it plenty of times in the privacy of her own bedroom, but never before an audience. It seemed fitting that her first time would be with Roderick, who'd also given her her very first underwater orgasm. No doubt she'd be experiencing many more "firsts" before the weekend was over.

Pulse pounding, Lena reached under her skirt and panties and tentatively touched herself. Of course she was already drenched. Her body remained in a perpetual state of arousal whenever Roderick was around.

Staring into his eyes, watching him watch her, she leaned back against the cushioned seat and slowly, provocatively, spread her legs. She licked two of her fingertips, which still tasted sweetly of fudge, then slid them into her wet, aching pussy. Her body arched, a soft sigh of pleasure escaping her lips. She pushed her fingers inside as far as they'd go, pressing the hot flesh of her inner walls, following the curve of her pelvis.

Holding her gaze, Roderick settled back against the seat and stretched out his long legs. But she wasn't fooled for a second by his relaxed pose. She could feel the heat and tension radiating from his body. And when the carriage passed under a streetlamp, she saw the unmistakable bulge of his erection straining against his fly.

The experience of being watched by him was unbearably arousing, unbearably erotic. Slowly, deliberately, she began moving her fingers in and out of her body. Her nipples hardened beneath her blouse, begging for attention. With her free hand she cupped her right breast, tweaking and tugging at the nipple until it felt as tight and achy as her engorged clitoris.

Roderick watched her, nostrils flaring, eyes glittering feverishly. She expected him to pounce on her at any minute, but he remained still, exercising the same willpower that had kept him tied to the bed last night.

Lena shoved her fingers deeper, feeling her wetness leak out onto her hand. Wanting to torment Roderick, to push him to the limits of his self-control, she withdrew her hand and held it up to a sliver of moonlight streaming through the carriage window. When Roderick saw the moisture glistening on her fingers, he sat forward, his fist clenching and unclenching on his thigh.

Lena felt a surge of wicked satisfaction. *Gotcha,* she thought.

She licked her fingertips, tasting herself before sliding her fingers back into the warm sheath of her body. Smothering a groan, Roderick slid down on the bench and spread his legs as if he could no longer keep them together, as if his erection had grown so massive inside his dark pants that he couldn't contain it. His reaction excited and electrified Lena, made her feel powerful and primitively erotic. When he began rubbing himself, she almost came apart.

Leaning her head back against the seat, she closed her eyes and worked her fingers faster, alternately thrusting them inside and running them in tight circles against her swollen clit.

Soon she was panting, and so was Roderick. The harsh rhythm of their breathing nearly drowned out the clattering of the carriage wheels and the clip-clopping of the horses' hooves.

Opening her heavy-lidded eyes, Lena saw that Roderick had moved closer to her on the bench. A current of electricity ran from his body to hers. As they stared into each other's eyes, Lena imagined him sinking to his knees in front of her, burying his mouth between her legs and sucking her clitoris as only *he* could do. She imagined wrapping her legs around his neck, holding him tightly in place as he laved and licked her, feasting on her pussy as if it were dipped in the finest imported chocolate.

And then she imagined his long, hot tongue thrusting deep inside her.

That pushed her over the top.

She cried out and dissolved, shivering from head to toe.

As the violent spasms gradually tapered off, she slumped against the seat and grinned weakly at Roderick.

Without a word he reached over and took her hand. As she stared at him, he drew her slick fingers into his mouth and sucked hard, his eyes closing in helpless ecstasy.

She almost lost it again.

When he'd sucked her fingers dry, he kissed them one at a time, then splayed her hand over his thudding heart and leaned his head back against the seat. Her belly quivered at the sight of his huge erection tenting the front of his pants. She wanted to unzip him, take him down the back of her throat and finish him off.

But she resisted, exercising patience. She could see the bright, glittering lights of the marina just up ahead. The gleaming white hull of the *Native Sun* towered above the other docked boats.

She sighed. "I think I'm going to buy shares in that fudge shop."

"Hell," Roderick growled thickly, "after tonight, I'll buy the damn company."

Chapter Sixteen

When Lena's cell phone rang early the next morning, she was sleeping so soundly that she almost didn't hear it. When the ringing finally registered in her brain, she felt a dagger of alarm that made her bolt upright, then snatch her purse off the floor and fumble out her phone. Her heart knocked when she saw her sister's number.

"Morgan?" she answered alertly.

Morgan began, "Don't panic—"

Which was the absolute *wrong* thing to say, because it kicked Lena's heart rate into full-fledged alarm mode. "What is it?"

"There's been an accident at the retirement home."

"What happened?" Lena demanded, her voice sharp with fear.

"Poppa's been injured. He broke his arm and—"

"What! How the hell did that happen?"

"I'm not sure," Morgan said quickly. "I'm on my way

to the hospital right now. I told the retirement home I'd call you myself. For some reason they couldn't get through to your cell phone. You must be somewhere with spotty reception."

Guilt assailed Lena. "I'll meet you at the hospital as soon as I can get there."

"Okay." Morgan hesitated. "Where are you anyway?"

"I'll tell you later," Lena evaded. "But do me a favor and call me when you arrive at the hospital. I want an update on Poppa ASAP."

"Yes, ma'am," Morgan promised.

Lena disconnected, her hand trembling as she clutched the phone, her thoughts racing a mile a minute.

"Lena."

She whipped her head around to see Roderick propped up on one elbow, watching her with a concerned expression. "What happened?" he asked gently.

"There was an accident. My grandfather broke his arm and—oh, God! I don't even know if that's the worst of it! I didn't let my sister finish. I have to call her back." She was already speed-dialing Morgan's number. When the call went through to voice mail, she cursed in frustration.

"Calm down," Roderick murmured.

"Don't tell me to calm down!" Lena snapped. "My grandfather is an eighty-year-old man who's already suffered a massive stroke that left him bound to a wheelchair. The last thing he needs is another injury to further weaken his body, not to mention his psyche!"

"I wasn't trivializing your concern," Roderick said evenly. "I told you to calm down because having a panic attack won't do you any good."

"Since when do you care about what's good for me?"

Lena jeered, her voice filled with bitter accusation. "This whole weekend was all about *you,* not me. You and your damn needs. I told you I had other obligations, but you wouldn't listen!"

Instead of defending himself, Roderick gazed at her with those dark, penetrating eyes that discerned way too much. "You shouldn't feel guilty because you weren't there, Lena. Unless you attach yourself to your grandfather's hip—"

Lena lunged to her feet impatiently. "I don't have time for this! I need to get back to Chicago."

As she strode toward the bathroom, she suddenly remembered that they were on a boat out in the middle of Lake Michigan. Swearing profusely, she drew up short and whirled around. "How long will it take us to get back to Chicago?"

"Not long," Roderick assured her, throwing back the covers and rolling out of bed. "We'll take the helicopter."

For once, she was glad he had a solution to everything.

Lena told herself to keep her emotions in check for her grandfather's sake. But when she arrived at the hospital and saw him lying in bed, looking frail and battered with one arm elevated in a cast and IV tubes snaking out of the other arm, her mind flashed back to the terrible day three years ago when she'd received the news about his stroke. Fearing the worst outcome that day, she'd caught the first flight home and rushed straight to the hospital, wondering whether she'd make it in time to say goodbye to her grandfather.

As if sensing her presence in the doorway, Cleveland opened his eyes and slowly turned his head to look at her. He mustered a feeble smile. "There she is," he greeted her in a thin, raspy voice. "There's my baby girl."

"Poppa." Tears blurred Lena's vision as she hurried to his bedside and leaned down to hug him as gingerly as her overwrought emotions would allow.

"Now, now," Cleveland soothed, reaching around to awkwardly pat her back with his good arm. "Don't you start all that boo-hooing or you'll get your sister going again. She's been in the bathroom for the past twenty minutes trying to compose herself."

Lena didn't know whether to laugh or sob. "I was so worried about you!"

Cleveland clucked a tongue. "No need for that. I'm just fine, as you can see."

Lena sniffed, taking in his ashen complexion, rheumy eyes, sunken cheeks and plastered arm. "With all due respect, Poppa, you look anything *but* fine."

He smiled softly at her. "Can't say the same about you, though. You look pretty as a picture, baby girl. And unless my eyes are deceiving me, your face is glowing."

"Your eyes are deceiving you," Lena retorted, even as heat suffused her cheeks. No way could her grandfather tell, just by looking at her, that she'd spent the past day and a half having the best sex of her life. And no way was she telling him.

She brushed a gentle hand over his warm forehead and frowned. "You have a fever."

He grimaced. "I know. And before you start fretting, the doctor says it's normal to run a fever after suffering an injury. It's the body's way of coping with the trauma."

"How did this happen, Poppa?" Lena demanded. "How on earth did you break your arm?"

Before he could respond, the bathroom door opened and Morgan walked out. Her puffy, red-rimmed eyes confirmed that she'd been crying.

Lena's heart constricted with tender sympathy. Morgan was the one who'd found their grandfather sprawled on the floor after he suffered a stroke, so receiving the emergency phone call from Lakeview Manor this morning had probably given her horrible flashbacks.

"Hey, you're here," she said to Lena.

"I'm here." When Morgan reached her, Lena hugged her around the waist and gently searched her face. "You okay?"

"Sure," Morgan said ruefully, hitching her chin toward their grandfather. "But *I'm* not the one in traction. So has he told you yet?"

"Told me what?" Lena asked, dividing a wary glance between her sister and grandfather.

"Has he told you how he broke his arm? I've been trying to get a straight answer out of him since he woke up from surgery."

Lena frowned at her grandfather. "What's going on, Poppa? You know I'm going to interview everyone at the retirement home to find out what happened this morning. If you're trying to protect someone—"

Cleveland grimaced. "No, no, no. Nothing like that. I was waiting for you to arrive so I could tell both of you at the same time."

"Tell us what?" the sisters echoed in unison.

An excited gleam filled Cleveland's eyes. "The Lord has answered our prayers. When I woke up early this morning, I felt a tingling sensation in my left leg. Oh, it's happened once or twice before, but this time it was different. Stronger. It reminded me of that burning sensation you get in your fingers and toes after they've gone numb from frostbite. But once you get inside where it's nice and warm, they start thawing out and tingling as the feeling returns." He paused, a broad grin sweeping across his face. "That's what I experienced this morning. I felt the numbness wearing off my bad leg."

"Oh, Poppa." A lump had lodged in Lena's throat. She and Morgan reached for each other's hands and squeezed.

"But that's not even the best part." Cleveland's voice had grown stronger, his eyes brighter. Even his coloring had dramatically improved. "I kept lying there in bed, staring up at the ceiling and waiting for the tingling sensation to go away. But it didn't. So you know what I did?"

Lena and Morgan leaned forward with riveted expressions.

Cleveland grinned. "I rolled myself into an upright position. Well, about as upright as I could manage. Then I took a deep breath, said a prayer—and pushed myself to my feet."

The two sisters gasped.

"Poppa!" Morgan cried excitedly. "You didn't!"

"I did," Cleveland asserted, beaming with pride. "I stood on that tingling leg for a good while, just waiting for it to give out on me. It didn't. So I took another deep breath, said another prayer. And I stepped forward."

Lena and Morgan squealed, tears streaming down their faces.

"Three," Cleveland said, holding up the corresponding number of fingers. "I took three steps across the room before the leg buckled under me. I went down like a felled tree. Unfortunately, I landed awkwardly on my arm and broke it."

"Oh, Poppa," his granddaughters chorused sympathetically.

Almost at once they began fussing over him, checking his IV fluids, giving him a drink of water, adjusting his blanket and making sure he was comfortable.

When the flurry of activity was over, Morgan settled into a visitor chair at the foot of the bed while Lena claimed the bedside one.

"So what did your doctor say?" Morgan asked Cleveland. "Does this mean you're going to walk again?"

He made a face. "You know how these doctors are. They don't want to get their patients' hopes up, so they downplay everything. He says he's cautiously optimistic, but even he admits that what I experienced this morning is one hell of a breakthrough. Now Margaret—er, Nurse Jacobs," he amended when Lena and Morgan exchanged knowing glances, "*she's* very excited about what happened. She's a God-fearing woman, so she knows miracles can happen. After she lectured me for trying to walk without anyone around to assist me, she promised to show me some safe exercises that we can do in therapy while I'm stuck wearing this cast. Once it comes off, it's full steam ahead."

"That's wonderful, Poppa," Lena said warmly. "I'm so happy for you. Of course, I wish you hadn't broken your arm in the process of making such an amazing breakthrough."

"So do I," Cleveland admitted with a rueful grimace. "But as the saying goes: No pain, no gain."

Lena smiled. "That's what they say."

"Anyway, enough about me. How was your trip?"

"My t-trip?" she stammered, flushing.

"Yeah. Morgan says you had to go out of town unexpectedly."

"Oh. Right. I did." *Not now. Please, God, not now.* "You know, Poppa, you should probably get some rest. You had surgery this morning, and I'm sure the painkillers they gave you are making you drowsy. You were dozing off when I arrived."

To her relief, Cleveland nodded in agreement. "It *has* been an eventful day. But I don't—" He broke off abruptly, staring over her shoulder in surprise.

Even before Lena turned around, she knew Roderick had appeared in the doorway. She'd specifically told him to stay in the waiting room, but she should have known he wouldn't listen to her, just as he'd insisted on escorting her to the hospital and taking her home afterward.

"Say, I know who you are," Cleveland exclaimed. "I see your picture in the paper all the time. You're—"

"Roderick Brand," Morgan breathed, her eyes wide as saucers in her face.

Roderick flashed a smile at her, but his attention was on Cleveland, who was staring at him with unabashed curiosity. "I hope I'm not interrupting—"

"Not at all," Cleveland said easily, though he had to be wondering why one of Chicago's wealthiest residents was standing in the doorway of his hospital room. He looked askance at Lena, who was blushing furiously and wishing some mythical creature would swoop in on giant wings and whisk her away from there.

As comprehension dawned, Cleveland gaped at Roderick, his snowy eyebrows shooting up to his hairline. "You're here with Lena?"

Roderick smiled. "Yes, sir. I am."

"Well." *I'll be damned,* the unspoken words echoed in the stunned silence that followed. This time Lena simply prayed for the ground to open up and swallow her whole.

"Well, don't just stand there." Recovering from his shock, Cleveland waved Roderick into the room with his good arm. "Come join the party."

Lena leveled a glare at Roderick as he approached the hospital bed.

Deliberately ignoring her, he reached out and grasped her grandfather's hand. "It's a pleasure to meet you, Mr. Morrison."

"Same here, young man. Got a good handshake there. Confident. Strong." Cleveland sounded as impressed as he looked.

"Thank you, sir," Roderick said lazily. "Yours ain't too bad either."

"For an old-timer, you mean?"

Roderick grinned, and Cleveland let out an appreciative bark of laughter.

Lena caught Morgan's meaningful look and just shook her head, as if to say *Don't ask.* She hoped Roderick had a damn good reason for doing this to her, though she couldn't fathom what would justify him putting her on the spot like this.

"Hi, Roderick." Impatient with her sibling's lack of manners, Morgan stood and initiated her own introduction. "I'm Lena's sister—"

"Morgan." He smiled, shaking her hand. "It's nice to meet you. I've heard so much about you."

"All good, I hope?" Morgan grinned, flirting shamelessly.

Roderick chuckled. "All good."

Morgan beamed at him. "Poppa was right. You *do* have a nice handshake."

Lena rolled her eyes. "Down, girl."

Morgan made a face at her.

Grinning, Roderick returned his attention to Cleveland. "I'm sorry about your accident, Mr. Morrison. How're you feeling?"

"Right now? I feel just dandy. Talk to me later when the meds wear off." His eyes twinkled with mirth. "You ever broken an arm or a leg, Roderick?"

"Yes, sir. Broke my arm playing football in high school."

Cleveland sized him up. "Wide receiver?"

"That's right."

"Were you any good?"

Roderick shrugged. "I was decent."

"Come on," Cleveland guffawed. "I bet you're just being modest. Guy your size? With those hands? I bet you were named All-State and had college recruiters fighting over you."

Roderick smiled. "I may have received one or two scholarship offers."

Cleveland grinned. "That's probably another understatement, but okay, I'll play along. So what happened? You broke your arm and decided football wasn't for you?"

"Poppa!" Lena chided, throwing an apologetic glance at Roderick. "I'm sure Mr. Brand didn't come here to be interrogated."

"I don't mind," Roderick drawled, his eyes glimmering with laughter. "To answer your question, Mr. Morrison, I never intended to pursue a career in professional football. It wasn't my passion. Running my own company someday? *That* got my juices flowing."

Out of the corner of her eye, Lena could see Morgan's lips curving in a slow, lascivious grin. Apparently Lena wasn't the only one whose hormones had reacted to Roderick's use of the words *passion* and *juices flowing* in the same breath. Her "juices" hadn't stopped flowing since she met him.

"I can definitely respect that," Cleveland was saying. "It takes a lot of courage to go after what you want."

"Persistence helps, too," Roderick added, flicking a glance at Lena that was so subtle she wondered if she was the only one who'd caught it.

Cleveland smiled affably. "It's rewarding when your persistence pays off, as yours obviously has."

Lena shot a stricken look at her grandfather, relieved when she realized that he was referring to Roderick's company—not her. "I understand that you've recently expanded into the Japanese energy market," Cleveland continued. "That was quite a deal you landed. Congratulations."

Roderick smiled. "Thank you, sir. I had an angel on my side," he murmured, giving Lena another one of those secret looks.

"One of my comrades at the retirement home is a big fan of yours," Cleveland said, seemingly unaware of the undercurrents between Roderick and his granddaughter. "Abraham's the one who got me into reading the *Wall Street Journal* and *Financial Times*. When you were named Businessman of the Year, Abraham was so excited you'd have thought his first grandchild had just been born. Come to think of it, I don't even think he broke out cigars for *that* occasion."

Roderick chuckled. "He sounds like quite a character."

"Oh, he is," Cleveland agreed with a laugh. "If you

ever met him, the first thing he'd do is give you pointers on how to run your business. Doesn't matter how much he admires and respects you. He just has to throw in his two cents. He does the same thing with Lena's singing."

"Singing?" A spark of interest lit Roderick's eyes as he looked at Lena. "I didn't know you could sing."

An embarrassed flush crawled up her neck. "Everyone can sing. Some better than others. I fall into the 'others' category."

"What?" Cleveland laughingly scoffed at the suggestion. "Don't listen to her, Roderick. She's just taking a page from your modesty playbook. My baby girl sings like a bird. Which is no surprise, considering who she's named after."

Roderick smiled slowly at her. "You're named after Lena Horne?"

She nodded, grinning wryly. "No pressure, right?"

"You should ask Lena to sing 'Stormy Weather' for you. Or 'Love Me or Leave Me.' *Ooo-wee.*" Cleveland laughed, shaking his head. "She'll have you wrapped around her little finger after that."

Roderick smiled faintly. "I think she already does," he murmured, holding Lena's gaze.

She swallowed, then swallowed again when the knot in her throat wouldn't dissolve.

Cleveland looked from one to the other with undisguised interest. "So where did you two meet anyway?"

The blood drained from Lena's head. "Meet?" she croaked.

"Yeah." Cleveland smiled whimsically. "No offense, baby girl, but I didn't realize you traveled in the same social circles as billionaire CEOs. So I'm just curious about how you and Roderick met."

"Oh." She licked her dry lips. "We, ah…"

Roderick watched her, a wicked gleam in his eyes.

"We met, um, at—"

From the foot of the bed, Morgan went into a violent coughing paroxysm that drew her grandfather's concerned gaze. "Are you okay?" he asked her. "You need some water?"

Morgan gasped, vigorously nodding her head.

"Lena, pour your sister some water."

Lena jumped up, only too happy to do as he'd told her. As she handed the plastic cup to her sister, she mouthed, *Thank you.*

Eyes glimmering with mischief, Morgan mouthed back, *You owe me.*

I know, Lena replied.

Turning back toward their grandfather, she announced briskly, "All right, Poppa, we're going to leave now so you can get some sleep."

Cleveland frowned. "But—"

"No buts. You've had a long day, and you really need to rest. But don't worry. Morgan and I will be here when you wake up later. We'll get something from the cafeteria and have dinner with you. Okay?" Not giving him a chance to argue, she leaned down and kissed his forehead, then gave Morgan and Roderick a look that warned them there'd be hell to pay if they didn't follow her out of the room. *Now.*

Roderick chuckled softly. "It was a pleasure to meet you, Mr. Morrison."

"Same to you, son. Say, do you have a pen? I'd love to have you autograph my cast."

Ignoring the dirty look Lena gave him, Roderick smiled. "Sure. I'd be honored."

Cleveland grinned broadly. "When Abraham finds out that I met you, he's gonna be so jealous. Lena, give the man a pen."

"Sorry, Poppa. I don't have one."

"I do!" Morgan piped up, earning a glare from her sister.

As Roderick began writing on the cast, Cleveland glanced up at his granddaughters. "He'll be out in a minute," he said, all but shooing them out the door.

The last thing Lena wanted was to leave Roderick alone with her grandfather, who was clearly up to something. But before she could object, Morgan grabbed her hand and dragged her from the room and down the hospital corridor.

When they were a safe distance away, Morgan squealed excitedly, "Oh my God! You're sleeping with him!"

"Shhh!" Mortified, Lena glanced up and down the hallway to make sure no one had overheard her. Thankfully, the only person around was well out of earshot.

Turning back to Morgan, she demanded, "What makes you think I'm sleeping with Roderick?"

Morgan snorted out an incredulous laugh. "You're kidding, right? It's so obvious!"

"How?"

"For starters, every time he just looked at you, Lena, I expected your clothes to go up in flames. It wasn't the lewd, crude stare you get from a guy at the club who's checking you out and wondering how he can get in your panties. No, girl, Roderick looks at you with pride of ownership."

"Pride of ownership?" Lena scoffed.

"Yeah. Like he's already *been* in your panties and has memorized every dip and curve of your body, so every time he sees you, it's like he's reliving the experience all over again." Morgan shuddered, fanning her face with her hand. "I'd *kill* to have a smokin' hot guy look at me that way!"

Lena knew "the look" her sister was talking about. Knew it all too well.

"You spent the weekend with him, didn't you?" Morgan persisted, a knowing gleam in her eyes. "You didn't go out of town on business. You were with Roderick. Fess up."

"Fine," Lena groaned in defeat. "You're right. We were together."

"I knew it!"

"No, you don't, Morg. It's complicated."

"I don't see why. Girl, that man is even finer than he looked on *Oprah*. Those eyes, those lips, those shoulders, those hands. That *voice*. And you were right—he smells delicious!" Morgan sighed deeply. "I never thought I'd say this, Lena, but I hate you. I really hate you."

"Hey!" Lena laughingly protested.

Morgan grinned. "I'll only forgive you if you tell me that he has a brother."

Lena chuckled. "Actually, he has a tw—" She broke off abruptly as Roderick emerged from her grandfather's hospital room.

He glanced down the corridor, his dark gaze latching onto hers.

"Like a heat-seeking missile," Morgan murmured.

Lena blushed. Not wanting to stand there ogling Roderick as he sauntered toward them, she turned away and pretended to admire a pastel seascape, the kind of generic painting that graced the walls of hospital corridors everywhere.

Morgan, on the other hand, had no qualms about ogling Roderick. As he drew closer, she intoned under her breath, "What a man, what a man, what a man."

"Shhh!" Lena hissed. "He'll hear you!"

Morgan grinned unabashedly.

When Roderick reached them, Lena turned and plastered on a gracious smile. "Thanks for bringing me to the hospital, Roderick. I really appreciate it. But you don't have to stick around any longer. I'm sure you have things to do."

He looked amused. "Are you trying to get rid of me?"

"No." *Hell, yes!* "It's just that I don't want to take up any more of your time."

"I don't mind. And I promised to drive you home, remember?"

"That won't be necessary. I can catch a ride home with Morgan."

"Actually," Morgan interjected, "my car's a mess, and you always complain—"

"I'll deal with it." Keeping her serene smile in place, Lena said to Roderick, "See? There's really no reason for you to stay."

"Unless you really want to," Morgan told him.

Lena skewered her with a look. "Would you mind giving us a minute?"

Morgan divided a glance between her sister and Roderick, then grinned. "No problem. I need to return a phone call anyway."

As she strolled off, Roderick smiled at Lena. "I like your family. I can tell how much you guys love one another."

"Thanks," Lena muttered, then added sullenly, "They seem to really like you, too."

His smile deepened. "You make that sound like a bad thing."

"I'm not so sure it isn't. By the way," she said accusingly, "thanks for letting me twist in the wind when my grandfather asked where we'd met."

Roderick grinned unrepentantly. "I was waiting to hear your answer. I wanted to see how good you are at thinking on your feet." He shook his head, tsk-tsking. "Not very good at all."

"Oh yeah? Well, I wouldn't have had to come up with any answer if you hadn't put me in that position in the first place! I thought I told you to stay in the waiting room!"

"You did," Roderick said mildly. "But I wanted to meet your grandfather."

"Why?" she burst out in exasperation. "It's not as if you and I are dating!"

"We're doing something."

"We're having sex. Wild, unbelievably hot sex. That doesn't warrant me introducing you to my family. Now they're going to have all these questions for me, questions I can't answer!"

Roderick's expression softened. For the first time, she detected a trace of guilt in his eyes. "Let me take you and your sister out to lunch," he gently suggested. "I'll have you back before your grandfather wakes up."

Lena shook her head, dragging a hand through her hair. "Thanks for the offer, but I'd prefer to stay here in case Poppa needs anything."

"That's what the nurses are for."

"I know. And they're perfectly capable. But I'd really rather not leave. In fact, I'm going to need my evenings free this week to stay with Poppa while he's hospitalized. Given his age and health issues, the doctor wants to keep him for observation for a few days before he goes back to the retirement home."

Roderick nodded. "I understand."

"So you don't mind that I might not be able to see you this week?"

He smiled at her surprised tone. "I'm not an ogre, Lena. I know that you have priorities, and your grandfather is one of them. If we have to postpone spending time together, then so be it."

She gave him a grateful smile. "Thank you for being so understanding."

"Of course." He paused. "But you should know that your grandfather asked me to take you to dinner and a show sometime this week."

"He did *what?*"

Roderick's lips twitched. "He asked me—"

"I heard you," Lena interrupted, frowning. "Why did he ask you that?"

"He said you're always going places alone. Museums, restaurants, movies. He thinks you're lonely."

"I'm not lonely," she snapped, flushing with humiliation.

"Your grandfather thinks you are. So he wants me to take you out on another date—"

"Another?"

Roderick grinned. "He seems to be under the impression that we've just started dating. And since you didn't correct him—"

"Neither did you, obviously."

His grin widened. "I didn't have the heart to do it. And it wasn't really my place."

Lena scowled. "Your 'place' was the waiting room,

where you were supposed to stay out of sight. But, *nooo,* you just had to go rogue." She groaned, slapping a hand to her forehead. "This is just the beginning. First he's planning our dates, next he'll be planning our wedding."

Roderick chuckled. "Come on now. Let's not get carried away."

"Okay, but don't say I didn't warn you." Out of the corner of her eye, she could see Morgan hovering near the end of the corridor, pretending not to watch them.

Lena sighed. "I should go. My sister's waiting."

Roderick glanced over his shoulder, met Morgan's stare and smiled. When Morgan grinned and fluttered her fingers in a wave, Lena rolled her eyes in disgust.

Turning back to her, Roderick said, "My lunch offer still stands."

"Thanks, but my answer's the same."

"Then maybe I should ask your sister."

She stared at him. "You wouldn't."

His eyes glinted wickedly. "I might."

Lena folded her arms across her chest. "Go ahead."

A slow grin curved his mouth. "Is that a dare?"

"Maybe."

He laughed softly. "You should never dare me, unless you're prepared to deal with the consequences."

Lena sniffed. "What consequences? Morgan thinks you're hot, but she also believes you and I are involved, so she wouldn't—"

"Encroach on your territory?"

"Exactly."

He smiled mischievously. "Are you sure about that?"

Lena didn't hesitate. "Positive."

"Okay." He reached out and stroked his knuckle over her cheek, a slow, lingering caress. "I'll be in touch."

She swallowed and nodded, then watched as he sauntered away. When he reached Morgan, he stopped to say something to her. Lena was too far away to make out the words, or Morgan's reply. She told herself it didn't matter. It didn't matter whether he invited her sister out to lunch, and it didn't matter whether or not Morgan accepted. They were both adults, and Roderick didn't belong to Lena.

So she had no reason to feel a stab of jealousy when Morgan rested a hand lightly on his arm, or when Roderick threw back his head and laughed in response to whatever she'd said.

And she definitely had no reason to feel a huge wave of relief when Roderick glanced over and met her gaze, winked at her, then left—alone.

When she caught up to her sister and suggested they grab a bite to eat, Morgan said, "Girl, you'd better be glad I love you. That man is too damn tempting for his own good."

"Let me guess," Lena said flatly. "He asked you out to lunch."

"No." Morgan looked puzzled. "Why would he do that?"

Lena shrugged. "I don't know. To be polite. To rescue you from hospital food."

"Wouldn't he ask *you* out to lunch?"

"He did. Invited both of us. I politely declined."

"Well, damn. *I'd* have gone with him."

"Alone?"

Morgan gave her a sly look. "Would you have minded?"

"No."

"Liar!" Morgan laughed, then linked her arm through Lena's as they headed for the cafeteria.

Yeah, Lena had no reason to feel relieved.

But, damn it, she did.

Chapter Seventeen

By the end of the week, Cleveland was back at Lakeview Manor, where he was welcomed like a conquering hero returning from battle. The staff pampered him even more than before, and the other residents filed in and out of his room to admire his cast and hear all about the miraculous breakthrough he'd experienced. Cleveland told and retold the story with great relish, shamelessly basking in all the attention.

Every evening, Lena got off from work and headed straight to the retirement home, where she kept her grandfather company until he nodded off around eight. And then she returned to an empty apartment, her chest filled with an inexplicable ache that told her something was missing.

With each passing day she expected to receive a call from Roderick, summoning her to the spot of their next tryst. But he didn't call.

At first she was relieved. She'd asked for time to look after her grandfather, so Roderick was respecting her wishes. Good for him.

But he'd also promised Cleveland that he'd take Lena out on a date that week. Although she'd resented her grandfather's meddling, she'd actually found herself looking forward to dinner and a show with Roderick.

But as the days wore on and her phone remained silent, she went from feeling relieved, to perplexed, to annoyed. Downright annoyed. So when Zandra called on Saturday morning to ask whether she was available to meet a new client that evening, Lena was tempted to accept out of spite.

"Lena?" Zandra prompted when she didn't immediately respond.

"I can't," Lena declined apologetically. She'd made a deal with Roderick, and a deal was a deal.

"Are you sure?" Zandra prodded. "The client specifically asked for you, and I'd really hate to refer him to someone else. He says he met you a few months ago at a party, and you two struck up a conversation he really enjoyed. Medium height and build, dark hair, green eyes, British accent. Do you remember?" She didn't use his name. It was one of her unwritten rules: Never identify clients over the phone.

Lena smiled. "I do remember him. Nice guy. Great accent."

"So you wouldn't mind going out with him?" Zandra asked hopefully.

"Not at all. But I can't. Not this weekend."

Zandra paused, undoubtedly surprised. Lena was always available on the weekends. She purposely kept her schedule clear to accommodate the agency.

"Is something going on, Lena?" Zandra asked, a note of concern in her voice.

Lena saw her opening, and seized it with both hands. "Actually, my grandfather just got out of the hospital."

"Oh, no," Zandra exclaimed. "Is he okay?"

Lena gave her an account of everything that had happened over the past week, omitting any mention of Roderick.

When she'd finished speaking, Zandra said gently, "Oh, Lena, I'm so sorry your grandfather had to go through all that. But that's exciting about him being able to walk again."

"Very exciting," Lena agreed. "We're all keeping our fingers crossed and praying for the best."

"Amen to that." Zandra paused. "Hey, do you want to grab a massage with me? I'll be heading out soon for my appointment, and I'd love your company."

"A massage, huh? I haven't had one of those in months."

"Then you're long overdue. My treat."

Lena grinned. "A free massage? I'm there."

Two hours later, after a lavishly relaxing massage, Lena and Zandra lounged in the upscale day spa's steamy sauna.

As Lena felt the final traces of tension melt from her body, she closed her eyes and sighed contentedly. "This was absolutely wonderful, Zandra. Thanks for inviting me."

On the bench beside her, Zandra murmured, "No need to thank me. You deserve some pampering after the week you've had."

"Mmm." A hazy smile touched Lena's mouth. "I didn't realize how much stress I was carrying around until your masseuse got her hands on me. She's *very* good."

"The best," Zandra agreed. "I have a standing appointment with her every week. You're more than welcome to join me any time."

Lena chuckled softly. "I just might take you up on that offer."

"I hope you do."

A companionable silence lapsed between them.

It didn't last long.

"So," Zandra began conversationally. "I spoke to Roderick yesterday."

"Oh?" Lena kept her tone neutral. "How's he doing?"

"Busy, as usual. He mentioned something about traveling to Japan next week to meet with his transition team and work out some kinks regarding the merger."

Lena nodded, remembering that he'd invited her to accompany him to Japan. As if.

"I think he's going to be dividing his time between Chicago and Tokyo over the next couple years or so," Zandra continued. "He already has a real estate broker looking for apartments."

"Really?" Lena's chest squeezed with an emotion she refused to identify.

As if sensing it, Zandra added smoothly, "But I don't think he'd ever decide to move there permanently. Chicago has always been his home. He has too many ties here, too many family members who'd start a revolt if he even *thought* about leaving."

Wondering where the conversation was leading, Lena cracked one eye open and peered sideways at Zandra. Long strands of black hair had escaped from her upsweep and clung damply to her face and neck. Like Lena, she was wrapped in a plush towel emblazoned with the spa's fancy logo. Beads of water glistened on her smooth brown skin and trickled down the valley between her full breasts. With little or no effort, she oozed sensuality like a perfume laced with pheromones.

And, remarkably, Roderick was immune to her. *Hallelujah!*

"Before we got off the phone," Zandra said casually, "Roderick made the strangest request."

Lena tensed. *Uh-oh. Here it comes.* "What?"

"He asked me not to send any clients your way until further notice."

Lena gasped. "He did *what?*"

Zandra met her outraged stare. "Is there something I should know about you and Roderick?"

Lena scowled, then covered her face with her hands and groaned. "He wasn't supposed to say anything."

"He didn't. Not much, anyway. Shortly after he made the request, he had to run to a meeting. So I didn't have a chance to follow up with any questions."

"I'm *so* gonna kill him," Lena muttered darkly.

Zandra chuckled, a low, throaty sound. "In all fairness to Rod, I sort of tricked him into saying what he did. I was fishing for information, trying to find out whether he wanted to see you again. He doesn't know that you told me what happened between the two of you the night of the party. I guess I wanted to rattle his cage a little. So at the end of our conversation, I casually mentioned to him that a new client was interested in going out with you." She grinned. "The first word out of his mouth? *Shit!* He muttered it under his breath, but it came through loud and clear."

Lena shook her head, mentally firing off a few expletives herself.

"That's when he told me not to set you up with any more clients until further notice," Zandra continued. "As you can imagine, my curiosity went through the roof after that. So I called you this morning to test the waters, to see whether you'd be willing to go out with a client." She paused, searching Lena's face. "Taking care of your grandfather isn't the only reason you declined, is it?"

Lena hesitated for a prolonged moment. "No."

Zandra nodded slowly. "So you and Roderick have some sort of...understanding?"

"Yes." Lena pushed out a deep breath, then reluctantly relayed the details of her arrangement with Roderick.

"Oh, my God." Zandra stared at her in stunned disbelief. "Talk about an indecent proposal."

"I know," Lena muttered self-consciously. "It's scandalous."

"Positively," Zandra agreed.

Lena eyed her cautiously. "Are you mad?"

Zandra frowned. "Honestly? I'm a little annoyed that you and Roderick made this secret arrangement without consulting me first."

"I figured you would be," Lena mumbled guiltily.

"Can you blame me? Considering that your deal with Roderick affects my bottom line, I think you at least owed me the courtesy of a phone call. As I reminded you before, the holiday season is always our busiest time of year. Not having one of my top escorts for three weeks will really cut into my profits. So, yeah, a heads-up would have been nice."

"I know." Lena sighed heavily. "I'm sorry, Zandra. I was afraid to tell you, especially after I'd just violated the agency's no-sex policy. I knew I was skating on thin ice."

"You're not alone," Zandra grumbled. "I can't wait to give Roderick a piece of my mind."

Lena gulped on his behalf.

After a prolonged silence, Zandra sighed. "That said, Rod's one of my closest friends, and using the agency was a one-time thing for him anyway. So it's not as if you'll be sleeping with one of our regular clients."

Lena flushed all over, grateful for the clouds of steam that obscured her body's reaction. "My college really needs the funds," she felt compelled to explain. "I wouldn't have agreed to Roderick's offer if—"

Zandra held up a manicured hand. "You don't have to explain yourself to me. Ultimately, a girl's gotta do what a girl's gotta do. Believe me, Lena, I'd be the last person to judge you. Hell, most of my friends and relatives think I run a brothel."

Lena grimaced. "That's not good."

Zandra grinned wryly. "At first it got under my skin. It made me feel like they were criticizing me and looking down their noses at me. Nowadays? I don't even bother correcting them. And wouldn't you know it? Some of those same judgmental people are the ones who're always hitting me up for money."

"Hypocrites," Lena muttered.

Zandra laughed. Leaning her head back against the sauna bench, she drawled in an amused voice, "So when does your, ah, arrangement officially begin?"

Lena blushed, studying her lacquered toenails with focused absorption. "It already has."

"Oh." Zandra chuckled, low and indulgent. "Wasted no time, did he?"

"Nope." Lena bit her lip, wondering if her face could possibly get any hotter.

"Before he got off the phone with me," Zandra said,

"Rod promised to compensate me for any revenue I'd lose as a result of not having you available. I told him to keep his money and send referrals my way instead. Within an hour the agency had two new clients—a billionaire philanthropist and a software tycoon, both of whom are close associates of Roderick's."

"I'm so glad to hear that," Lena said sincerely. "I felt really guilty about costing you money, Zandra."

"I know you did. But I'm not the only one you should be concerned about. You earn a substantial amount per month, Lena. Roderick should be compensating you for your time as well."

"He offered to, but I turned him down. I don't need his money—the college does."

Zandra slid her a wry, teasing grin. "Taking one for the team, huh?"

Lena heaved the long, dramatic sigh of a martyr. "It's worth the sacrifice."

"Sacrifice. *Riiight.*" Zandra laughed. "Well, look at it this way. If you're going to be anyone's sexual companion, you could do a whole lot worse than Roderick Brand."

"*That's* an understatement."

The two women grinned at each other.

Sobering after a few moments, Zandra murmured, "Just be careful, okay?"

"With Roderick?"

Zandra nodded.

"I will." Lena hesitated, then couldn't resist asking, "Are you trying to tell me something?"

Zandra looked pained. "I probably shouldn't have said anything."

"Too late."

Zandra pushed out a long, deep breath. "Okay, here's

the thing," she began, choosing her words carefully. "Roderick is a wonderful guy—"

"Uh-oh. That's never a good way to start off."

"No, it's true. He *is* wonderful. Absolutely. I told you before how much I cherish his friendship, and I meant that. But he, ah, doesn't exactly have the best track record with women."

Lena smirked. "You're saying he's a player. What a shock."

"No, that's not what I'm saying. He's *not* a player. Yes, he's dated a lot of women, but he's never intentionally set out to hurt any of them. The thing about Roderick is that he has very high expectations. Maybe unrealistic expectations." Zandra sighed. "You know how some guys are scarred by not having positive examples of relationships in their lives? Like if they grew up without a father, they often don't know how to treat women? Well, Rod has the opposite problem, if you can call it that. His parents have a wonderful relationship. They've been happily married for forty years, and they're still going strong. I used to wish they were *my* parents," she admitted ruefully.

Lena gave her a sympathetic smile.

"Anyway," Zandra continued with another sigh, "I think their amazing marriage may have led Roderick to develop impossible standards for women. Oh, I'm not talking about shallow stuff, like he's gonna be checking your feet for bunions in the middle of the night."

"Whew!" Lena said, wiping her brow in exaggerated relief.

Zandra laughed. "Girl, Roderick isn't your typical billionaire playboy. Sure, he's dated models here and there, but I can honestly tell you that he prefers regular women. He's gone out with females that some of his friends considered *too* ordinary, but Rod didn't care. He's totally an around-the-way boy."

Lena smiled, and felt her appreciation for him go up a notch. So far, Zandra hadn't told her anything that would send her screaming for the hills.

"When I say Roderick has impossible standards, I'm talking about relationship matters. He brings his own rigid set of expectations to the table, and if they're not met, he can get turned off quickly. He's very stubborn—"

Lena snorted. "*That's* an understatement."

"—so it's not easy for him to compromise. He's been known to break up with girlfriends over things that could have been easily resolved, if only he'd been more willing to give and take." She shook her head in exasperation. "It's like he has this idealized version of the perfect woman, but I'm not even sure *he* knows what he's really looking for. He just knows he hasn't found it yet, and he puts women through hell in the process." She paused, frowning. "His brother's the same way."

"The twin?"

"Yeah. He told you about Remy?"

Lena nodded, wondering if Zandra knew about Remington Brand's feelings for her.

A shadow crossed Zandra's face. Or maybe it was just a cloud of steam. A moment later she blew out a deep breath and said, "Look, the bottom line is that I think you and Roderick could be good for each other. That's why I set you up on a date together. Honestly? I was hoping you two would hit it off and start seeing each other—gradually."

Lena eyed her speculatively. "You really *don't* approve of our arrangement, do you?"

Zandra grimaced. "I don't, to be perfectly honest

with you. But it's not my place to approve or disapprove. You guys are mature, consenting adults with healthy libidos. Believe me, I totally understand that. But I just want to make sure you both know what you're doing. This arrangement of yours could get pretty complicated. Dangerous." Her voice gentled as she regarded Lena. "I just don't want to see you get hurt. Either of you."

Lena swallowed hard, then nodded. "Thank you for being so honest with me, Zandra."

"You don't have to thank me. Since I'm the one who introduced you to Roderick, I just felt it was my responsibility to give you a heads-up, woman to woman."

"I really appreciate that," Lena said sincerely. She hesitated, then added, "If at any time I think I'm getting in over my head with Roderick, I'll call the whole thing off."

Zandra gave her a soft, intuitive smile. "Hopefully it won't be too late by then."

Chapter Eighteen

After leaving the spa, Lena drove to Lakeview Manor for her Saturday afternoon visit with her grandfather. She'd been there for an hour when Morgan arrived, the heels of her stiletto boots barely touching the ground as she floated across the terrace to reach Lena and Cleveland.

"Hey, you two!" Morgan kissed her grandfather's cheek and hugged her sister before dropping into the vacant chair at the table and sighing contentedly. "What a beautiful day!"

Lena and Cleveland exchanged knowing glances and chorused, "What's his name?"

Morgan laughed, her cheeks flushing prettily. "What're you talking about?"

Cleveland guffawed. "You know what we're talking about."

"Who's the new guy who has you floating on cloud nine today?" Lena added.

Morgan grinned. "I can't get anything past you two, can I?"

Lena chuckled dryly. "Not when you show up here practically levitating off the ground. So who is he?"

Morgan sighed again. "His name's Isaiah. I met him this morning when I was waiting in line at the bank. He's an attorney at one of the top law firms in Chicago."

Cleveland arched a snowy brow. "An attorney, huh? That's quite an upgrade from your last boyfriend, who was always between jobs."

Morgan scowled. "Which is the main reason he wanted me to move in with him—to help pay his rent. Good riddance to *that* loser."

"Amen," Lena and Cleveland agreed.

Morgan laughed. "Isaiah's nothing like Jason, I can tell you that. He's taking me out to dinner tonight— someplace fancy. Jason *never* did that."

Lena grinned. "So what does Isaiah look like?"

"Girl, he's fine," Morgan gushed. "He's about six-one, brown-skinned, with bedroom eyes and a gorgeous smile." A sly grin curved her mouth. "Of course, he's not as mouthwatering as Roderick, but since *he's* already taken…" She trailed off pointedly.

Lena's face heated. "Roderick's not 'taken.' Not by me anyway."

Morgan and Cleveland traded dubious glances. "He sure looked taken to me," Morgan countered.

"Me, too," Cleveland agreed.

"Then you're both mistaken," Lena told them.

Before either could argue, Margaret Jacobs appeared on the terrace. The sixty-year-old nurse was petite and slightly stocky, with smooth skin the color of maple and dark eyes that twinkled with warmth and humor.

Reaching the table, she clucked her tongue and draped a thick afghan around Cleveland's shoulders. "I knew you'd be out here with no coat on. You know better than that."

"I don't need a coat," Cleveland asserted, waving off her concern with his good hand. "It's a perfectly nice day. No wind in sight."

Margaret shook her silvered head in mild exasperation before turning her attention to Lena and Morgan. "Hello, girls," she greeted them with a warm smile. "It's good to see you again."

"Hi, Nurse Jacobs," the sisters chorused. "How are you?"

"Got my health and sanity, so I can't complain." She winked, drawing more smiles out of Lena and Morgan.

Like their grandfather, Margaret Jacobs was widowed, having lost her husband to prostate cancer several years ago. She had three grown sons but no daughters, so she'd unofficially adopted Lena and Morgan as her own. It was no secret that Cleveland was her favorite patient at the retirement home. She doted on him so much that Lena often wondered whether Margaret returned Cleveland's feelings.

"So," Margaret began conversationally, smiling at Lena and Morgan, "do you girls have any special plans this evening?"

Morgan grinned broadly. "I have a date with an amazing guy I met this morning."

Margaret's smile widened. "That's wonderful, baby. I'm so glad you got rid of that other young man you were seeing. He wasn't right for you at all."

Morgan grimaced. "That's what everyone kept telling me. I wish I'd listened a whole lot sooner."

"Better late than never," Margaret and Cleveland said in unison, then grinned at each other.

Lena and Morgan shared a knowing glance.

"So what about you, baby girl?"

Meeting her grandfather's inquisitive gaze, Lena asked cautiously, "What *about* me, Poppa?"

"Do you and Roderick have any special plans tonight?"

She shook her head. "Roderick's been very busy—"

Cleveland frowned with displeasure. "He'd better not be too busy to make time for you. The two of you just started dating. How are you supposed to get better acquainted if you hardly spend any time together?"

Lena blushed, wondering what her grandfather would say if he knew just how "well acquainted" she and Roderick were.

"That reminds me," Cleveland said, his eyes narrowing thoughtfully on hers. "You never did tell me how you and Roderick met."

Lena darted a furtive glance at Morgan, hoping she would come to her rescue again. But her sister was preoccupied with sending text messages on her cell phone. Lena was on her own.

"We, uh, met at a party, Poppa."

"Really? I didn't realize the two of you had the same acquaintances. I've read magazine articles about Roderick hobnobbing with Oprah and the Obamas." He grinned teasingly. "Are you leading a double life I should know about?"

Lena choked out a laugh. "Of course not, Poppa! What a crazy thing to say!"

Margaret clucked her tongue at him. "Why don't you

leave the poor girl alone, Cleveland? She's almost thirty years old. She doesn't need you interrogating her about her love life."

Lena gave the woman a grateful smile as she briskly continued, "Anyway, the reason I came outside was to take you on your daily stroll through the gardens. Are you ready?"

Cleveland's eyes lit up. "You'd better believe it." He always looked forward to spending quiet time with Margaret as she wheeled him around the property's lush, labyrinthine gardens.

Lena rose from the table, eager to escape just in case he decided he'd rather continue his interrogation. She bent, kissing his cheek and smiling at him. "I'll see you tomorrow, Poppa. In the meantime, stay out of trouble."

He grinned. "Don't worry. Margaret will keep me in line."

She chuckled. "*Somebody* has to."

As Margaret positioned herself behind Cleveland's wheelchair, Morgan glanced up from her texting and peered around the table. "What'd I miss?"

Everyone just laughed.

Chapter Nineteen

Later that evening, Lena was walking back to her apartment after making a trip to the neighborhood drugstore. Out of the corner of her eye, she saw a dark SUV pull up alongside her. No stranger to being hassled on the street by leering, obnoxious men, she kept moving, intending to ignore the driver. But when the passenger window rolled down and the opening notes of "Stormy Weather" drifted out to her, she stopped dead in her tracks. Her heart lurched, and a foolish grin spread across her face before she could check it.

"Hey, beautiful," came the deep, sexy drawl she'd been expecting—hoping—to hear all week.

Schooling her features into a neutral mask, Lena turned slowly to find Roderick seated behind the wheel of a gleaming black Escalade. His mouth curved in that slow, lazy smile that always took her breath away.

She swallowed. "Hey, yourself."

He looked her over, taking in her white V-neck T-shirt worn beneath a cropped blazer and skintight jeans tucked into black knee-high stiletto boots. His eyes glinted with appreciation. "Get in."

Lena shook her head. "No, thanks. I can walk the rest of the way."

"Let me give you a ride."

"I'm good. Really."

As she continued down the sidewalk he pulled up ahead, double-parked and climbed out of the truck. And then he was right there, blocking her path, smelling and looking too damn good in a black sweater, black jeans and black Timberland boots. Dark stubble shadowed his jaw, giving him a rakishly sexy look. All he needed was a gold hoop in his ear and a sword dangling at his side, and he'd be transformed into a swashbuckling pirate.

He cupped her chin, brushing his thumb across her lower lip. "Did you miss me?"

"No." *God help me, YES!*

Laughing softly, he slid his hands under her blazer and into the back pockets of her jeans, pulling her closer. "Okay," he murmured, smiling into her eyes. "I'll say it first. I missed you."

She hated that her heart flipped over and her insides melted. "You could have called," she said, instantly wishing she could snatch the words back. She sounded petulant. Worse, she sounded needy.

"I was trying to give you some space," Roderick drawled, bending his head to nuzzle her neck. "Isn't that what you asked for this week? So you could look after your grandfather?"

"Y-yes," she stammered, shivering at his touch. "I wasn't complaining. I was just pointing out that you could have called to set up our, ah, next appointment."

"Appointment?" He smiled against her throat. "We'll have to come up with a better word."

Forcing herself to pull away, Lena threw a self-conscious glance up and down the quiet, residential street. She blushed when she met the amused stares of a young white couple walking toward them.

Roderick chuckled, enjoying her discomfiture. "Told you you should have gotten in the truck."

Lena shot him a dark look. "It'd serve you right if you got a ticket for double-parking."

"Wouldn't be the first time. How's your grandfather doing?"

"Much better. But I'll have you know that I spent the whole week dodging questions about you and our relationship."

Roderick grinned. "Have you gotten any better at thinking on your feet?"

"Let's just say I benefited from the constant flow of visitors into his room and an act of mercy by his nurse."

Roderick laughed. Gently skimming his knuckle over her cheek, he asked, "Have you eaten yet?"

"No." She smiled. "And you still owe me dinner and a show, remember?"

"I know. We're going on Monday night. I've already got the tickets."

"Really? To what show?"

"You'll find out Monday." He smiled softly. "What do you want to eat tonight?"

You, she thought wickedly. *I want to dip you in honey and sop you up with a biscuit.*

Aloud she said, "Let's eat someplace casual, where we can just go as we are. I don't feel like getting dressed up."

"I know just the place. Ever been to Michael's?"

"Nope, never heard of it."

Roderick gave her a look of grave disappointment. "You're not a true Chicagoan until you've developed an appreciation for a good hot dog."

Lena laughed. "I hoof it practically everywhere I go. Doesn't *that* make me more of a Chicagoan?"

He grinned. "Naw, sunshine, it's all about the dog." He took the plastic bag out of her hand and started toward the truck, asking over his shoulder, "What'd you buy? Anything that needs to be refrigerated before we go?"

"Naw." She grinned. "Just some feminine products."

Wordlessly he passed the bag back to her, and she laughed.

Roderick took her to a place called Michael's in Highland Park.

Lena agreed to try a char dog, then had second thoughts when she got an eyeful of the monstrosities that were brought out to them. The hot dogs were nestled between poppy seed buns and loaded with chopped onions, sport peppers, mustard, neon-green relish, tomato, pickles and celery salt. They were appallingly fattening—and surprisingly delicious.

Lena, who'd always made a practice of sitting face-to-face to her clients, didn't bat an eye when Roderick joined her on the same side of the booth. They sat close together, their thighs brushing under the table as they shared a plate of cheese fries, dabbed mustard from the corner of each other's mouths and laughed as Roderick showed Lena how to eat the messy hot dog without having it fall apart.

It was the most fun she'd had since…well, since the

previous Saturday at Mackinac Island. She thoroughly enjoyed being with Roderick. Whether they were having a romantic candlelight dinner aboard his luxurious yacht or gorging on overstuffed franks in some outdated-looking diner, every minute spent in his company made her crave more. So when he suggested going to the Navy Pier to walk off their meal, Lena jumped at the chance to prolong their evening.

They held hands as they strolled along the scenic pier, which was packed with tourists and abuzz with noise and bright lights. They took a ride on the Ferris wheel, which swept them high into the air and dazzled them with spectacular views of the city. It wasn't Lena's first trip to the Navy Pier, nor was it Roderick's, who'd been coming here since he was a child. But when they looked at each other and smiled, Lena knew she wasn't the only one who thought the place had never seemed more magical.

When they weren't holding hands, she loved the warmth of Roderick's palm at the small of her back as he guided her through the crowds, the way he pulled her protectively against his side whenever someone strayed too close. Although the evening had cooled, the heat of his touch kept her skin tingling, her body humming with sexual awareness.

Before she realized it, he was leading her toward the back of the pier. Away from the bright lights and—more importantly—away from the crowds. Once they'd turned a dark corner and ducked behind a deserted boathouse, Roderick hauled Lena into his arms and kissed her.

As their hungry lips meshed and parted, she whispered, "Don't tell me."

"Tell you what?" He licked into her mouth, sensually twirling his tongue around hers.

She shivered. "You used to sneak back here every summer and make out with girls."

His grin was a flash of white. "How'd you guess?"

"Mmm," she purred, arching back as his mouth fed on her throat. "You're such a naughty boy."

"And you love it."

She did. Thoroughly.

He reached between their bodies. She heard the soft rasp of a zipper, followed by his muffled groan of frustration. "Why'd you have to wear jeans today?"

She laughed. "Sorry. You've gotten spoiled."

"That's okay. Where there's a will—" He yanked the tight jeans just past her hips, taking her panties with them. She felt the cool air on her skin, then the heat of his hands as he cupped her bare bottom. A soft moan escaped her.

She unfastened the button of his jeans, dragged down the zipper and wrapped her hand around his hot, pulsing erection. He groaned.

Slipping his fingers between her legs, he stroked her slick folds. "You're so wet," he murmured approvingly.

She smiled. "I *stay* wet for you."

He made a sound—a deep, rough sound that bordered on a growl. And then he removed his hand and nudged his penis between her thighs, rubbing back and forth against her clitoris until the tantalizing friction made her moan. She curled her arms around his neck and widened her legs as far as her jeans would allow. Roderick lifted her slightly off the ground, then slid into her wetness. She gasped sharply.

He began thrusting upward, strong, steady thrusts that sent stabs of pleasure slicing through her. Unable to wrap her legs around him, unable to really move, she could only clench her teeth to keep from screaming as her body began to convulse.

They came together, crying out just as fireworks exploded in the night sky.

Lena raised her head from his shoulder and they grinned at each other, their faces illuminated in bright flashes of color.

"Talk about perfect timing," Lena murmured, and they both laughed quietly.

Roderick lowered her feet to the ground, and they quickly composed themselves before returning to the noise and the crowds. Lena was flushed, her legs feeling as wobbly as if she'd been guzzling tequila.

Roderick smiled down at her. Tightening his hold around her waist, he leaned close to murmur in her ear, "That was just a teaser. Wait till I get you back home."

A delicious shiver of anticipation ran through her.

"Lena?"

At first she didn't recognize the voice.

She stopped and turned around, her gaze sweeping the crowd to identify the owner.

And that's when she saw him.

The man who'd callously used and humiliated her three years ago. The one man she'd hoped and prayed she would never see again.

Glenn Donahue.

As he separated from the crowd, her heart nose-dived.

"You know him?" Roderick murmured, a subtle edge to his voice.

Lena nodded tightly.

Whatever You Like

As Glenn approached, she briefly catalogued skin the color of toasted almond, attractive features and a trim physique outfitted in a beige sweater and blue jeans.

"Lena," he greeted her with a warm smile. As if he hadn't looked right through her the last time they ran into each other. "I *thought* that was you."

"Glenn." Her smile was cool, detached.

"You look beautiful. But that's nothing new."

"Thanks," Lena murmured. "Glenn, this is Roderick—"

"Brand," Glenn finished, his smile broadening as he grasped Roderick's hand. "Glenn Donahue. It's a pleasure to meet you. I'm a huge fan."

Roderick inclined his head, coolly sizing Glenn up. Lena also couldn't help comparing the two men. Roderick was at least three inches taller and fifty pounds heavier. And in terms of who exuded more virility, there was no contest—Roderick won by a landslide.

As Glenn stood there grinning at him, Lena suddenly understood why he'd gone out of his way to speak to her tonight. He'd wanted to meet Roderick, not catch up on old times with *her*.

As if to confirm her suspicion, Glenn told Roderick, "The next time you're undertaking an expansion project, be sure to look up Donahue Development. That's my company. I'm now one of the largest real estate developers in Chicago."

"Congratulations." There was a hint of mockery in Roderick's voice.

Glenn's smile faltered. As he divided a speculative glance between Roderick and Lena, she saw a malicious gleam enter his eyes a moment before he asked innocently, "So, Lena, are you working tonight?"

Heat rushed to her face. Just when she'd thought

Glenn Donahue couldn't humiliate her any more than he already had, he proved her wrong.

Beside her, Roderick stiffened. If he'd suspected that Glenn was just an old boyfriend, he now knew better. And the truth was just as embarrassing, just as damning, as it had been three years ago.

Summoning every ounce of dignity she possessed, Lena smiled sweetly at Glenn. "Working tonight? Oh, no. I'm just enjoying the company of a handsome, wonderful man who knows how to show a woman a good time." She sighed. "If only *all* my dates worked out that way."

As Glenn's face tightened at the veiled insult, she felt a small surge of satisfaction. But it didn't matter. The damage had already been done.

"Are you here alone, Glenn?" she inquired, glancing around curiously.

"No," he said quickly. "My date's in the restroom."

Lena smiled. "I hope you're both having as good a time as we are. Now if you'll excuse us," she said smoothly, "Roderick and I were just leaving. Nice running into you again."

"You, too," Glenn muttered sourly.

Lena could feel the tension rolling off Roderick's body as they left the Navy Pier and made their way to where he'd parked his truck. He didn't speak, and neither did she.

As they headed onto the JFK Expressway, the tense silence stretched between them, straining her nerves to the breaking point. When she couldn't take it anymore, she drew a deep breath and blurted, "I'm sorry. I know that was awkward—"

"He was one of your clients?" Roderick's voice was brittle.

"Yes." Lena swallowed with difficulty. She knew what was coming next.

"You slept with him?"

She averted her face to the window, closing her eyes. "Yes."

She knew what he was thinking. He was recalling every hypocritical speech she'd given him about not becoming sexually involved with her clients. He was remembering the way she'd reacted with such shame after they made love that first night, as if she'd never crossed the line before. As if he and he alone had caused her downfall.

"So I'm not the first client you've ever slept with," he said flatly.

Her stomach twisted sickeningly. "No," she whispered.

She braced herself for an angry barrage of insults and accusations. But Roderick grew silent, and somehow that was far more devastating than anything he could have said to her. She remembered Zandra's warning about how quickly he got turned off when a woman fell short of his expectations, and it made her feel worse. Like she'd let him down.

When they reached her apartment building, Roderick parked and walked her to her front door. Lena felt as though she should say something, *anything,* to defend herself. She should tell him that what they'd shared meant more to her than anything she and Glenn had done. Because it was true.

But she couldn't get the words past her constricted throat. And when Roderick leaned down and brushed a kiss across her forehead, she couldn't shake the sense that something precious was slipping away from her.

"Good night, Lena," he murmured.

She tried to read his expression, but it was indecipherable. "Good night," she said softly.

He turned and walked away without a backward glance, leaving Lena to wonder whether she'd seen him for the last time.

Chapter Twenty

To keep her mind occupied the next day, Lena threw herself into a whirlwind of activity. After popping two aspirin to combat menstrual cramps—courtesy of an overnight visit by Mother Nature—she proceeded to clean and vacuum her apartment from top to bottom. Next she baked a lemon pound cake for her grandfather and delivered it to him. After leaving the retirement home, she ran errands she'd been putting off for weeks. And at the end of the evening, she pulled out her laptop and caught up on work.

The day came and went without a word from Roderick.

Lena told herself that any concern she felt was on the college's behalf. If Roderick decided to renege on his deal with her, the college wouldn't receive the grant money, which was the most important thing at stake here. So it was only natural that his prolonged silence would make her nervous. She was worried for her employer's sake, that's all.

Or so she told herself.

The next day at the office, she couldn't concentrate on work. She tried to get started on a new grant proposal, but her mind kept wandering. She was staring off into space when a knock sounded on her door.

Startled, she glanced up to find her boss standing in her doorway. "E-Ethan," she stammered, embarrassed because he'd caught her daydreaming when she was supposed to be working. "What can I do for you?"

"I just came by to see how you were doing." Gentle, concerned blue eyes searched her face. "Is everything okay, Lena? You've seemed distracted all morning."

"I'm fine." When Ethan looked unconvinced, she added honestly, "I just have a lot on my mind."

"Your grandfather," Ethan surmised with a sympathetic nod.

"Mmm." Lena felt a pang of guilt for using her grandfather as a crutch.

"I know how rough last week was for you." Ethan paused. "If you need to take some time off, just let me know. It's not as if you haven't accrued plenty of vacation days."

Lena nodded slowly. "Thanks, Ethan. I'll keep that in mind."

"Good." He propped a shoulder against the door. "How are those revisions coming along for the performing arts grant?"

"Great," Lena said brightly, inwardly cringing at the bald-faced lie. "I expect to have it resubmitted by the end of the day."

"Wonderful." Ethan beamed with approval. "I've been champing at the bit to tell Dr. Dukes about

Roderick Brand's visit and his generous offer to approve an additional five hundred thousand dollars. I still can't believe our good fortune."

"Neither can I," Lena murmured, grateful that Ethan hadn't spilled the beans to the college's president.

"It hasn't been easy to keep such great news to myself," he admitted with a grin. "Every time I've seen Dr. Dukes around campus or had a meeting with her, I've been tempted to tell her. I know how thrilled she's going to be, and I don't have to tell you how much publicity we're going to receive as a result of this major grant award. But I want to wait until everything's finalized. And I have every confidence that you'll get the deal done." He laughed, winking at her. "No pressure."

Lena forced a weak laugh. "No pressure."

After Ethan left her office, she groaned softly and dropped her head onto her desk. If Roderick decided not to keep his end of the bargain, she was royally screwed. And she'd also be royally pissed.

Her cell phone rang, startling her.

She jerked upright, then dove for the bottom desk drawer to retrieve the phone from her handbag. When she saw Roderick's private number on the caller ID, her heart slammed into her rib cage. She paused to take a deep, calming breath, then answered with a cool, "Hello?"

"Lena. This is Roderick."

Her stomach knotted. She rose unsteadily from her chair, crossed the room and closed the door before she spoke again. "Roderick. How are you?"

"I've been better." His voice was heavy. With exhaustion? Or with residual anger? "Listen. Something's come up, and I won't be able to take you to the show tonight."

Hurt flared in Lena's chest. "If this is about Saturday night—"

"It's not," Roderick said brusquely. "I have to leave for Japan earlier than I'd planned. In fact, I'm flying out this afternoon."

"Oh." Disappointment swept through her. "How long do you expect to be gone?"

"I don't know. Two weeks, at the minimum. Longer, if necessary."

"I see." She leaned back against the door and closed her eyes against an odd stinging sensation. "Well, have a good trip. I'm sure you have important business matters to attend to."

"I do," he muttered grimly.

Tell him, Lena's conscience urged. *Tell him that Glenn meant nothing to you. Set the record straight... before it's too late.*

She inhaled a deep breath. "Roderick, there's something I—"

"Hold on." She heard a woman's voice followed by dead air, as if Roderick had pressed the mute button.

Lena waited tensely, telling herself that the female voice she'd heard belonged to Roderick's secretary—not a new lover.

After a full two minutes, he came back on the line sounding more aggravated than before. "Sorry about that. Look, something else has come up, so I have to run."

"Okay. I understand. Have a safe trip."

"Thanks."

Lena hesitated, then blurted, "Will you call me when—"

But Roderick had already hung up, severing the connection between them. Perhaps for good this time.

* * *

Lena returned to her apartment that evening with a heavy heart.

After changing into an old UCLA sweatshirt and black leggings, she trudged back to the living room, turned on the television and plopped down on the sofa to eat the takeout meal she'd picked up on the way home. But she found herself poking disinterestedly at the lasagna and salad. She had no appetite, because her thoughts were consumed with Roderick and the brief conversation they'd had that morning. It bothered her that he'd be out of the country for two weeks—maybe even longer—and things were still unresolved between them.

Sighing heavily, she shoved aside her mostly untouched meal, grabbed the remote control and leaned back against the sofa cushions. As she began channel surfing, her cell phone rang. She retrieved it from the coffee table and checked caller ID.

Her heart skipped several precious beats.

It was Roderick.

"Hello?" she answered, not caring how eager she sounded.

"Hey," Roderick said softly.

"Hi." She willed her pulse to stabilize. "I thought you were leaving for Japan today."

"I did," he confirmed. "I'm calling from the jet."

"Oh." She'd foolishly hoped that he was still in Chicago, maybe even on his way over to her apartment. *Hope springs eternal.*

"There's something I wanted to ask you earlier, before my secretary interrupted our call."

Lena moistened her dry lips. "What's that?"

"I want you to join me in Japan."

"What?"

"You heard me. I want you to fly out to Japan to be with me."

Her heart went into overdrive. "I—I can't," she whispered. But she was tempted. *Oh, how she was tempted.*

"You don't have to leave tomorrow," Roderick said. "I realize it's short notice, and you'd need time to pack and put in your leave request at work. But if you could be ready by Wednesday morning, I'd make all the arrangements with my pilot."

Lena blew out a shaky breath and dragged a trembling hand through her hair, mussing it. "I don't know, Roderick. This…this is a lot to consider. I mean, you're asking me to go out of the country with you."

"I know," he said quietly.

"And what am I supposed to do with myself while you're tending to business? And don't you dare say go shopping," she warned.

He laughed softly. "You can do anything you want, Lena. Pamper yourself at the spa, go sightseeing, visit museums and palaces, enjoy a show at the Kabuki theater. You speak Japanese. Have you ever been to the country?"

She sighed. "No. I've always wanted to visit, though."

"Well, here's your chance. And you wouldn't be on your own the entire week," Roderick assured her. "Believe me, I wouldn't ask you to join me if I intended to neglect you."

Lena groaned, even as she felt her resistance weakening. "I couldn't stay more than a week."

"I'll take whatever I can get." There was a smile in his voice. He could sense victory.

"My grandfather—"

"Is in very good hands at the retirement home, and you know it."

She sighed. He was right, of course. Her grandfather was more than well cared for at Lakeview Manor. And she'd only be gone for a week anyway.

I can't believe I'm actually considering this, Lena thought as she rose from the sofa, walked over to the windows and gazed out at the night skyline. The idea of spending a week alone with Roderick—anywhere—was both exhilarating and terrifying. She had no doubt that they'd have a wonderful time together. They always did. And therein lay the problem. This arrangement between them was only temporary. In two weeks Roderick would cut the college a nice check, and he and Lena would go their separate ways. She couldn't lose sight of that fact, or she'd be in a world of trouble.

If she wasn't already.

"Lena." Roderick's low, husky voice tempted her beyond all reason. "Please say you'll join me."

She closed her eyes, drew a deep breath and took the plunge. "I'll be there."

Chapter Twenty-One

After a twelve-hour flight aboard Roderick's plush private jet, Lena arrived in Tokyo around seven-thirty on Wednesday evening. Since Roderick had a late business meeting, he'd arranged for a chauffeured car to take her to the hotel where he was staying.

Though fatigued from her long flight, Lena felt a buzz of excitement as she stared out the window at the passing scenery. Tokyo was a sprawling, dazzling kaleidoscope of neon lights, giant plasma screens, noisy markets and futuristic skyscrapers that rose above bustling streets. It was as vibrant, crowded and intoxicating as Lena had always imagined, an assault on the senses that left her a little dizzy.

After wending through bumper-to-bumper traffic, the car arrived at The Peninsula Tokyo, a luxury hotel located in the prestigious financial district of Marunouchi, which was opposite the Imperial Palace and minutes from the renowned Ginza shopping mecca.

Lena boarded an elevator that whisked her all the way up to the Peninsula Suite, the hotel's crème de la crème of suites. It boasted an opulent décor, an enormous dining room, a grand piano and breathtaking views of Tokyo and the Imperial Palace Gardens.

On the console table, a bottle of wine sat next to a crystal vase filled with a lovely assortment of chrysanthemums. Nestled among the fragrant flowers was a small card. Lena picked it up and read the note dictated in Roderick's bold, masculine handwriting: *Welcome to Tokyo. Sorry I couldn't be there to greet you, but I'm so glad you came. Relax, have a glass of wine, enjoy the view. And know that I'm hurrying back to you.*

Lena shivered, anticipation fluttering in her belly.

"Will there be anything else, ma'am?" the concierge asked her in halting English.

Lena glanced up and smiled. "No, thank you. *Doumo arigatou gozaimasu.*"

The man beamed with pleasure, then bowed gracefully and departed.

Feeling as if she were in some sort of utopian dream, Lena wandered from room to room, marveling at ultramodern features that included nail polish dryers and fingertip bedside panels that allowed guests to control everything from temperature settings to levels of mood lighting.

When she'd finished exploring the suite, she got undressed and stepped into the marble bathroom, which boasted a built-in plasma television and a rain shower that turned into a spa at the touch of a button. She stood beneath the hot spray of water, head tilted back, eyes closed as she luxuriated in the heat and steam that enveloped her.

She felt him before she saw him—big, strong hands sliding up her thighs and over her breasts, drawing her nipples into tight buds.

She opened her eyes to meet Roderick's dark, glittering gaze. And then she smiled, as if she encountered naked, fully aroused men in her shower every day. "Hi."

His lips curved, slow and sexy. "Hi, yourself."

He slanted his mouth over hers, sending electricity sizzling through her veins. Her breasts swelled, her sex pulsed and throbbed. The man could bring her to orgasm with just one kiss.

"I was hoping to find you in the shower when I got back," he murmured, his tongue dipping into her mouth, stroking hers.

"Mmm, I bet you were." Drawing away after several pleasurable moments, she smiled into his eyes. "Could you hand me the shampoo? I forgot to bring it inside with me."

As he turned and opened the shower door to retrieve the bottle, she openly admired the way his broad, muscular back tapered down to the taut, round butt she loved to grip during sex. He turned to pass her the shampoo bottle, chuckling softly when he caught her ogling him. She grinned unabashedly.

She poured shampoo into her hands and massaged the creamy herbal concoction into her hair. With her arms raised above her head, her breasts were thrust forward. Taking this as an invitation to feast, Roderick pressed her nipples together and drew them into his hot, hungry mouth. Choking back a moan, Lena laughingly told him to do something productive with himself before she wound up getting shampoo in her eyes.

Smiling wickedly, he lathered up the loofah and gently began bathing her. Warmth spread through her limbs as his hands glided over her skin, leaving soap bubbles in their wake. She rinsed out her hair, then turned and reached for the bar of soap. They washed each other in lazy silence, their fingers brushing, their eyes meeting as hot water rained over their faces.

When they were finished, Roderick leaned down and kissed her. It was slow and sweet and slippery. She opened her mouth and took his tongue deep. He reached down and slid one, then two fingers inside her. She moaned softly, pushing her hips forward. His thumb swirled tenderly around her clit while he stroked her sensitive inner flesh. She came within seconds, shuddering and crying out as her wetness ran down her legs.

Still kissing her, Roderick palmed her butt, lifted her off the floor and pinned her against the marble wall. Her arms went around his neck, her legs around his waist. He slid inside her. Her pussy felt swollen as it stretched around his thick erection, taking him all the way into her body. He began thrusting, water pooling between their bodies in a steamy, sensual river.

She moaned as he lowered his mouth to her throat, nibbling and suckling her. As his hips ground slowly against hers, she reached behind him and squeezed his butt, which caused him to shudder and thrust faster, pumping into her until they both came with rapturous shouts.

Moments later they emerged from the shower and dried each other off, stealing kisses in between. Lips curving in a coquettish smile, Lena dropped her towel to the floor and sashayed naked from the bathroom.

She squealed with laughter as Roderick caught her

around the waist and scooped her into his arms. He reached the king-size bed in three powerful strides and set her down on her hands and knees. When he entered her from behind, her laughter dissolved into a moan.

Afterward, they shared a glass of wine and an exotic platter of sushi sent up from one of the hotel's five-star restaurants. Wrapped in a beautiful silk kimono Roderick had given her, Lena sat on his lap and fed him with a pair of chopsticks. Candles glowed invitingly on the living room table, and a wall of windows treated them to a panoramic view of the glittering night skyline. It was perfectly enchanting, perfectly romantic.

"Mmm," Roderick murmured as Lena slid another piece of sushi into his mouth. "That's good."

"Best I've ever had," she agreed, helping herself to the next bite. After the sumptuous dinner she'd been served aboard Roderick's private jet, she hadn't expected to find herself hungry again that night. But, as usual, they'd worked up an appetite.

"Ready for more?"

Roderick nodded, and she fed him another piece of sushi. As he chewed and swallowed, she arched an amused brow at him. "I didn't know if you would be happy with the sushi I ordered."

He grinned. "I trust you, baby. You make everything taste better."

She snorted out a laugh. "Yeah, right. You and your lines."

"No, it's true. For example, I've never been a huge fan of fudge, but after that night…" He trailed off meaningfully, and Lena flushed from head to toe. Which, of course, made him laugh.

"Damn, I love making you blush," he told her.

"So I've noticed," she muttered, fighting the tug of a grin. "Anyway, it's good for you to develop a taste for sushi. Now that you've taken over a Japanese company, it probably wouldn't hurt you to learn how to speak the language either."

"Actually, I've been thinking the same thing," Roderick said, smiling at her. "Think you could teach me?"

"Oh, I don't think so," Lena demurred, absently toying with the last piece of sushi.

"Why not?"

"Japanese is a complicated language. It can take a while to learn it."

"So…what's the problem?"

She glanced up and met his gaze. It was on the tip of her tongue to remind him that she'd be out of his life in less than two weeks. But her throat had grown strangely tight, and she couldn't bring herself to vocalize the words.

Averting her gaze, she plucked their wineglass off the side table and took a long, fortifying sip. When Roderick pointedly licked his lips, she hesitated, then lowered the glass to his mouth to let him drink. He held her gaze, his eyes silently communicating a message she was afraid to interpret. Afraid to receive.

Her hand trembled as she pulled the glass away and set it back on the table.

"Lena—"

"This hotel is amazing," she said brightly, throwing an appreciative glance around the suite. "The driver who brought me from the airport said it's only three years old. No wonder everything's so sparkly and new. Have you stayed here every time you've traveled to Tokyo?"

"Yes," Roderick replied, giving her an amused look that told her he wasn't fooled by her evasion tactics.

Undeterred, she continued cheerfully, "I guess if you have to live out of a suitcase, you couldn't find a nicer home away from home than The Peninsula."

"Actually, I'm looking for a place of my own."

"Oh, that's right. Zandra mentioned something about that on Saturday. Find any promising leads yet?"

"Not yet. My real estate agent has some properties he'd like to show me while I'm here." Roderick hesitated. "Maybe you could tag along. I wouldn't mind having a woman's input."

Lena swallowed, then forced a nonchalant shrug. "Sure. I'll go." As if there were nothing remotely intimate or "couple-ish" about going house hunting with him. "Tomorrow?"

He shook his head. "I was thinking Friday. I don't want to drag you all over Tokyo a day after you just got here. You should relax tomorrow, sleep in late, get a massage downstairs at the spa. It's supposed to be really nice. World-class."

"Mmm, sounds good. I just had a massage, though. With Zandra."

"So get another one. There's no such thing as too much pampering, is there?"

"Definitely not."

He smiled. "In the evening we can hit the Kabuki theater."

Lena grinned. "Dinner and a show?"

"A promise is a promise."

"Woo-hoo!" She clapped, nearly dislodging the plate on her lap. As Roderick caught and righted it, she asked him, "Want the last piece of sushi?"

"Naw," he drawled, "you can have it."

When she picked it up and popped it into her mouth, he scowled. "Well, damn. If I'd known you were going to use your fingers, I would've taken it."

She laughed. "I'm sorry. Did you have a problem being fed with chopsticks?"

"Not at all." His eyes glinted. "But use your fingers next time. I like tasting you."

Need tightened low in her belly. Slowly she licked the spices from her fingers, watching his gaze darken, feeling his penis twitch beneath her thighs.

"Don't start something you can't finish, woman," he warned softly.

She chuckled, delighted by how easily she could arouse him. Setting aside the empty plate, she asked, "So how'd your day go? Have you taken care of those troublemakers at the office?"

Roderick had told her about two of Kawamoto's top-level executives who'd been resistant to the acquisition. Afraid of getting squeezed out of their jobs, and resentful that their new employer was a brash young American—a *black* American, at that—they'd refused to cooperate with Roderick's transition team, which had forced him to return earlier than planned to personally resolve the matter.

Lena smiled at him. "Were you able to squelch the mutiny?"

"Of course," Roderick drawled, making an exaggerated show of cracking his knuckles. "You know I had to show 'em who's boss."

"Uh-oh," Lena intoned with mock dread. "Don't tell me you went all Chicago-gangster on them."

His grin was crooked. "What can I say? You can take the boy outta the South Side…"

She burst out laughing. "I knew it!"

"Knew what?"

Grinning and shaking her head, she explained, "One of the first impressions I had of you was that you'd be downright formidable if you were ever crossed. You've got a ruthless streak, Mr. Brand."

He shrugged. "Guess it comes with the territory. You need killer instincts to survive in the cutthroat world of business, especially when the odds are stacked against you."

Lena nodded understandingly. No one could have predicted the success story that Roderick's life would become. One of six children born to working-class parents, and raised in one of the toughest neighborhoods on Chicago's South Side, he'd defied the odds by excelling in school and going on to attend a prestigious university. Now, at the age of thirty-five, he headed one of the country's largest energy conglomerates, and he showed no signs of slowing down.

Lena smiled softly. "Your parents must be so proud of you."

"They are," Roderick agreed with a quiet, reflective smile. "But they've always set the bar high for me and my siblings, so they expect nothing but the best from us."

"Good parents," Lena murmured.

"Most definitely."

She grinned playfully. "If your life's story is ever made into a movie, Idris Elba *has* to play the lead role."

"Idris? Nah."

"Why not?"

"We look nothing alike."

Incredulous, Lena sputtered, "Are you kidding me? Have you *looked* in a mirror lately? You could be his younger—" Seeing the amused gleam in Roderick's eyes, she broke off and laughed. "I knew you couldn't be serious. You probably hear all the time how much you resemble Idris."

He chuckled. "I hear it often enough."

"It's a compliment, you know."

"I know. And I appreciate it." He grinned, and Lena decided not to inflate his ego by telling him that he was even finer than Idris.

"So, am I flying solo tomorrow?" she asked him.

"Just for a few hours. I have a couple meetings in the morning."

Nodding, she covered her mouth to stifle a yawn.

"Getting sleepy?"

"Yeah." She sighed. "It's been a long day. I think jet lag is catching up to me."

Smiling, Roderick gathered her into his arms. She cuddled against him, tucking her head beneath his chin and marveling at how right it felt. How…perfect.

He stroked a hand up and down her back. "I can't promise you that I won't be tempted to have my way with you in the middle of the night," he murmured teasingly.

She let out a soft, drowsy laugh. "Do I need to sleep in the other room?"

"That's not even an option."

"Then be a good boy and let me rest."

He sighed. "It's gonna be a *long* night."

She smiled. Lulled by his soothing caresses, the deep timbre of his voice and the warm strength of his body, she felt her eyelids grow heavy. Before she drifted off to sleep, she heard him whisper into her hair, "I'm glad you're here, Lena."

And she thought, *So am I.*

Chapter Twenty-Two

She took Roderick's advice and slept in late the next morning. By the time he returned from the office, she was showered, dressed and raring to go sightseeing.

Their first stop was the Imperial Palace, situated within a large plaza surrounded by moats and massive stone walls. Although the palace buildings and inner gardens weren't open to the public, they were able to view and take photos of the two main bridges that formed an entrance to the imperial family's private residences.

From there they headed to the East Garden, where they strolled the beautifully manicured grounds, admired the vibrant profusion of Japanese flowers and wandered through former guard lodgings and tea rooms that had been carefully preserved for centuries. A gently sloping bridge led them to a pond with lanterns and a bubbling waterfall. It was a postcard-perfect photo spot, so they laughingly took turns posing on the bridge while the other snapped pictures.

"I want one of us together," Roderick said.

Before Lena could stop him, he flagged down another tourist, who graciously agreed to take their picture. As they moved into position, Roderick curved an arm around Lena's waist and smiled into her eyes, murmuring, "I want as many souvenirs as possible."

Her heart turned over, and she felt a deep ache of longing. Longing for something she knew better than to want—a future with Roderick.

Somehow she managed to smile cheerfully for the photo.

As the tourist returned the camera to Roderick, he smiled at them and said, "You two make a beautiful couple."

Lena flushed. "Oh, we're n—"

"Thanks," Roderick spoke over her. "We're very happy together."

"I can tell."

Once the friendly man had moved off, Lena gave Roderick a puzzled look. "Why'd you tell him that?"

He shrugged. "He's a stranger. What difference does it make whether he thinks we're a couple? Anyway," he said, grinning as he took her hand, "let's go see if we can catch a sumo wrestling match."

Lena laughed. "I don't think so!"

After leaving the East Garden, they took bullet trains that whisked them around to several other tourist attractions, including the Tokyo National Museum and Tokyo Tower. From the moment they exited the train station at the famed Shibuya district, they were bombarded by the sight of neon-lit skyscrapers, teeming throngs of people, giant video screens and flashing advertisements projected onto the sides of buildings. They strolled to Center Gai, a bustling pedestrian zone lined with CD stores, high-tech game centers, boutiques and nightclubs.

Lena didn't know whether to be appalled or fascinated by the eclectic fashions worn by Japanese schoolgirls, who paraded the streets in heavy Goth makeup, rainbow-hued ensembles and monstrous platform boots.

She and Roderick stopped for lunch at a cozy restaurant tucked into the basement of a hotel. They drank sake and dined on shabu-shabu, a delicious Japanese dish featuring thin slices of beef cooked with vegetables.

After lunch, they were standing at an intersection waiting to cross the street when they were mobbed by a group of Japanese teenagers pointing excitedly to Roderick and yelling, "Stringer Bell! Stringer Bell!" Who, of course, was the drug kingpin famously portrayed by Idris Elba on *The Wire*.

Lena and Roderick took one look at each other and burst out laughing.

Needing a reprieve from the hyperactive pace of Shibuya, they headed to Asakusa to visit Sensoji, Tokyo's oldest and most architecturally stunning temple.

By the time they returned to the hotel that evening, Lena was completely worn out. After kicking off her flats and dumping her bags of souvenirs on the floor, she staggered to the bed and collapsed with an exhausted groan. A moment later Roderick joined her, draping an arm around her waist as he spooned her from behind.

"Don't get too comfortable," he told her, chuckling. "We still have plans tonight."

"What plans?" Lena moaned protestingly.

"Dinner and a show. Remember?"

She shook her head wearily. "Not tonight. Please, I beg of you. My feet can't take any more walking."

Roderick laughed, his warm breath fanning the side of her face. "Hey, no one told you to overdo it with the sightseeing. We could have come back hours ago, but you insisted on visiting more places."

"I was greedy. I wanted to take in everything at once. You should have talked some sense into me."

He chuckled softly. "So now it's my fault, huh?"

"Basically." She grinned, closing her eyes and sighing contentedly as he nibbled her earlobe. "Let's just stay in tonight and order room service."

"We did that last night."

"Only because I got in so late. Anyway, do you have a problem spending a quiet evening alone with me?"

"That depends," Roderick murmured.

"On what?" she demanded indignantly.

He smiled against her ear. "On how 'quiet' you want the evening to be."

Heat curled through her veins. "I suppose it doesn't have to be *that* quiet."

"Mmm. I'm listening."

She turned in his embrace, wreathing her arms around his neck and smiling into his dark eyes. "Let's start with a hot shower, and see how loud the evening gets from there. Sound good?"

"*Very* good." Lowering his head, Roderick kissed her deeply and intimately, letting her know how much he desired her.

And for now, that was enough.

"Well? What do you think?"

Lips pursed, Lena wandered slowly around the luxurious penthouse, which was indistinguishable from the last four penthouses she and Roderick had already visited that morning. Each property had boasted lavish interiors and the requisite floor-to-ceiling windows that offered sweeping views of Tokyo's cityscape.

"Lena?" Roderick prompted.

She turned around to face him. "It's nice."

Across the living room, the real estate agent made a strangled sound in his throat and gaped at her. *"Nice?"* he echoed incredulously.

"Very nice," Lena amended, lips quirking.

He frowned. "You *do* realize that this is one of the most expensive properties in Tokyo?"

Lena smiled sweetly. "You may have mentioned that once or twice before."

The short, wiry Japanese man flushed with indignation. "Mr. Brand is a wealthy, prominent businessman," he said in an imperious voice. "Where he resides should be a reflection of his status."

"I realize that," Lena said mildly. "But I also think it should reflect more than the size of his bank account."

The man gave Roderick an aggrieved look, as if to ask, *Why is she here?*

Eyes glimmering with amusement, Roderick said smoothly, "Would you mind giving us a minute?"

The real estate agent frowned with displeasure. "We're on a very tight—"

"This'll only take a minute."

The man hesitated, then drew himself up to his full height—all four feet eleven inches—and marched off in a huff.

Lena and Roderick looked at each other, then covered their mouths with their hands and cracked up laughing.

"Where'd you *find* that guy?" Lena whispered between giggles.

"Kawamoto recommended him," Roderick whispered back. "He's supposed to be one of the top real estate brokers in Tokyo."

"Well, he has lousy people skills."

Roderick grinned. "I'm sure he ain't too pleased with you either. If he could physically look down his nose at you, he would."

Lena's peal of laughter was muffled against Roderick's chest as he pulled her swiftly into his arms.

"Is everything all right?" the real estate agent inquired suspiciously from the doorway.

Roderick glanced up. "Hmm? Oh, yeah, everything's fine. She's just…overcome by the beautiful view."

"Do you need more time?"

Stroking Lena's shaking shoulders, Roderick replied, "A few more minutes. Thanks."

After the Realtor had gone, Lena hiccuped and raised teary eyes to Roderick's amused face. "I'm sorry. Maybe I should have stayed back at the hotel. You know that man's gonna talk bad about you and your atrocious taste in women."

"Probably." Roderick grinned. "But I'm glad you came anyway."

"Are you? I know I haven't been much help."

Roderick chuckled. "Now that you mention it, you *have* found fault with every property we've looked at so far."

"I know." Lena sighed, glancing around dispassionately. "It's just that these penthouses all look the same to me. Don't get me wrong. They're absolutely gorgeous. The ultimate in luxury living. But they lack… What's the word I'm looking for?"

"Personality?" Roderick suggested.

"Exactly! They lack personality. And they're so Westernized," she complained. "I mean, what's the point of living in another country if you're gonna buy a place that looks like something you could easily find back home?"

Roderick followed her gaze around the penthouse. "I can definitely see what you mean. But I'm only going to be living in Tokyo a few months at a time. The most important thing to me is proximity to the office."

"I know. And your real estate agent is right about one thing. You have an image to uphold, and your home should reflect that. You're going to be entertaining a lot of clients, so you can't exactly invite them to a dinner party in the slums."

"That probably wouldn't be good for business," Roderick agreed wryly.

Lena pursed her lips, critically appraising the penthouse. "Why did you choose to stay at The Peninsula? What's your favorite thing about it?"

Roderick shrugged. "It has the best views of the Imperial Palace East Garden."

Lena snapped her fingers. "That's it! That's what you need."

She called the real estate agent back into the living room. Once she explained to him what she was looking for, they headed to another high-rise in Tokyo Midtown. But the moment they stepped through the door of the apartment, Lena knew they'd found a winner. The spacious, ultramodern residence had an open floor plan with glass wall dividers that created private nooks within each room. Everything about the Japanese-inspired design exuded simple elegance—the black-and-cream color scheme, exposed timber planks in the ceiling, high-tech lighting, Japanese silk screens and exotic bamboo flooring. And the pièce de résistance? A private rooftop terrace that featured a tranquil, lushly landscaped Zen garden.

Gazing around in awed admiration, Lena said, "Now *this*—"

"—has personality," Roderick finished, and they smiled at each other.

"The property just came on the market," the real estate agent told them, sounding very pleased with himself. As though it had been *his* idea to find the place.

Lena and Roderick traded another grin.

"I'll take it," he said.

Chapter Twenty-Three

That evening they attended a show at a Kabuki theater and had dinner with Ichiro and Natsumi Kawamoto, along with a few of the couple's close acquaintances. At one point during the meal, Lena found herself the center of attention when someone asked her how she'd learned to speak Japanese.

"When I was in high school," she explained, "a Japanese family moved into my neighborhood. I became friends with the girl who was my age. In exchange for teaching her how to swim, she taught me Japanese."

Approving nods and smiles went around the table. Ichiro Kawamoto humorously advised Roderick, "You'd be wise to marry this woman and take her with you wherever you go in Japan. That way if someone is badmouthing you, she can translate the insults for you."

As everyone laughed, Lena and Roderick stared at

each other. The piercing intensity of his gaze made her knees knock together so hard she had to reach under the table and put a steadying hand on her legs.

Before leaving the restaurant, she excused herself to use the ladies' room. When she emerged, she stumbled upon Roderick and Kawamoto conversing in a corner near the restaurant's foyer. She was about to keep walking when she heard Roderick laugh and say to the other man, "Thanks, my friend, but I'm not in the market for a wife. I won't be for a very long time."

Something twisted in Lena's stomach, and she hurried away before Roderick saw her standing there.

Good thing she hadn't looked forward to him proposing after dessert.

Later that night, Lena lay awake in bed staring up at the ceiling, mentally replaying Roderick's words. She didn't want to examine why she was so bothered by what she'd overheard. She had no illusions about their relationship. She'd known the rules from the start. And after everything Zandra had told her about Roderick, tonight's comments shouldn't have come as such an unpleasant surprise to her. But they had. And she was afraid to ask herself why.

"Lena."

She jumped slightly. She'd been so absorbed in her thoughts that she hadn't noticed Roderick watching her quietly, his face cast in moonlit shadows.

"I thought you were asleep," she murmured.

"I was." A note of wry amusement laced his voice. "All the commotion woke me up."

"What commotion?"

He reached over and gently tapped her temple. "From the thoughts tumbling around in there."

She smiled, but said nothing.

"You're not going to tell me?"

"Tell you what?"

"What you were thinking about."

She shifted, resting her head on her folded arm and closing her eyes. "I was thinking about your new apartment and how great it is that you can move in right away."

"Liar," Roderick said softly.

She didn't deny it.

A long silence lapsed between them. Just when she thought he'd drifted back to sleep, he murmured, "Why did you become an escort?"

The question, and the timing, caught her off guard. She opened her eyes and stared at him, but it was too dark to decipher his expression.

"Why do you want to know?" she countered calmly.

"There's nothing about you I *don't* want to know."

That shut her up for several moments. God, the things he *said* to her sometimes. The things he *did*. What was a woman supposed to think?

"Lena," he prompted.

She moistened her lips. "I wanted to make some extra money."

"To take care of your grandfather," Roderick stated.

"Yes."

"You wanted to put him in the best retirement home money could buy."

She nodded. "It was the least I could do for him."

Roderick said quietly, "You're a wonderful granddaughter, Lena. Incredibly generous and unselfish."

She flushed, embarrassed by his praise. "I try to be."

"You are." His tone brooked no argument.

She smiled a little. "Thank you for saying that."

"I'm just speaking the truth." He paused. "So your grandfather doesn't know that you work as an escort. That's why you couldn't tell him how we met."

Her smile faded. "No. He doesn't know. And I'd prefer to keep it that way."

"Because he wouldn't approve."

Lena sighed. "No, he wouldn't."

Roderick fell silent. But she knew he still had questions for her. She'd been waiting for him to bring up Glenn for the past three days. On one hand she welcomed an opportunity to explain her behavior. On the other hand, she resented the fact that she felt compelled to explain anything. She'd made a terrible mistake by sleeping with Glenn, but that didn't mean she owed Roderick an explanation *or* an apology.

So why did she feel like she did?

"Do you enjoy it?"

His voice pulled her out of her musings. "Enjoy what? Being an escort?"

"Yeah."

She hesitated. "I do, actually."

"Why?"

She wondered if she'd only imagined the note of censure edging his voice. Striving not to sound defensive, she answered evenly, "I enjoy meeting new people, having new experiences." She paused. "I had a wonderful childhood. My grandparents were very loving and attentive, and Poppa worked tirelessly to ensure that we'd never want for anything. But as great as my upbringing was, it was also very…sheltered. I didn't realize how big the world was until I started college at UCLA, and even then I commuted from home to save my grandfather money on housing."

She sighed. "I guess what I'm trying to say is that being an escort has opened up a whole new world to me. You're rich, so maybe you take for granted what it's like to be at a party attended by Oprah, or the governor, or even a Saudi sheikh."

"I wasn't always rich," Roderick said shortly.

"But you are now, and chances are you will be for the rest of your life."

He said nothing.

She could feel the tension emanating from his body. Tension fueled by some unnamed emotion. The words he'd spoken to Kawamoto echoed through her mind, and suddenly she was struck by the thought that Roderick would never consider her potential wife material—or even girlfriend material—as long as she worked as an escort.

Why should that matter to you? her conscience challenged. *You're not interested in becoming his girlfriend or his wife.*

But it bothered her that she was good enough to bed but apparently not good enough to wed.

Frowning, she rolled over, turning away from him.

After several moments, he said in a low voice, "I wasn't criticizing you, Lena. I hope you know that."

She didn't respond.

"If you weren't an escort," he added huskily, "we never would have met. So I'm feeling pretty grateful right now."

Her chest squeezed. She closed her eyes, and wasn't surprised when two warm tears leaked out, rolled across her face and melted into her pillow.

She was officially in over her head.

Chapter Twenty-Four

By Monday afternoon, Roderick had completed all the necessary paperwork to receive the keys to his new apartment. He wanted Lena to spend at least two nights there before she returned home, so they transferred their belongings from the hotel to his new digs.

Against her better judgment, Lena wished there was a way she could prolong her visit. Every time she thought about leaving Tokyo—leaving Roderick—her throat and chest tightened until they ached. Two days before her scheduled departure, she made a decision not to squander the rest of her time with Roderick by wallowing in sadness and regret. Instead, she'd do something special for him. Something they would both remember long after they'd gone their separate ways.

When he returned from the office that evening, she was waiting for him.

He didn't see her, because the apartment was dimly

illuminated by candlelight and she was hidden behind a shoji screen in the living room. As she watched through the narrow opening, Roderick paused in the foyer, his gaze drawn to the note she'd placed on the table next to two burning sticks of incense. Glancing around, he reached for the note and read the words she'd by now memorized: *Welcome home. A night of pleasure awaits you in the teahouse.*

His lips curved in a slow, sensual smile that quickened her pulse from across the room.

As she watched, he tucked the note inside his breast pocket and left the foyer, heading down the hallway toward the room that had been modeled after a Japanese teahouse. The sliding doors were made out of authentic balsa wood and covered with translucent Japanese paper that allowed light to enter the small room. Inside, the simple décor consisted of a scroll painting and tatami rice-straw mats that covered the floor. The "teahouse" was just one of the many rooms that had captivated Lena's imagination.

Most captivating of all, of course, was the apartment's new owner.

Lena slipped quietly from her hiding place and walked to the kitchen to retrieve a tray of refreshments she'd prepared earlier. She lingered another minute, giving Roderick a chance to get settled in the room, letting his anticipation build before she went to join him.

As she neared the closed doors, she saw that he'd removed his shoes and left them by the entrance in accordance with Japanese custom. She smiled to herself, pleased that he'd remembered such a detail. Enacting a fantasy was so much more enjoyable when both parties really got into it. Not that she had much experience to draw upon.

Balancing the tray on one hand, she slid the doors open and entered the candlelit room. The scent of flowers wafted from incense sticks burning in every corner.

Roderick sat cross-legged in the middle of the floor, his hands clasped loosely in his lap. He'd been watching the entrance intently, waiting for her arrival. When he saw her, his eyes widened, then slowly raked over her from head to toe. Dressed in a beautifully embroidered red kimono with flat brocade sandals and her hair artfully arranged in a bun, she'd transformed herself into a geisha. But instead of the traditional white makeup, she'd opted for smoky eyes, rouged cheeks and lips painted a matte red.

She could tell by Roderick's stunned expression that she'd achieved the dramatic result she was going for.

"Wow," he whispered, staring at her. *"Wow."*

Lena gave him a demure smile. Carrying the tray, she crossed the room with the small, meek steps she'd practiced for over an hour after watching *Memoirs of a Geisha* that afternoon. When she reached Roderick, she sank down gracefully and set the tray between them on the floor.

"You look amazing, Lena," he said in a husky, awestruck voice.

"Arigatou." She smiled at him. "In case you didn't know, that means thank you."

He smiled lazily. "I think *I'm* the one who should be thanking you. When did you plan all this?"

"I'm not giving away my secrets." She smiled enigmatically. "May I pour you some tea?"

"Yes, please."

She reached for the teapot on the tray and filled a small cup with Japanese green tea. As she served him their fingers brushed, making her skin tingle. She bowed gracefully.

When Roderick just gazed at her, she whispered under her breath, "You're supposed to bow, too."

"Oh." He dipped forward obediently, then raised the teacup to his lips. "Did you brew this yourself?"

Lena nodded. "It's called Sencha. It's one of the most popular green teas in Japan. It's raised in the sun and harvested in the early season."

Roderick took a sip, making a slight face. "Interesting."

Her lips quirked. "It's an acquired taste. One that you should probably acquire now that you're going to be spending part of the year in Japan."

"Good point." He smiled and took another sip. "Aren't you going to have some?"

"No." She smiled demurely. "I'm here to cater to you."

"Is that right?" His voice went low and husky.

She swallowed dryly and licked her lips. "Are you hungry?"

"Very." His heated gaze made it clear he wasn't interested in food.

Ignoring the way her pulse skittered and jumped, Lena began fixing him a plate that consisted of Japanese finger foods. He set aside his teacup, and she moved closer to slide the first offering into his mouth.

"Mmm," Roderick murmured, chewing.

"You like that?"

"Yeah. What is that?"

"It's called daigakuimo. It's Japanese candied sweet potatoes."

His eyes twinkled. "So even in Tokyo, I can get some soul food."

Lena laughed, feeding him another piece. As his warm, silky mouth closed around her fingertips, her breasts throbbed and her loins quivered. She wondered just how long she'd be able to remain in character.

"I like it when you feed me with your fingers," Roderick said huskily.

"Do you?" There was a breathless catch to her voice.

"Mmm-hmm. I like the taste of you in my mouth."

The deliberately provocative remark licked at her like flames. It was all she could do not to strip naked and straddle his face.

Instead she fluttered her lashes and gently rebuked him. "You're being very improper, Mr. Brand."

"Am I? I'm sorry." His wolfish grin was anything but remorseful. "It's just that you're so beautiful, and I've never been served by a geisha before. This is a very special treat for me."

She smiled softly. "The purchase of your new home was cause for celebration."

"Yeah? So this is kinda like a housewarming party?"

"You could say that."

"Well, this is one housewarming party I'll *never* forget."

I'm counting on it, Lena thought.

Gesturing to the plate of food, she asked, "What do you want to try next? You can have whatever you like."

"I'll take whatever you give me."

Their eyes met and held, and Lena knew he wasn't talking about what she should feed him next.

That was her undoing.

She set aside the plate, then slowly rose and stood over him. Her nipples had grown hard and her clit was engorged, slick with her arousal.

Roderick gazed up at her, a sexy smile teasing the corners of his mouth. "You really *are* my American geisha."

Her lips curved in a sultry smile. "Oh, I don't know about that."

"What do you mean?"

Holding his gaze, she untied the belt of her kimono and pulled it open to reveal her body sheathed in a red lace negligee.

Roderick swore hoarsely, looking her up and down with devouring eyes.

"This isn't quite what geisha wear under their kimonos," Lena purred.

"Probably not," Roderick whispered.

Before she could draw her next breath, he grabbed her around the waist and pulled her down to the floor. His body covered hers as he seized her mouth in a hot, voracious kiss. She moaned, her hands curling around the nape of his neck. Their tongues tangled and danced, an erotic glide of wet and heat.

Groaning, he drew away and began peeling off her negligee, murmuring almost apologetically, "It's sexy as hell but I want to see you. All of you."

He tossed aside the scrap of lace, then swept his dark, glittering gaze over her naked body. "Beautiful," he whispered in a husky, worshipful voice. "I can't get enough of you, Lena."

She quivered with pleasure, then closed her eyes with a deep, purring sigh as he began kissing his way down her body. The heat of his mouth electrified her, trailing fire everywhere he touched. He licked and sucked her nipples until they ached, then ran his mouth down her trembling stomach.

The moment she felt the hot wetness of his lips and tongue on her sex, she went off like a rocket, arching her head back with a shocked cry. He lapped at her, drinking her up until she'd stopped convulsing.

Rearing back from her, he made quick work of undressing himself. And then he was leaning over her again, his dark, powerful body backlit by candlelight. His hands gripped and spread her thighs as he settled between them. Bracing himself on both arms, his palms flat on either side of her head, he thrust into her. She cried out, her hips arching upward to meet his, her legs wrapping around his waist.

He pressed her down to the floor and began pumping into her, his hips rocking against hers, his butt muscles flexing beneath her calves. She clung tightly to him, her nails raking his back as she gasped out her pleasure.

"Damn," Roderick groaned, his eyes blazing fiercely as he stared down into hers. "Damn, sweetheart, what're you *doing* to me?"

She wanted to ask him the same thing, but all she could get out was a broken moan. So she pulled his head down to hers and kissed him, pouring all that she couldn't say into the kiss. And he kissed her back as if he understood, and felt the same way.

She matched him stroke for desperate stroke, never slowing, never stopping, thinking she might die if she did. Every breath she took was ripe with the animal musk of their lovemaking, mingled seductively with the scent of incense.

She wanted to make this moment last forever. But Roderick had increased the tempo of his thrusts, his hips pummeling hers until she went flying over the edge. Wave upon wave of electric sensation exploded through her groin, and she screamed his name in a way she'd never done before.

As her body spasmed, Roderick slid halfway out of her, then plunged deep and hard, one last powerful thrust that locked their bodies together. And then he came, calling her name like a prayer, his body shuddering so violently that Lena climaxed again.

They collapsed against each other, panting and shaking in the aftermath of their passionate coupling. Lena drew his body even closer to hers, holding him tenderly in her arms as he nestled against her. Naked and sweaty, their limbs entwined, his penis snug inside her, she felt an overwhelming sense of rightness wash over her.

And she knew, like never before, that leaving him would be the hardest thing she'd ever had to do in her life.

Chapter Twenty-Five

Two days later, they were seated in the plush lounge of a small airport primarily used by private jet carriers. They'd been served a light breakfast and were now nursing mimosas as they waited for Roderick's Gulfstream to be refueled and prepared for takeoff.

Neither was feeling very talkative.

Eye contact had been minimal, as well.

"You really didn't have to see me off this morning," Lena said, breaking the prolonged silence that had lapsed between them. "I know you have pressing matters to attend to at the office."

"I do," Roderick agreed in a mild tone, "but they can wait."

Lena smiled shyly. "I had a wonderful time this week."

"I'm glad to hear that." Roderick paused. "I enjoyed having you here with me."

They stared at each other, the longest they'd maintained eye contact since arriving at the airport.

"Roderick—"

"Lena—"

They spoke at the same time, then chuckled quietly. Almost sadly.

"You go first," Roderick invited.

Lena swallowed. "I was just going to ask whether you have a better idea of when you'll be back home."

He grimaced. "I don't, unfortunately."

"Oh." Disappointment made her throat and chest ache.

"I'm still shooting for Monday," he told her. But he didn't sound very optimistic.

A heavy silence followed.

"What were you going to say?" Lena prompted.

He gave her a blank look.

"A few minutes ago," she reminded him. "When we said each other's names at the same time."

He shook his head slowly. "I don't remember."

For some reason, Lena didn't believe him. Before she could press the issue, however, his pilot arrived to inform them that the jet was ready for departure.

Lena's throat tightened painfully, as if invisible fingers were suddenly strangling her. When she stood, her legs didn't feel steady enough to support her weight. In silence, she and Roderick followed the pilot to the exit that led out to the tarmac, where the Gulfstream glistened in the morning sunlight alongside several other aircraft.

When Lena stopped at the doors, Roderick signaled to his pilot to give them privacy, then looked down at Lena. "I was going to walk you out to the plane."

She shook her head, offering him a tremulous smile. "I hate long goodbyes."

He hesitated, quietly searching her face. She wondered if he could tell that she was desperately fighting back tears. God, she hoped not. She needed to walk away from this—from him—with her pride intact.

After another moment he nodded. "All right. No long goodbyes then."

"Thank you."

Their eyes held for several seconds.

And then Roderick leaned down, brushing his lips across hers.

Lena closed her eyes, savoring the tender kiss as if it would be their last. Because she knew there was a chance it might be.

All too soon Roderick pulled away. "Have a good trip," he murmured.

She opened her mouth to speak, but the words got trapped in her throat. So she merely nodded, then allowed the smiling pilot to escort her toward the waiting plane.

They were halfway across the tarmac when Roderick's voice rang out above the noise of idling jet engines. "Lena!"

She turned around to look at him.

His expression was gentle. "I miss you already."

Tears rushed to her eyes, blurring his image. She wanted to run back to him, throw her arms around his neck and beg him to return home with her now, business be damned.

But of course she did none of those things.

Instead she summoned a teary smile and called back, *"Doukan!"* Which was Japanese for "ditto."

Roderick nodded slowly.

And somehow Lena knew he'd understood.

Understood even more than she'd intended to reveal.

Chapter Twenty-Six

Lena stood at the windows staring out at the rain that had been falling steadily since early that morning. She was back home. Back in her own apartment, back in her own world. But as she gazed through the rain-streaked glass, it wasn't Chicago's familiar skyline she was seeing. It was Tokyo's. Worse, she couldn't stop humming the words to "Stormy Weather."

Don't know why there's no sun up in the sky...

"Wow, Lena! These photos are amazing!"

Lena's gloomy musings were interrupted by her sister, who sat cross-legged on the sofa clicking through photos on Lena's laptop.

As she turned from the windows, Morgan sighed enviously. "Aw, man. These pictures make me want to visit Japan more than anything."

"You should go. I think you'd really enjoy yourself."

Lena grinned. "Between the Ginza and Shibuya districts, you'd be in retail heaven."

"Don't tease me," Morgan groaned. "That's so mean."

Lena laughed. "Mean? Aren't I the one who brought back bagloads of clothes and shoes for you?"

"You sure did." Morgan grinned, preening in one of the new designer shirts that she'd insisted on wearing immediately. "Those bitches at work are gonna be so jealous."

Lena grinned, clucking her tongue. "Now, now, that's not very nice. Besides, I thought you patched things up with them."

Morgan scowled. "I thought so, too. Until they stabbed me in the back again."

"What happened?" Lena asked, joining her on the sofa.

Morgan waved a dismissive hand. "We'll talk about it later. Right now I want to hear all about your trip to Japan. It looks like you and Roderick had a wonderful time together."

Lena smiled softly. "We did."

"Mmm-hmm. I bet you did." Morgan grinned lasciviously. "You still haven't told me why you changed your mind about seeing him again. As I recall, you were adamantly opposed to the idea. And then the next thing I know he's showing up at the hospital, then whisking you off to another country. What happened?"

Lena smiled wryly. "Let's just say he made me an offer I couldn't refuse."

Morgan looked intrigued. "What kind of offer?"

Lena instantly regretted the slip of tongue. "It's a long story. I'll tell you about it later. Now finish looking through those photos so we can go grab dinner."

Morgan glanced dubiously out the windows. "I ain't going back out in that downpour."

"You have to," Lena said with a chuckle. "I haven't had a chance to go grocery shopping yet, so I don't have any food."

"Ever heard of takeout?"

"Wimp."

Morgan chuckled, returning her attention to the photos. "You certainly did a lot in one week. Oh, look at those beautiful mountains!" She turned the laptop toward Lena. "Where was that?"

Lena glanced at the screen and smiled. "That was an island called Hokkaido. Very scenic lakes and forests. We went hiking through one of the national parks and bathed in the hot springs."

"Out in the open? Naked?"

Lena bit her lip, blushed and nodded.

Morgan grinned, and began clicking eagerly through the slideshow.

"What're you doing?" Lena asked.

"Trying to see if Roderick shows up naked in one of these pictures."

Lena laughed. "You wish!"

"I do. I *really* do."

Grinning and shaking her head, Lena rose from the sofa and started toward the kitchen. "I'm getting a takeout menu. What're you in the mood for?"

"Japanese food, thanks to these pictures. But I'll settle for some deep-dish."

"Pizza it is, then. Do you want the usual—"

Suddenly Morgan gasped.

Alarmed, Lena spun around. "What? What is it?"

Morgan lifted her head from the laptop and stared at Lena. "Come look at this photo."

With a puzzled frown, Lena retraced her steps to the sofa and peered over her sister's shoulder. The moment her gaze landed on the photograph in question, she understood why Morgan had reacted so strongly.

It was one of the pictures that had been taken by the friendly tourist at the Imperial Palace East Garden. He must have snapped off a shot before Lena and Roderick were ready, because they weren't looking into the camera. Roderick was smiling tenderly at Lena. And she…oh, God. In that brief, unguarded moment she'd gazed at him with her heart laid bare.

With just one press of a button, a complete stranger had exposed a truth Lena had been trying to outrun for days.

"Oh. My. God." Morgan gaped at her. "You're in love with him."

Lena pressed her fist against her mouth, but the choked sob escaped anyway.

Morgan's expression softened with concern. "Lena?"

She shook her head helplessly, tears scalding her eyes and blurring her vision. "I don't know what I'm going to do," she whispered.

"What do you mean?" Morgan asked gently.

"I thought I could handle it, but I was wrong."

"Handle what?"

"Our arrangement." Lena gulped painfully. "The damn deal we made."

Morgan rose from the sofa, draped a comforting arm around Lena's shoulders and steered her back to the sofa. "Tell me what's going on."

And just like that, the story came pouring out of Lena, along with the tears. She told her sister everything, starting from the night she and Roderick met to their bittersweet goodbye at the airport yesterday morning. By the time she was finished, she'd gone through half a box of tissues and sobbed through Morgan's new designer shirt. Morgan, God bless her, didn't seem to mind.

"Oh, sis," she soothed, gently rubbing Lena's back. "I'm so sorry. I had no idea."

"I know," Lena mumbled miserably. "I was ashamed to tell you. Not only had I slept with a client, but then I agreed to *continue* sleeping with him for money. I could only imagine what you'd think of me."

"I would have thought that you're human," Morgan said with wry amusement. "Only a superhuman could have resisted such a tempting offer from Roderick Brand. As you may recall, *I'm* the one who told you to let him be your sugar daddy."

Lena managed a teary laugh. "You weren't serious about that."

"Says who?"

Shaking her head, Lena drew away and leaned her head back against the sofa. Staring up at the ceiling, she whispered hoarsely, "God, I'm such a mess."

"Yes, you are," Morgan agreed softly. "So what are you going to do about it?"

"I don't know. I honestly don't know."

"You could start by telling him how you feel," Morgan suggested.

Lena swallowed hard. "I could. But I don't think I could handle it if he didn't return my feelings."

"Well," Morgan said speculatively, glancing at the laptop screen, "judging by the way he's smiling at you in this photo, I'd say your chances are pretty good. After all, a picture is worth a thousand words."

Lena followed the direction of her sister's gaze. Her heart squeezed at the memory of what Roderick had said to her as they posed on the bridge. *I want as many souvenirs as possible.*

Did she dare hope that he felt the same way about her?

"Even if you don't tell him yourself, he'll know the moment he sees this picture." Morgan smiled quietly. "I did."

She had a point.

Lena pushed out a shaky breath and raked a hand through her hair. "Okay. Suppose I tell him how I feel, and he asks me to quit my job at the agency?"

"I'd fully expect him to," Morgan said pragmatically. "Why would a guy like that want to share his girlfriend with other men?"

Lena frowned. "But what about Poppa? Even if you and I pooled our resources, we couldn't afford to pay for Lakeview Manor on our salaries. We explored that option before, remember? We couldn't make the numbers work."

"Okay," Morgan said slowly. "Here's another thought. If you and Roderick were dating, *he* could pay for the retirement home. Hell, he could build Poppa his own private facility, something even bigger and better than where he is now."

Lena's frown deepened. "Poppa's my responsibility, not Roderick's. There's no way I'd ask him to foot the bill just because we're dating—"

"And he happens to be filthy rich." Morgan grinned.

Lena scowled.

"Anyway," Morgan pointed out, "you probably wouldn't have to ask Roderick to do it—he'd do it on his own. For you, and for Poppa. Didn't you see the way they bonded?"

Lena groaned. "Let's not get ahead of ourselves. I haven't even told the man how I feel about him."

"When does he get back from Japan?"

"I don't know. Monday, at the earliest."

"That's almost a week away! You can't wait that long to tell him, Lena."

She sighed heavily. "I know." Hell, if she waited another hour—let alone five days—she'd lose her nerve and talk herself out of saying anything.

Rising from the sofa, Morgan said, "I'd better let you get to it."

On second thought. "No, Morg, don't go yet."

Her sister hesitated. "Why not?"

"You braved the nasty weather just to come over here and have dinner with me, so that's what we're doing. I'll call Roderick later."

"Are you sure?"

"Positive." Lena mustered a wobbly smile. "Family first."

Morgan's dark eyes twinkled. "If my hunch is right about Roderick's feelings, he'll soon be family, too."

After Morgan left, Lena summoned the courage to call Roderick. She knew it was after 7:00 a.m. in Tokyo. With any luck, she could catch him before he headed to the office.

Her heart thudded while she waited for him to answer the phone. One ring, two, three—

"Hello." His deep voice sounded clipped, distracted.

Lena swallowed and tried to calm her shaking nerves. "Good morning."

There was a pause. Then, in a gentler tone, he said, "Hey, beautiful."

Her knees went weak, and she sank to the sofa. "Hey, yourself. I thought I'd try to reach you before you left for the office."

"I'm on my way now. Just marinating in traffic."

"Oh." She felt a pang of guilt. "I guess if you'd taken one of those other penthouses, you'd have been closer to the office."

"Pretty much." He paused, then added softly, "But none of those other places had a teahouse."

Her heart soared. "I'll never forget—"

The rest of her declaration was drowned out by the sudden cacophony of blaring horns, followed by Roderick's muffled expletive. A moment later he came back on the line sounding disgusted. "Sorry about that. Damn crazy drivers."

"Worse than Chicagoans?"

"Most definitely."

She grinned. "How'd I know you'd say that?"

He hummed a noncommittal note, distracted again.

She heard papers rustling in the background. She envisioned him in the backseat of his chauffeured car, dressed in one of his impeccably tailored suits, leather briefcase open on his lap, his black brows furrowed in concentration as he perused documents on his sleek, high-tech laptop.

"If this is a bad time, I can try you later," she offered.

"No, this is fine. I'm in meetings all day, so this is probably the only chance we'll get to talk." She heard tapping as his fingers flew rapidly across the computer keyboard.

Inwardly she sighed. *Great.* She'd called to pour out her heart to him, to tell him that she loved him and didn't want to live without him. And he was multitasking.

"I'm sorry," he muttered darkly. "It's been one of those mornings."

"I understand. Really, I can just call you tom—"

"No, it's okay. I just had to send off that last message. The rest can wait until I get to the office." He blew out a deep, ragged breath. "How are you?"

"I'm fine." *I miss you. I miss hanging out with you. I miss falling asleep in your arms and waking up with you inside me. I don't think I'll ever be the same without you.*

"Did you go to work today?" he asked her.

"I did."

"You should have stayed home. You got in late from a twelve-hour flight."

"I know, but I had that professional development training that I promised Ethan I'd attend if he gave me the week off. Tomorrow's Friday, so at least I have the weekend to catch up on sleep."

"You won't, though. You're like the Energizer Bunny."

She laughed. "Look who's talking."

He chuckled softly. She waited for him to make a suggestive remark about his staying power, but instead he asked, "How's your grandfather?"

Ignoring a stab of disappointment, she replied, "He's doing great. I called him when I got back and told him I'd see him on Saturday to give him his souvenirs."

"Cool."

"Of course," Lena drawled wryly, "Morgan couldn't wait till Saturday to receive the gifts I brought back for her. All I had to do was mention clothes, and she rushed right over after work."

Roderick chuckled. "A clotheshorse, just like my sisters."

Lena grinned. "They'd probably get along fabulously."

"Probably."

Lena found herself holding her breath, hoping he'd suggest that their sisters should meet. But he said nothing more.

She cleared her throat. "I was just, um, showing Morgan the photos from my trip." She hesitated, biting her lower lip. "Have you looked at them yet?"

"Honestly, I've been so busy I haven't had a chance. All hell broke loose after you left yesterday."

"Really? I'm sorry to hear that." Guilt gnawed at her. Maybe things had slipped through the cracks while he was spending so much time with her. "What's going on?"

"Kawamoto's company—*my* company—just got slapped with a patent lawsuit by one of our competitors."

"Oh, no," Lena exclaimed. "That's terrible, Roderick."

"The lawsuit is baseless," he said grimly, "but trying to unsnarl this mess is going to cost time, money and resources I hadn't anticipated. I've been on the phone with the lawyers and company execs since the crack of dawn."

"No wonder you sounded so tense when you answered the phone," Lena murmured sympathetically.

"Yeah." He heaved a long, deep breath.

A knot of dread tightened in Lena's stomach. "With all that's going on," she said quietly, "it doesn't sound like you're going to be able to return home on Monday."

There was a heavy pause. "I'm not. In fact, it may be a while before I'm back in Chicago."

Her heart plummeted. She was afraid to ask, but she knew she had to. "How long?"

"I can't say right now. At least three months. Maybe more."

Lena closed her eyes. She felt as if she were drowning, slowly suffocating.

"I've authorized the release of the grant funds. Your college should receive the check next week." His tone was suddenly brisk, impersonal. As if he were merely concluding one of his business transactions. Was that all she'd been to him? A business transaction that had served its purpose, but had now run its course?

"Thanks," she murmured. "Ethan will be very pleased."

"I'm sure. How soon will you receive your promotion?"

"I don't know...I haven't given it much thought."

"Of course." His tone was faintly mocking. "You have other sources of income."

Anger flared in her chest. "That's right," she said tartly. "I do. And now that our little arrangement is over, I can go back to earning my 'other sources of income.'"

"Right," he drawled sarcastically. "New people, new experiences."

Taken aback by the unexpected assault, she whispered harshly, "Why are you doing this? Why are you saying these things to me?"

He fell silent for so long she wondered whether they'd lost their connection—literally and figuratively.

"Roderick—?"

"Look, I need to go," he said abruptly. "I'm at the office, and they're waiting for me to start a meeting. I'll call you tomorrow."

"Don't bother," Lena snapped.

"Excuse me?"

"You heard me. It was fun while it lasted, Roderick. We both got what we wanted out of the deal, so there's no need to drag this out any longer."

"Is that what we're doing?" His voice was chillingly soft.

"Take care of yourself, Roderick." She forced the words past a throat clogged with raw emotion. "I wish you the best."

He paused for a long moment. "So that's it."

She swallowed. "Yes."

"Whatever you say, Lena." The line went dead.

Calmly and deliberately, she disconnected, then dialed another number.

On the second ring, Zandra answered, "Hello?"

"Zandra. It's Lena."

"Hey, Lena. What's up?"

She took a deep breath. "I'm ready to come back to work."

There was a pregnant pause. "Are you sure?"

Lena closed her eyes to prevent the tears that threatened. "As sure as I'll ever be."

Chapter Twenty-Seven

Nursing a glass of champagne, Lena swept a disinterested glance over the crowd of fashionably dressed strangers. It was another Saturday night. Another elegant ballroom. Another swanky function attended by some of Chicago's movers and shakers.

And she couldn't wait to go home.

"Having a good time?" asked her companion, Dylan Chapman, an attractive, dark-haired Englishman who was in Chicago on business.

Lena forced an upbeat smile. "Of course. You?"

Amused green eyes met hers. "About as good a time as you're having," he said with a smooth, cultured British accent.

A guilty flush heated Lena's face. "I'm sorry," she murmured sheepishly. "I'm afraid I haven't been very good company tonight, have I?"

"It's not you. It's this bloody soiree." He raked a

distasteful glance around the room. "I'd rather swim buck naked across the English Channel in the middle of February than be forced to endure another one of these dull, pretentious gatherings."

Lena nearly spit out her champagne. "Dylan!" she gasped.

He grinned at her. "I'm sorry—was that too candid?"

"Well, no, not really." She laughed, using a napkin to dab at her mouth. "But I don't understand. If you don't want to be here, why did you come?"

"I didn't have much of a choice," Dylan admitted with a wry grimace. "The company I work for expects me to attend these dreadful functions and schmooze with all the right people."

Lena gave him a rueful smile. "And schmoozing's not really your thing."

"Not by any stretch." He smiled winsomely. "My only consolation is that you were able to accompany me this evening. I was crushed when I contacted the agency three weeks ago and Miss Kennedy told me you'd be unavailable for a while."

Lena arched an amused brow. "Crushed?"

"Inconsolable." He grinned. "I'm glad I took a chance and called the agency again. Let that be a lesson to anyone who says persistence doesn't pay off."

Lena chuckled. "I'm flattered that I made such an impression on you, Dylan, considering that our previous encounter consisted of a ten-minute conversation at a party held over four months ago."

"The best ten minutes of that whole dreary evening, I assure you." He smiled at her. "Since neither of us seems to be enjoying ourselves, what do you say we cut out early and grab a cup of coffee somewhere?"

Lena smiled. Dylan was a smart, funny, attractive man whose company she enjoyed. But the way he'd been flirting with her throughout the evening made it obvious that he was interested in more than sharing coffee with her. The *last* thing she wanted to do was lead him on. God knows she'd had more than enough drama with clients.

"Not that your offer doesn't sound tempting," she answered smoothly, "but I'm afraid I'll have to pass."

Dylan chuckled. "It's just as well. The gentleman who's been glowering at us for the past five minutes would probably take great satisfaction in dismembering me if I tried to sneak out of here with you."

Lena frowned. "What gentleman?"

"Tall, good-looking fellow. Killer tux. Lethal glare."

Lena followed the direction of Dylan's gaze across the crowded ballroom—and froze.

Roderick.

Her heart jammed in her throat.

What was he doing in Chicago? Just over a week ago he'd told her he wouldn't be home for months. And now here he was at the same party, his dark eyes simmering with leashed fury as he glared at her and Dylan.

Averting her gaze, Lena took a hasty gulp of champagne and coughed when the bubbles shot straight up her nose.

"Are you all right?" Dylan asked.

She nodded quickly, throat burning, eyes tearing up.

"Old flame?"

"Not old enough," she mumbled.

Dylan nodded wisely. "Want me to tell him to bugger off?"

That wrung a hoarse, mirthless laugh out of her. "I wouldn't recommend that."

"Indeed. I've grown rather fond of having my limbs attached to my body."

Lena grinned wryly at him before she braved another glance in Roderick's direction. He was now conversing with a beautiful woman whose breasts were spilling out of her low-cut dress. His date? Lena wondered, then told herself she shouldn't care. Even though she did.

Dylan was also studying Roderick, his eyes narrowed speculatively. "He looks familiar."

"Hmm." Lena didn't volunteer Roderick's name. She'd spent the past week trying her damnedest to forget about him. Why did he have to show up tonight? Had he known that she would be there? Did he intend to make his way over to her, or would they spend the whole evening pretending to be strangers?

She needn't have worried.

When she glanced around the room again, Roderick was gone.

She and Dylan toughed out the party until ten-thirty. After dropping him off at his hotel, Lena implored the chauffeur to drive around the city for a while so she could clear her head. By the time she returned to the empty silence of her apartment, midnight had come and gone. She went through the motions of changing into a nightgown, brushing her teeth and cleansing her face. And then she crawled into bed and prepared to lie awake for hours, as she'd done every night since leaving Tokyo.

It was after one when she heard the doorbell ring.

She didn't pretend not to know who it was.

She'd been expecting him.

But that didn't stop her heart from hammering wildly as she slid out of bed, slipped on a robe and made her way to the front door.

He was in shirtsleeves, the shirttail untucked from his pants and his tie jerked loose around the collar. Without waiting for an invitation, he shouldered past her into the apartment.

Closing and locking the door behind him, she said tightly, "It's late—"

"Did you have a good time at the party?" he asked curtly.

"Yes, I did," she lied, defiantly folding her arms across her chest and glaring at him. "Did you?"

"I think you know the answer to that question."

"Actually, I don't. One minute you were talking into a woman's cleavage. The next minute you were nowhere to be found."

"Jealous?" he taunted.

Her temper flared. "Go to hell, Roderick."

As she stalked past him he grasped her upper arm, pulling her around to face him. She hated the way her body shivered in response to his touch.

His eyes blazed into hers. "I didn't leave with her."

"I don't care!"

"Liar," he snarled.

She tried to yank her arm away, but he tightened his hold. Not hurting her, but making it impossible for her to escape.

"Who was that man you were with?"

"Who do you *think?*" she hissed. "He was a client."

"Did you sleep with him?" Roderick demanded.

Her jaw went slack, and she stared up at him in wounded outrage. "How *dare* you ask me that question?"

"Did you?"

"None of your damn business!"

"The hell it isn't!"

"Why?" she jeered. "You think you *own* me? Just because we had an arrangement for three weeks, you think that gives you the right to barge in here and ask me whatever the hell you want?"

"Don't play with me, Lena," he growled warningly. "I drove by here an hour ago, and you weren't home. So answer my damn question. Did you sleep with him?"

Something snapped inside her, and she shouted, "Yes, damn you! I slept with him!"

Roderick's face contorted with fury, even as a whispered denial burst from his lips, "I don't believe you!"

"No? Well, it's true. I fucked him," Lena spat, deliberately crude. "I was rattled after I saw you at the party, so he suggested that we leave and go somewhere to talk. He was a very good listener. One thing led to another, and we wound up back at his hotel room."

Roderick closed his eyes and ground out through clenched teeth, "You're lying."

"I assure you I'm not. He has a strawberry birthmark on the inside of his right thigh. I told him the shape reminded me of the British royal crest. He said it was proof that he was the rightful heir to the throne, and we laughed. And then he kissed me—"

Roderick released her arm abruptly and stalked toward the living room as though he couldn't stand to be anywhere near her.

But she wasn't finished with him. She wanted to hurt him as much as he'd hurt her with his unjust accusations.

"Ever since the first time I heard Idris Elba speak,"

she continued tauntingly, "I've had a thing for British accents. So I was in trouble the moment Dylan opened his mouth. While we made love he talked dirty to me. The things he said with that accent… Oh, man, it drove me wild." She laughed, a harsh, nasty laugh she didn't even recognize as her own.

"Poor Glenn," she said, shaking her head with mock sympathy. "It took him *three* dates to get me into bed. You and Dylan? One and done. At this rate, my next client won't even have to wait—"

"Enough!" Roderick roared. He spun around and advanced on her, looking enraged enough to hit her. But he did something potentially worse. He cupped her face in his hands and seized her mouth with fierce, hungry possession.

"Damn you," Lena whispered furiously, even as she threw her arms around his neck and kissed him back with equal ferocity.

She heard a crash as he swept the small foyer lamp to the floor, plunging them into moonlit darkness. He then lifted her against him and planted her on top of the table. In a frenzy of impatience, he unzipped his pants and shoved her silk robe and nightgown out of the way, growling when he discovered that she wore no panties.

His mouth ground bruisingly against hers as her thighs locked around his hips. He drove into her, swallowing her sharp cry as he buried himself to the base.

He began thrusting, rocking the table against the wall with the force of each deep, savage stroke. Within moments they were both crying out and erupting together in a violent rush.

Lena's body was still vibrating with the aftershocks

of orgasm when Roderick struck the wall behind her with his fist, then dropped his head forward, aligning his cheek with hers. His breathing was as loud and ragged as her own. Tears welled in her eyes, but she refused to shed even a single one.

If he'd told her right then and there that he loved her, that he *didn't* believe she was a whore who slept indiscriminately with her clients, she would have recanted everything she'd said.

But a moment later he pulled out of her, tucked himself back into his pants and zipped up. He didn't speak, didn't meet her eyes in the moonlight. Instead he turned and walked slowly to the door, as if his legs had become lead weights. Her breath stalled as he paused with one hand on the doorknob, head bent, broad shoulders hunched as he wrestled with the decision to stay or go. She waited, heart pounding frantically, every fiber of her being clamoring to call out to him, to beg him not to leave her. But she remained proudly silent.

After an agonizing eternity, he opened the door and departed without a backward glance.

And this time Lena knew she'd seen the last of him.

Slowly she drew her legs up to her chest, dropped her face onto her knees and finally let the tears fall, a bitter deluge of heartache and regret.

Chapter Twenty-Eight

As October slipped into November, Lena's days settled into a predictable routine that she almost welcomed for the sake of her sanity. She got up every morning and drove an hour to work, where she'd been recently promoted to assistant director of grants and corporate development, a position that put her in charge of two grant writers and an intern. She'd also received a ten-thousand-dollar salary increase and gushing accolades from the college's president, who'd waxed eloquent about Lena's accomplishments during the grant dedication ceremony heavily attended by the media.

As she posed for the requisite photo op with the giant cardboard check, Lena smiled brightly and forced herself not to think about what she'd had to do to procure the grant money, the ultimate price she'd had to pay. She was relieved when Roderick sent a company executive to represent him at the ceremony. She couldn't have maintained her composure if he'd been there, couldn't have smiled through the charade.

After the way her last date had ended, she dreaded the idea of going out with another client. Fortunately, she had enough money saved up to cover her grandfather's care expenses for the next six months, so she didn't need the extra income right away.

When she called Zandra and told her she was taking some time off, Zandra didn't ask any questions.

She didn't have to.

Thanksgiving rolled around, arriving at a time in Lena's life when she was feeling anything *but* thankful. She wanted nothing more than to spend the day in bed, wallowing in her misery. But she knew she couldn't do that. She had a feast to prepare, a family tradition to uphold.

That afternoon, she was removing a picture-perfect turkey from the oven when her grandfather wheeled himself into the kitchen, looking refreshed from his catnap. She'd taken him out of the retirement home for the next four days so they could spend the holiday together as a family.

"It sure smells wonderful in here," Cleveland exclaimed, appreciatively eyeing the turkey. "My, what a beautiful bird!"

"Thanks, Poppa." Lena threw him a knowing grin. "But you'd say that even if I'd just pulled a charred carcass out of the oven."

He chuckled, not denying it as he surveyed the array of food covering every available surface of counter space. "Everything looks delicious, baby girl. I can't wait to eat."

Lena could. She hadn't had an appetite in weeks, and

the thought of gorging on all this food made her feel decidedly ill.

As if he'd read her mind, Cleveland jabbed a finger at her and warned sternly, "Don't think I'm gonna sit by and let you get away with picking at your food. You've been losing too much weight as it is."

A rueful smile touched Lena's mouth. "Remember how Grandma used to ration my portions at Thanksgiving? She used to say to me, 'Now, baby, you know I'm only doing this for your own good. You have the most beautiful face, but it'd be a shame if folks only saw a chubby girl every time they looked at you.'"

Cleveland's expression softened. "You know she meant well. She just didn't know what to say out of her mouth sometimes, God rest her soul. But she was very proud of you. Used to brag about you all the time."

Lena smiled softly. "I know. I never doubted that."

"Good," he said gruffly. "Anyway, don't change the subject. We were talking about how much weight you've lost."

"No, *you* were," Lena corrected, turning to remove a pot of collard greens from the burner.

"I'm worried about you, Lena."

The gentle concern in his voice made her throat tighten. But she'd promised herself she wouldn't cry today, or any other time during her grandfather's stay.

"Now, you know I don't like to pry in your personal life—"

Lena snorted out a laugh. "Since when?"

Cleveland had the decency to look abashed. "Well, I *try* not to," he amended. "But I can't help it if I worry about you, especially when I have plenty reason to." His gaze followed her around the kitchen as she bustled about putting the finishing touches on dinner. "What happened between you and that nice young man?"

"Roderick?" Lena kept her tone neutral. "I thought I told you that I'm not seeing him anymore, Poppa."

"You didn't tell me—your sister did."

"Oh. Where *is* Morgan anyway?" Lena wondered aloud. "I sent her to the corner store to pick up a few things I needed, and that was over an hour ago."

"Knowing your sister, she probably took a detour to the shopping mall, or snuck across town to see Isaiah. Things seem to be going pretty well between them. And there you go again, trying to change the subject."

"I'm not, Poppa." Lena lingered in the pantry so she wouldn't have to lie right to his face. "There's not much to say about me and Roderick. We hadn't been, ah, seeing each other for very long. We weren't that serious."

Cleveland grunted. "That's not the impression *I* got from him."

"With all due respect, Poppa, you only met him once."

"Twice, actually."

"What?" Lena whirled around in surprise. "When?"

"He came to see me again a week later. It was Sunday night. I remember because you'd brought me a lemon pound cake earlier that day, and I shared it with Roderick when he stopped by that evening. He couldn't get enough of it. I told him, 'Wait till you try her German chocolate cake,' and he said something about how you'd gotten him to appreciate fudge."

Lena blushed from her scalp to her toes.

"Anyway, he brought two six-packs of beer, which made him very popular with the fellas. They propped me up in bed, and we all sat around playing cards and watching the Bears game." Cleveland grinned. "Most fun I've had in a long time."

Lena couldn't believe what she was hearing. Roderick had paid a visit to her grandfather the day after the whole Glenn fiasco? While *she'd* spent the day driving herself crazy over whether she would ever see him again, he'd been yukking it up with her grandfather at the retirement home?

Incredulous, she shook her head. "Why didn't you tell me, Poppa?"

Cleveland shrugged. "He asked me not to, and given the way you tried to hustle him out of my hospital room, I guess I can understand why he didn't want you to know. Anyway, that's when I realized he must be pretty serious about you, baby girl. Why else would he spend a whole evening hanging out with a bunch of old coots at a nursing home?"

"Why, indeed?" Lena murmured, staring at the bag of flour in her hand as if she couldn't remember how it had gotten there.

"So you can understand why I was surprised when your sister told me that you and Roderick broke up."

Lena heaved a weary sigh. "We didn't break up, Poppa. We were never really together to begin with."

Cleveland gave her a pointed look. "Is that why you went to Japan with him?"

She said nothing.

Cleveland wheeled himself over to the breakfast table, picked up a small plastic plate and began adding items from a fruit and vegetable tray. When Lena hurried over to help him, he waved her off, saying gruffly, "If I can play cards with one arm in a sling, I can damn well fix myself a plate of carrots and celery sticks. Now go on and finish what you were doing so we can eat soon. I'm starving."

Swallowing a grin, Lena dutifully returned to her simmering pots on the stove.

"I was thinking," Cleveland said casually.

"Thinking what?"

"Now that you got that nice promotion at work, maybe you can quit that second job of yours."

Lena froze for a moment, then spun around and stared at him. "You…you know about that?"

He met her gaze calmly. "Your sister told me that you got a part-time job to supplement your income so that you could afford the retirement home."

Lena scowled. "I'm going to kill her," she muttered under her breath.

"That won't be necessary," Cleveland said mildly. "I'm glad she told me. I've always suspected you were working two jobs to keep me at Lakeview, but every time I tried to ask you, you shot me down. Morgan dodged my questions, too." He paused. "But not this time. She seems to be under the impression that the long hours you work are interfering with your personal life. Specifically, your relationship with Roderick."

"That's not true," Lena protested with a vigorous shake of her head. "My—"

"I want you to take me out of Lakeview Manor."

Aghast, Lena stared at him. "But you love it there!"

"I do," he calmly agreed. "But I love *you* more."

Tears pricked her eyelids. "Poppa—"

"I've talked to Nurse Jacobs and asked her to look into more affordable retirement facilities for me. She's familiar with the terrain and has several contacts who can supply good referrals. Another option she suggested is home care assistance. She knows of some affordable providers, and even offered her own services if we're interested." He smiled. "She told me to let you know that her rates would be very reasonable."

Stunned, Lena shook her head slowly at him. "You've really given this a lot of thought, haven't you?"

"I have for a while," Cleveland admitted. "I was just waiting for the right opportunity to discuss it with you."

Lena blew out a deep, shaky breath. "This is a lot to consider, Poppa. I need more time to think it over. And I want you to stay at Lakeview until your arm completely heals. Don't argue with me," she warned when he opened his mouth to protest. "I've already paid the bill for the next six months, so that's that."

His eyes twinkled. "Yes, ma'am."

She gave him a knowing look. "So you want Nurse Jacobs to be your personal caregiver, huh?"

He nodded. "She's going to help me achieve my ultimate goal."

"What's that?"

His expression grew tender. "To walk you down the aisle on your wedding day."

That undid her.

When Morgan returned to the apartment, she was greeted by the sight of Lena curled up in their grandfather's lap, tears streaming down her face as she softly crooned the words to "Stormy Weather."

Chapter Twenty-Nine

At the end of January, Lena decided it was time to quit her job as an escort. She hadn't gone on a date in months, so she figured there was no sense in prolonging the inevitable. Because she and Zandra had become good friends, she wanted to give Zandra the courtesy of resigning in person.

On her day off from work, she drove to the downtown building that housed Elite For You Companions and parked in the rear lot. As she stepped through the doors of the escort agency, she skidded to a halt, her heart slamming against her chest.

Standing in the lobby was a tall, broad-shouldered man in a dark suit, his hands tucked casually into his pockets as he studied a painting on the wall.

"Roderick," Lena breathed before she could stop herself.

The man turned to face her, his mouth quirking at

the corners as he met her yearning gaze. "Not quite," he murmured.

Realizing her mistake at once, Lena blushed furiously and stammered out an apology.

"No need to be sorry," Remington Brand drawled. "I get that all the time."

Lena couldn't help staring at him. Although she'd known that Roderick had a twin, she was still stunned by the striking resemblance between the two brothers. She could only imagine the games of switcheroo they must have played on friends and unsuspecting strangers. Their features were identical, even right down to the thickness of their black lashes. To the untrained eye, the most obvious—and only—difference between them was the trim goatee that framed Remington's full, sensual lips. But because Lena had memorized Roderick's face, she could detect other differences, subtle things that she'd picked up while watching him sleep, or gazing at him across the dinner table.

She suddenly realized that Remington was returning her appraisal, his dark eyes narrowed as if he were trying to place where he'd seen her before. "So you know my brother?"

Lena swallowed, then jerked her head in a nod.

A slow, lazy smile curved Remington's mouth. "Well, any friend of Rod's is a friend of mine." He slid his hand forward. "Remy."

Lena shook his hand. "Hi, I'm—"

Her introduction was interrupted when Zandra suddenly emerged from the back. "Sorry to keep you wait—"

She stopped short at the sight of Lena and Remington standing in the lobby. She looked from one to the other before her gaze settled on Lena. Her sympathetic expression spoke volumes. Coming face-to-face with Roderick's twin had been a shock to Lena's system, and Zandra understood that.

"Hi, Lena," she greeted her gently.

At the mention of her name, recognition dawned on Remington's face. Lena didn't know whether to be ecstatic or sad that he'd apparently heard of her before.

Zandra said, "Lena, this is Roderick's brother—"

"I know." She smiled at him. "We were just introducing ourselves."

He smiled back at her. "So you're Lena, Roderick's—"

"Friend," she finished.

She didn't know how to interpret the look that passed between Remington and Zandra. It was followed by a long, awkward silence.

Pointedly clearing her throat, Zandra said to Remington, "Before she headed out, my receptionist told me you were waiting in the lobby. What're you doing here?"

"I came to take you out to lunch."

Zandra shook her head. "Not today. I'm busy."

"So take a break." The determined set of his jaw let her know that it wasn't a request. Lena remembered the look all too well.

Zandra frowned, her eyes narrowing on Remington's face.

He just stared her down.

"Fine," she relented, huffing an exasperated breath. She turned to Lena, whose mouth was twitching with laughter. "I'm so sorry, Lena. You came all the way down here—"

"That's okay. I should have called first anyway. I know how busy you are."

"I'm never too busy for you. Are you free on Saturday? We can get a massage and do lunch afterward."

Lena smiled. "That sounds good. See you then."

Zandra nodded, then shot a dark glance at Remington. "I'm going to get my coat."

"You do that," he said silkily.

She stalked off, muttering under her breath about pushy, overbearing brothers who thought the world revolved around them.

Remington grinned, and the sight of that lazy grin was so achingly familiar to Lena that her heart squeezed. As his gaze wandered back to her, she cleared her throat and pasted on a bright smile. "Well, it was nice to meet you, Remington."

"Remy," he corrected her.

"Sorry. Remy." She smiled, then turned and walked to the door.

"The whole family's flying to Japan next week," he announced to her retreating back.

Lena stopped, but didn't turn around. "Oh? The whole family?"

"Yep. My parents, grandparents, siblings, nieces and nephews. The Brand clan is invading Tokyo." He chuckled.

Lena smiled softly. "I'm sure Roderick will be happy to see all of you."

"He'd better be. He left right after Thanksgiving, and Mama's been depressed ever since. Even our old family dog has been moping around. Everyone really misses him."

"I bet." *I know the feeling,* Lena mentally added.

"We also figure he could use some cheering up. He

hasn't been himself in quite a while." Remington's voice softened. "Mama says he's staying away from home so he can lick his wounds in peace."

Lena closed her eyes, and for the first time in weeks, she felt a tiny glimmer of hope.

"Is there a message you'd like for me to pass along to him while I'm there?" Remington asked gently.

Lena swallowed hard. There were so many things she wanted to say. But words failed her. Courage failed her.

Glancing over her shoulder, she shook her head and said quietly, "Enjoy your trip."

Later, though, she had second thoughts. After staring at her cell phone for over an hour, she worked up the nerve to type what she hoped would be a game-changing message: *I didn't sleep with Dylan, and Glenn was a mistake. You weren't.*

She sent off the text and anxiously waited for him to respond.

By the end of the week, she still hadn't heard from him.

And that was when she finally abandoned the last shred of hope she'd been foolishly clinging to.

Chapter Thirty

At the end of February, Lena received a frantic phone call from Zandra. "Do you have any plans tonight?"

Lena chuckled dryly. "Is that a joke?" Zandra, of all people, should know that she'd been living practically like a recluse for the past four months.

"So…does that mean you're free?"

"Yes." A wary note crept into Lena's voice. "Free for what?"

Zandra sighed. "I need a *huge* favor."

Now Lena was downright suspicious. "How huge?"

"Well, I have a new client—"

"Zandra."

"I know, I know. You're retired from the business. Believe me, I wouldn't ask you for this favor if I had other options. But the girl who was supposed to go out with this client had a family emergency, and no other escort meets his specifications. He's hosting a private dinner party for some clients and he wants someone who speaks Italian. You are—*were*—the only other escort who does. So can you help me out?"

Lena groaned, wavering. "I don't know, Zandra. I really wasn't planning—"

"Please, Lena?" Zandra implored. "You'd really be doing me a favor."

And because Zandra had been there for her these past four months, always giving her a shoulder to cry on, Lena relented with a deep sigh. "All right. I'll go. But just this once."

"I'll never ask again," Zandra assured her.

So there Lena was on another Saturday night, preparing to meet her first client in months. She stared listlessly out the window as the limo glided down Lake Shore Drive, traveling past a stretch of elegant houses situated on pristine lawns before reaching a sprawling lakefront property.

The driver pulled into the circular driveway, then climbed out and opened the back door. Lena murmured an absent thanks as she stepped out and started up the cobblestone walk toward the imposing stone house.

She'd just raised her hand to press the doorbell when the door suddenly swung open.

She froze, stunned to find herself staring into the face of the man she'd been trying to forget for the past four months. Four of the longest, most excruciating months of her life.

"I don't believe this," she whispered, shaking her head slowly. "She set me up."

Roderick gazed at her. "Lena—"

She spun on her heel and started back down the walk.

"Don't go," he called after her.

Her heart twisted at the raw desperation in his voice, but her wounded pride kept her feet moving determinedly forward.

"I love you."

That stopped her cold.

But she didn't turn around. She didn't want him to see the tears glistening in her eyes, blurring her vision.

"I love you," Roderick repeated in a husky, ravaged voice. "I can't live without you anymore. I don't even know why I tried to in the first place."

Lena dragged in a shaky breath that burned in her lungs.

"Living in that apartment has been pure hell," he continued raggedly. "Everywhere I look I see reminders of you. And the teahouse? I haven't stepped foot inside that room since you left. I can't even walk past the closed doors without remembering the night we spent in there. I saw a geisha hurrying down the street one day, and I had to excuse myself from a tableful of Japanese businessmen just to get my bearings. When I came back, they looked at me like I'd lost my damn mind." He paused, a note of wry humor entering his voice. "If you'd been there, you could have told me just how bad they were talking about me."

That coaxed a reluctant smile out of Lena.

"I've been going out of my mind without you," he confessed. "You can't even begin to imagine."

Oh yes, I can, she thought.

"I love you, Lena Morrison," he said thickly, coming closer. "And the best part is, I know you love me, too."

"You don't know anything," she mumbled.

"Yes, I do." His voice softened. "I saw the picture."

That, finally, broke her.

The tears she'd been keeping in check spilled down

her face. As her shoulders began to shake with helpless sobs, she felt his strong arms go around her and haul her against his chest.

"I shouldn't have stayed away so long," he whispered fiercely. "I was so stubborn and *stupid!*"

"Me, too," Lena cried.

He crushed her to him, kissing her forehead, nose and lips, then rubbing his cheek back and forth against her hair as if he just wanted to absorb her into his body all at once.

"I couldn't bring myself to look at the photos we took together," he confessed. "I wish to God I had. Maybe I would've come to my senses a helluva lot sooner."

Lena smiled through her tears. "I couldn't bring myself to delete them. Came pretty close several times, but I just couldn't hit that button."

"I'm glad."

She lifted her head to meet his tender gaze. "So am I."

As he gently brushed the tears from her face, she blurted accusingly, "I sent you a text message."

"You did?" He looked surprised. "When?"

"A month ago. You never even bothered to respond."

He groaned with frustration. "That's because I never got it. Some asshole hacked into my phone, so I had to get the number changed. I swear to you, Lena, I *never* would have ignored a message from you."

A wave of relief swept through her, and she gave him a soft, tremulous smile. "I believe you."

"Good." He stroked a hand down one side of her hair. "What did your message say?"

"The truth." She looked into his eyes. "I didn't sleep with my client that night. I only said those things to hurt you, because you'd hurt me. I couldn't believe you'd accuse me of being with another man so soon after everything we'd been through."

Deep regret filled Roderick's eyes. "Words can't express how sorry I am for doing that to you. The thought of you being intimate with another man—*any* man, client or not—just drove me out of my damn mind. I flew home that weekend to talk to you, to see if we could work things out. I couldn't get in touch with you, so I cornered Zandra and made her tell me where you were that night."

He shook his head, his expression turning grim. "When I got to the party and saw you with another guy, it just sent me into a tailspin."

"Because I slept with Glenn," Lena stated flatly. "If I didn't already have a track record, you wouldn't have jumped to conclusions about me and Dylan that night."

Roderick frowned. "I didn't think you had a 'track record,' Lena."

"But you *were* angry about Glenn."

He hesitated, then nodded reluctantly.

"Glenn was a mistake. I'd just started—"

"You don't have to explain anything, Lena."

"Yes, but I want you to know." She cupped his face between her hands, pinning him with a direct gaze. "I'd just started working at the agency. I was inexperienced, and I was still a bit dazzled by the idea of rich, successful men paying for my company. Glenn was very sweet and charming. But he had no interest in me beyond that one night."

Roderick's expression softened with understanding. "I didn't realize he'd hurt you."

"How could you have? I never told you the whole story."

"I never asked." He grimaced. "I didn't want to know."

"I sensed that. And I was too embarrassed to tell you anyway."

He searched her eyes. "Is that why you were so resistant to me? Because you thought I was only after one thing?"

"Weren't you?" she countered, giving him a pointed look. "You propositioned me for sex, Roderick."

He had the decency to look sheepish. "Maybe that's what I was after at first," he admitted, "but it didn't stay that way for very long. I fell hard for you, Lena, and it scared the hell out of me."

She smiled softly. "I know the feeling."

He caught her hands and began kissing her fingertips one by one. "Do you know when I realized that I was in love with you?"

She shook her head, shivering at the warm brush of his lips.

"It was the day we went looking for apartments."

"Really?" She grinned impishly. "Because of the way I handled your snooty real estate agent?"

Roderick chuckled. "That *was* enjoyable."

"Very."

"But, no, that wasn't it. What got to me more than anything was that you cared about my happiness. It mattered to you that my home should be just that—a home, not a showplace. I don't know of any other woman who would've turned up her nose at a luxury penthouse. But you did, and that meant more to me than you can ever imagine."

Smiling tenderly, Lena curved a hand against his cheek. "I love you."

He lowered his head and kissed her as deeply and

intensely as he'd kissed her that night in the teahouse. And this time, there was no mistaking the depth of his feelings.

Linking her hands behind his neck, Lena nibbled his lower lip. "You were supposed to keep me warm this winter," she reminded him.

"Well, technically," he drawled, low and husky, "winter's not over yet."

"That's true."

"So what do you say we go into hibernation for a couple weeks, starting tonight?"

Her belly quivered. "We *do* have a lot of lost time to make up for," she purred.

"A *lot*," he agreed, his erection nudging her stomach.

Lena stepped away with a low, naughty laugh. "Down, boy. We don't want to scandalize your neighbors. Speaking of which," she said, motioning toward the house behind him, "is this your new home?"

He nodded, holding her gaze. "I was hoping you'd share it with me."

Her heart went into overdrive. She stared at him, afraid to misinterpret what he was asking. "You want me to move in with you?"

He lifted her face in his palms and looked into her eyes. "I want you to marry me."

Fresh tears welled in her eyes, and she swallowed hard. "Okay," she whispered simply.

Roderick hesitated uncertainly, as though he hadn't heard her. "Was that a yes?"

"Absolutely."

Looking both relieved and overjoyed, Roderick hugged her like he'd never let go. She wouldn't have complained if he didn't.

At length they drew apart and smiled warmly at each other.

"So what do you think of our new home?" Roderick asked her. "Did I do okay?"

Lena surveyed the large, beautiful house and grinned. "I'll let you know after I've been inside."

Roderick chuckled. "On that note…" Glancing over her shoulder, he signaled to the driver that he could leave. As the limo departed, Roderick swept Lena up into his arms, then frowned.

"What?" she asked.

"You've lost a lot of weight."

She shrugged. "Nursing a broken heart will do that to you."

His frown deepened. "We've gotta fatten you up," he muttered, striding up the walk toward the house.

Lena laughed. "No man's ever said *that* to me before. But since you mentioned feeding me, I could go for some Japanese food."

"I've already got you covered."

"You do? Is that what we're having tonight?"

"Yep." Reaching the front door, he said, "I can't wait to show you the garden. And I think you'll be very pleased with the centerpiece."

Lena stared at him, her heart stirring hopefully. "You built a teahouse? A real teahouse?"

Roderick slanted her a slow, mysterious smile. "You'll see."

And then he opened the door and swept her across the threshold. Into their new home. Into their new life.

Epilogue

Four months later

"Wake up, sleepyhead."

Lena groaned softly. "Go 'way. You promised to let me sleep in after you kept me up all night."

Roderick chuckled, gently kissing her bare shoulder. "I *did* let you sleep in. It's almost noon."

"I don't care," she mumbled groggily. "I need more rest."

"Okay," Roderick drawled, his warm breath caressing her nape, "but we'll be arriving at our destination soon, and ready or not, this love boat's gonna be overrun with our family members."

Lena rolled over in bed and stared up at him. "Why didn't you say so?"

He grinned. "I just did."

"You should have said that at first."

"Why? It wouldn't have gotten you up any faster—you're still lying there, lazybones."

She poked her tongue out at him, and he laughed.

Sobering after a moment, he gazed down at her. "Good morning, wife."

Pleasure coursed through Lena's veins, and she smiled shyly at him. "Good morning, husband."

A broad grin swept across his face. "God, I *love* how that sounds."

"So do I." She sighed contentedly. "I still can't believe we're on our honeymoon."

"It's been amazing."

"It really has."

After an unforgettably romantic wedding, they'd embarked on a Caribbean cruise aboard Roderick's yacht. The past two weeks they'd spent alone together had been sheer bliss, making up for the long, torturous months they'd been apart. Lena almost wished they hadn't invited their families to meet them in St. Lucia.

As if he'd read her mind, Roderick chuckled. "Just remember, it was *your* idea."

Lena grinned sheepishly. "I know. I'm just being greedy, wanting to keep you all to myself a little longer. But I'm glad we invited them. Morgan really needs a vacation from her job. And Poppa deserves a reward for working so hard in therapy."

Although her grandfather hadn't been able to walk her down the aisle on her wedding day—he'd wheeled alongside her with tears of joyous pride streaming down his face—he was making good progress, thanks to the assistance of Margaret Jacobs.

Everyone believed Cleveland would walk any day now, and because Lena didn't want to miss the momentous occasion, she'd begged him to accept

Roderick's invitation to move in with them. But Cleveland had chosen to remain at Lakeview Manor, wanting to give Lena and Roderick a chance to settle into their new home as husband and wife. He'd even hinted that they should get right to work on giving him great-grandchildren.

Roderick smiled, tenderly stroking Lena's cheek. "I love the way you always look out for your family."

"I'm not the only one." She gave him a knowing smile. "Isn't that why you invited Zandra on this trip? For your brother's sake?"

Roderick blinked innocently. "Zandra's always been like a member of the family. She goes everywhere with us."

"Uh-huh." But Lena knew better. If the dynamic duo of Roderick and Remy Brand teamed up against Zandra, the poor woman didn't stand a chance.

Chuckling at the thought, Lena said, "This ought to be a *very* interesting week."

"I'm counting on it," Roderick murmured under his breath.

"What was that?"

"Nothing." He grinned at her. "Now are you gonna get up, woman, or do I have to drag you out of that bed and carry you over my shoulder to the bathroom?"

Lena sighed in resignation. "Fine, bossy. I'll get up. But first—" She pulled him down for a kiss, then quickly shoved him onto his back and straddled him, startling a laugh out of him.

"Nice moves, samurai," he told her.

She grinned, blowing her tousled hair out of her face. "Think we have time for a quick game of Capture the Pirate Captain?" she purred seductively. "I brought handcuffs this time."

"What? Fresh out of manacles?"

She winked. "A girl's gotta improvise."

Roderick grinned. "And here you've got my mom thinking you're such a sweet, wholesome young lady. *Tsk-tsk.*"

Lena grinned mischievously. "Everyone has their secrets."

"So true." His hands roamed up her thighs and cupped her bare bottom. "I suppose it's not too late to ask the captain to slow down."

"Mmm. That'd be good." Lena kissed her way down his bare chest, feeling his muscles quiver at her touch. She grasped the waistband of his dark shorts and tugged.

Without warning Roderick flipped her over, pinning her beneath his heavy body.

"Hey!" she sputtered indignantly.

A wicked gleam filled his eyes. "I've got an idea. How about we play Capture the Maiden instead?"

Lena shot him an exasperated look. "I swear, you're such a control freak."

He grinned. "And you adore me anyway."

"I do. God help me."

Sobering, Roderick stared down at her, his eyes tracing her features in a way that made her feel positively reborn. "I love you so much," he said huskily.

"I love you, too, sweetheart." Lena closed her eyes, her lips curving in a dreamy smile. "Now stop talking, and get to capturing my vessel."

"Yes, ma'am." Without further ado he slid inside her, only too happy to oblige.

* * * * *

They're making power moves that can only lead to one thing…

Lovers Premiere

Essence bestselling author
ADRIANNE BYRD

Limelight Entertainment is Sofia Wellesley's whole life. When she discovers her agency is about to merge with its biggest rival—which is run by her childhood crush-turned-enemy Ram Jordan—she thinks her anger will get the best of her. So why is her traitorous heart clamoring for the man she hates most in the world?

LOVE IN THE LIMELIGHT

Fantasy, Fame and Fortune…Hollywood-Style!

"Byrd showcases her unique talents with this very touching and memorable tale."
—*RT Book Reviews* on *LOVE TAKES TIME*

Coming the first week of November 2010 wherever books are sold.

KIMANI™ ROMANCE

www.kimanipress.com

EVERY FAMILY HAS ITS SECRETS...

NATIONAL BESTSELLING AUTHOR

ROCHELLE ALERS

BECACE of YOU

From the author of the bestselling Hideaway novels comes the first in a dazzling, sexy new series, The Wainwright Legacy, chronicling the lives and loves of two prestigious New York families.

On Sale October 26, 2010, wherever books are sold.

www.kimanipress.com
www.myspace.com/kimanipress

KPRABOYSP

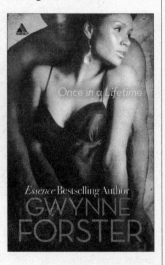

REQUEST YOUR FREE BOOKS!

2 FREE NOVELS
PLUS 2 **FREE GIFTS!**

KIMANI™
ROMANCE

Love's ultimate destination!

KROM10R

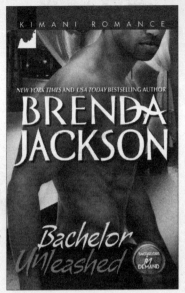